RELIANCE

RELIANCE: A Novel
Book One of the Reliance Trilogy
Heliosphere Books®

Copyright © 2019 by Kaitlyn Andersen
Published by arrangement with the author.

LCCN: 2019938040
ISBN-13: 978-1-937868-73-4 (trade paperback)
ISBN-13: 978-1-937868-80-2 (EPUB)
ISBN-13: 978-1-937868-81-9 (Kindle)

Cover design by chrisodesign.com.

Planet image by Thomas Breher via Pixabay.
Spaceship image by "NTNVNC" via Pixabay.
Girl image by Myicahel Tamburini via Pexels.

This is a work of fiction. Names, characters, places, and events either
are the products of the author's imagination or are used fictitiously.
Any resemblance to actual persons, living or dead, corporations,
or other entities, is entirely coincidental.

Heliosphere Books are published by Endpapers Press,
a division of Author Coach, LLC.

Heliosphere Books is a registered trademark of Author Coach, LLC.

RELIANCE

Book One of the
Reliance Trilogy

Kaitlyn Andersen

Heliosphere
BOOKS

San Diego

ONE

Finn No Last Name startled awake, greeted by waning darkness. Five stories below, the sounds of the city echoed and bounced off of thin, cracking walls, the Mud Pit's very own lullaby, composed of despair and harmonized with misery. Finn rubbed the back of her head and sighed, reveling in the symphony.

She hated sleeping, hated the lack of control and hazy images that felt too real to be dreams. At least when she woke up she always knew where she was.

Drunken yells, some of them in unintelligible alien tongues, drifted up to her, followed by gunfire. Whether a warning shot from the rifle of a Reliance soldier, or just another ticked-off Mudder, she couldn't be sure. This far out into no-man's land, chances were fifty-fifty.

Safe.

Finn repeated the word in her mind, closing her eyes and forcing the rapid drumbeat of her heart to slow. When her ears finally stopped ringing, and the claws of the past seemed to release her, she pushed herself up and off the threadbare mattress. As had become her habit of late, she tried to burn off some of the lingering unease with exercise, coaxing her exhausted body into the routine she'd been practicing. After a while, her limbs got up to speed, the muscles in her arms and legs burning.

She finished just as dawn began to break, pulling on a pair of fingerless gloves and a set of leather cuffs over her wrists. Her eyes scanned the tiny apartment she called home: one room barely two hundred square feet, a sink, and a tiny closet with a steel toilet—no lid.

Gray light began to seep through tattered curtains, drawing her to the only square window in the place, and she threw them back to catch a glimpse of the world outside. On Altara (or the Mud Pit as its residents had taken to calling it), ten months out of the cycle were winter months. As far ahead as Finn's eyes could track, masses of bodies huddled so closely together for warmth it became impossible to distinguish where one ended and the next began. They moved together as one, scurrying from overhang to overhang like rats in the rain. They would find no sunlight, no reprieve from the bitter cold, only gray and brown gloom as far as the eye could see.

Finn didn't know why she always looked each morning, as though one day she would throw aside the curtains to reveal sapphire-blue skies and jade meadowlands stretching to the edge of infinity. She never did. She never would.

A secret part of her longed to grow plants on the windowsill, some sage or maybe big, juicy tomatoes like the ones she'd seen in Grim's books, but they would never grow in a place like the Mud Pit.

Altara was only one of eight planets making up the outer rings of the system commonly known as the Farthers. Residents of the Farthers considered themselves lucky to catch a glimpse of *one* of the three suns their planets orbited, let alone enjoy the benefits the suns' rays could offer.

Finn snatched the crumpled piece of paper she'd stuffed into her pocket the night before.

She re-read the careful script *requesting* her presence inside the Dirty Molly, lips twitching as she fought a smile at Grim's choice in words. She was fairly certain her presence was more of a *requirement* than a *request*.

Securing a scarf around the lower half of her face, she grabbed her coat, sheathed knife, and the holstered pulse gun where she'd left them in a heap. When she'd first arrived on the Mud Pit, the mere thought of guns terrified her. She shrank from the very sight of them. Grim had offered no pity, forcing Finn to learn how to handle one. Guns were a necessary part of survival in the Farthers, and Grim said he'd be damned if he let someone who feared them work for him. In her own stubborn way, Finn grew determined to overcome her crippling fear. Though she still preferred knives and a pulse gun to an actual firearm, she'd become quite the skilled sharpshooter over the cycles.

Leaving her apartment behind, Finn made her way downstairs. As she passed the holes in the walls, the scent of wet rot and mildew wafted in from outside, filling her nostrils through the thick scarf. Throwing on her hood and positioning the holster around her waist, she headed out into the thick of it.

Finn's memories began and ended with the Mud Pit, but every once in a while (usually when she'd first awaken for the day) she'd hear the patter of drops before the sour scent of decay could hit her, and she'd swear she could feel a pang of longing in her chest, the distant recall of something sweet cloying in her nostrils. As though in yearning, her heart would stutter a beat, the phantom sensation of damp grasses caressing her toes as rivulets cascaded down her face.

Strangest of all, if she concentrated hard enough, she could see a man in her mind's eye: lines of worry that seemed to ease with the rain covering his handsome brow. A little girl sat in his lap, giggling as she told him of the shapes the raindrops formed: a whale's tail on his forehead, bird's wings fanning out from each eye.

The longer Finn tried to concentrate on them, the more translucent they became, slipping away and dissolving from her mind like specters in the night.

Today, the specters remained out of sight, her senses overloaded with the barrage of sewage the day's downpour sent flooding down the streets around her.

Finn's boots sank to the laces as she made her way down the mud-covered street. She tugged the hood of her coat tighter over her face as the rain came down in acidic torrents. Taking care not to breathe in the noxious steam that arose from its contact with the thickening grime, she made her way farther into the city.

The entire block ahead was a mass of gray, crumbling stone, each building bleeding into the next. The only break in monotony came from randomly placed graffiti dotted here and there, but even that had started to look uniform, the culprits always using the same palette of browns, grays, and blacks.

Finn would surrender a whole block of gold for just a touch of color in her world. Of course, she'd have to actually get her hands on a block of gold first.

Giant, iridescent holojectors mounted to the sides of every building she passed flashed in time to her steps; their smart displays adjusting to her stride as she forced her heavy boots through the muck. Reliance soldiers usually only turned them on for special announcements or reprimands, but today their digital speakers blasted the Union of the Planets' grating six-note anthem proudly, their displays projecting images of Inner Rings' splendor so bright they were tear inducing.

Today marked the anniversary of the Arcturians' arrival.

The holojector popped out of focus and then back in again, and Finn stuttered a step at the image projected on every screen.

A stunning upper-caste reporter filled each one, her image cast out as far as the eye could see, replicated infinitely, in an infinite array of sizes. Finn kept moving her feet to avoid sinking, but her eyes stayed riveted on the woman's red-sequined gown. The soft material fell in shimmering waves to the ground like a glittering river of fire.

A golden statue of an Arcturian loomed over her lean frame. Aside from its golden hue and bald head, the creation looked inauspiciously human.

Finn had never seen an Arcturian before. Very few, if any, of the people in the Farthers had. Most of the time, they chose to communicate through the diplomats and government officials constantly surrounding them, hiding away in their Inner Rings glass castles and refusing to interact with the masses. For most of the lower castes, the brief glimpses their streets' holojecters allowed of the Inner Rings statues, fountains, and skyscrapers made in monument to the mysterious golden colonizers were the closest they'd ever get to the Arcturians themselves.

According to the stories, Arcturian skin shone like spun gold and their eyes glowed red like the embers of a fire.

The reporter's voice cut through the chill in the air, filling up every empty space with the echo of her saccharine, slightly accented drone.

"Good morning Union citizens. Blessed be the Gods for sending our beloved Arcturian forefathers to our planets. Today marks the beginning of our annual unionization celebrations and the victory of our Reliant ancestors over the Disobedience. Our reliance and trust in our forefathers was rewarded one-hundred and fifty cycles ago when the war was fought and won. On this momentous occasion, we give thanks to the Arcturians for bringing peace to our planets."

"Finn, is that you? Wait up."

Finn cursed the bright auburn locks peeking through her hood and giving away her anonymity as Nova, a young woman in her early twenties and one of dozens of doxies on the Mud Pit, scrambled across the street as fast as her knee-high boots would carry her. When Nova reached her, Finn took in the woman's ragged brown skirt and the tiny shreds of material barely covering her bony chest. Her normally pale skin had started to take on a bluish hue.

"Nova, it's freezing out here. Where's the coat I gave you last week?" Finn reprimanded.

Nova grinned between shivers.

"I traded it for Red Faze." Before Finn could interject, Nova was already cutting her off. "Coats are bad for business. You would understand if you ever got off your high horse and joined ranks."

Finn shot the girl a disbelieving look and laughed.

"That won't happen . . . ever."

Nova didn't take exception to her distaste. Like Finn, she was a member of one of the lowest social castes in the Farthers. Girls in their positions didn't exactly have a lot of options for survival. If Grim hadn't taken Finn under his wing seven cycles ago, she could very well be standing next to Nova each night, trying to lure Reliance soldiers into parting with some of their coin. Though she was not a fan of the doxies' methods, she couldn't say she completely disapproved of their results; the intimate nature of their relationships with the men they serviced made them privy to the kinds of secrets people dropped a lot of gold for.

Finn set off again, and Nova did her best to keep pace, her stringy brown hair hanging in wet hunks around her face.

"Are you going to the Dirty Molly?" she asked with a hopeful expression.

Finn smiled.

"Is it raining?"

It took Nova several moments to understand. When she did, she grinned.

"Can I come with you? Business is always good there during the celebrations, but I don't want to walk alone. The screaming started even earlier than usual this morning."

"Just make sure you don't fall behind, yeah?"

The streets got more than a little wild this time in the cycle. Between the constant barrage of Reliance hoopla, the drunken lower castes' short tempers, and trigger-happy soldiers, Finn couldn't say she blamed the woman. Finn herself had already picked up on the ratcheting levels of turbulence in the city this morning. It made her skin itch and the air practically pulse with the force of it.

Thanks to Grim, the other Mudders tended to give her a wide berth. Working for the most renowned middleman in the Farthers had its perks. He'd taught her well, and she knew how to hold her own. She was the first apprentice he'd ever taken on, and that, coupled with a unique talent for stealing things, had garnered her a healthy reputation.

One she cherished like a dear friend.

"Maybe later you could take me to the black market?" Nova's tentative question broke through Finn's thoughts. She cast a confused look the doxie's way.

"What the hell could you possibly need at the black market?"

The place was a veritable breeding ground for all things illegal, including Reliance weapons and tech otherwise impossible to get a hold of in the Farthers.

Nova shrugged her shoulders casually.

"I hear customers talking. I'm curious."

"Yeah, well get used to curiosity," Finn scoffed. "There's no way I'm taking you there."

As they passed another collapsed concrete monstrosity, several Anunnaki called out in garbled English from beneath the cover of their vendor carts. They were a striking race to be sure, known for their long, jet-black hair and radiant, pearly skin.

Nova, as usual, couldn't help but stare, and Finn tripped her with a boot to get her attention.

"Don't look into their eyes, Nova. You know that's how they get you. One look and they'll have taken everything but your underwear."

No matter what product an Anunnaki peddled, they could make anyone think it worth its weight in gold with their hypnotic multi-hued eyes. She'd seen it happen a million times to first-timers on the Mud Pit: upper-caste Reliance folks who thought it made them seem worldly and roguish to visit a planet in the Farthers. They'd find themselves lost in the swirling reds, greens, and purples until they left an hour later, their arms full of impractical junk they had no use for and their pockets suspiciously empty.

For the most part Finn considered the Anunnaki to be bottom-feeders, but every once in a while she couldn't help but feel a little grudging respect for the gold-grubbers.

They'd found a way to survive just like the rest of them.

"It's not the Anunnaki, Finn. Look," Nova whispered, moving closer in to her side.

Finn followed her gaze and saw a young man with sallow, graying skin and sunken cheeks hunched motionless behind a dilapidated, makeshift stand. His glassy eyes (very much human and not Anunnaki) stared off into the distance, and she briefly wondered what he saw there that had him so transfixed. Then her eyes landed on his wares. Dozens of tiny vials in every shape and color imaginable, most of them marked simply by a little red *F* across their front, littered the top of his stand.

Meteor extract: better known to residents of the Farthers as Faze.

The Inner Rings may have had all the riches, splendor, and technology they could ever want, but the Farthers had one thing they didn't: the Meteor Belt. It surrounded their planets and offered a lucrative business opportunity for the more enterprising Mudders who had discovered a whole host of benefits from mining the meteors' rocks. Depending on the rock origin, potency, and a variety of secret chemical processes, peddlers sold extracts that could tint a person's skin or increase a person's strength. They even sold one called Red Faze that doxies like Nova used as hypnotic perfume when they could afford it.

Then of course there was the most coveted extract of all: Purple Faze.

Highly addictive, its contents granted the buyer an almost instant state of euphoria lasting upwards of twenty-four hours. Most of the upper castes considered Faze in all its various forms taboo, but the lower castes didn't have the same qualms. Taboo was a small price to pay for the reprieve from reality one small vial could offer them. Finn had long ago grown accustomed to the sight of her planet's streets littered with far-off gazes in hollow eyes, the ghost of a smile on cracked lips, and drool dripping from chins.

"Can we stop and look, Finn? Please?"

She met Nova's hungry gaze.

"Not today, Nova. If I didn't know better, I'd swear you were turning into a meteorhead."

Nova's lips puckered in a pout, but she kept her pace.

They passed a cart selling brown wool capes with hoods. The garments were definitely secondhand, as evidenced by the holes near the seams and the tattered edges (not to mention the stains), but the wool looked warm. Finn nodded to the vendor and flicked a gold coin his way, grabbing a cape and putting it around Nova's shoulders as they walked.

"If you trade this one, you'll be walking alone from now on," she warned the doxie.

Nova's lips began to move again, and Finn braced herself for whatever ridiculous thing she was about to say, when the volume on the holojector intensified and she was no longer able to ignore the sound.

"Citizens." The upper-caste reporter appeared onscreen again, crying out to the heavens as the camera zoomed in. *"Blessed be the forefathers. Blessed be our reliance on their wisdom, foresight, and innovation. Let us observe a moment of silence in honor of our Arcturian forefathers."*

At her jubilant command, the surrounding Mudders lost their loose hold on the seething undercurrent of outrage Finn had felt buzzing amidst them since she'd stepped outside that morning.

Several vendors of varying races left their carts unattended as they braved the rain, lifting angry fingers to flick the barcode markings at their necks and spit on the ground at their feet. A few even lobbed their heavier secondhand wares and broken bricks at the nearest holojector, all the while making lewd hand gestures at the reporter's closed eyes and hands clasped in prayer. Finn's own hand moved to rest over the holster at her waist.

The vendors' little show of rebellion didn't go unnoticed, and a handful of Reliance soldiers left their post on the street corner to deliver retribution. The sound of thick, wooden clubs thwacking against bare flesh mingled with pained groans.

It took less than a minute for the soldiers to chase the protesting vendors back to their carts.

Her trigger finger twitched of its own volition when a cloaked Anunnaki looked like she might take a stand. An overzealous soldier sent the female to her knees with a swiftly delivered blow to the head. The surrounding Mudders watched impassively as he kicked her to the ground.

As two of her friends darted forward to drag her out of the street, the soldier yelled to be heard over the rain.

"The next Mudder who disrespects the forefathers won't be walking for a week. Now you'll all bloody well observe a moment of Godsdamned silence."

A hush fell over the crowd at his threat.

Finn's pulse pounded in her ears, but with two carefully drawn breaths she tore her gaze from the scene and moved on. Just like Grim taught her.

There was nothing she could do. Nothing any of them could do.

As it was every cycle, chastened by the violent show, the remaining vendors returned to their posts. The soldiers lined up to resume watching the celebrations, their left hands coming up to rest over the red and gold badges protecting their hearts. One of the younger ones, most likely only a few years older than Finn and Nova, watched the proceedings on screen with such deference, honest to Gods tears sparkled in his red-rimmed eyes. His behavior was laughable but not entirely surprising, considering most of them would trade their firstborn for a planet transfer to the Inner Rings.

The two women made it three more blocks before Nova's steps slowed again. Finn sighed and crooked her neck, following Nova's gaze to a fresh cluster of signs Reliance soldiers had posted in the night. The Mud Pit's resident graffiti artists seemed to be having a wonderful time with their new canvasses. The posters encouraging Mud Pit dwellers to *Report All Half-Breeds* had been relatively mundane before a few Mudders had gotten creative with some red and brown clay. Now, beneath big, blocky letters reading MUTTS, they'd fashioned an image of old-fashioned, rickety gallows and the disfigured outline of a half-breed hanging limply from a rope.

At least Finn thought they meant for it to be a half-breed. It looked more like a shapeless blob than any living thing she'd ever seen.

She happened to think the signs were a waste of time, considering most Mudders couldn't read. They sure liked to talk though, and she supposed they'd learned how to spell *Mutts* well enough. The word had spread throughout the planet like crater-pox.

The Reliance had only recently introduced the term, and it didn't take long for every member of the Union to embrace the slur, upper and lower caste alike.

As it turned out, the Arcturians had finally found something that could bring the masses together: their hatred of half-breeds.

Finn shifted on the balls of her feet to avoid sinking.

"C'mon, Nova, it's just a half-breed sign. If you're going to tag along, I'm putting a ban on pit stops. We'll be hip deep in mud by the time we make it to the Dirty Molly if you have your way."

As if she hadn't heard her, Nova's head cocked to the side, studying the images.

"Have you ever seen one?"

"What, a half-breed? No. No one has for a long time. They're practically extinct."

Thanks to signs like these.

"I have."

It took her a moment, but eventually Finn registered her friend's whispered claim. She couldn't help the surprise that crept into her voice as she asked,

"You have?"

Nova nodded, her doe eyes solemn as she gazed upward.

"A long time ago. I must have been five or six cycles. I was waiting outside while my mother serviced the soldiers in their barracks. I saw a boy limping through the mud toward me. He was young, maybe twelve, and even skinnier than I was. When my mother came out, he hid behind some barrels. He looked so scared. I didn't want to get him into trouble, so I didn't say anything. A few hours later everyone smelled the smoke. They said the boy was a half-breed. They said he was half Solidarian and he could make fire with his hands. He burned the bunker to the ground with everyone inside. Every time I think about it, it gives me the creeps."

Nova shivered, as if to emphasize her words.

Finn remembered the hushed whispers of old men in the Dirty Molly, drunk on moon whiskey and feeling nostalgic as they recounted the story of the half-breed who took down a company of Reliance soldiers in one night with nothing more than his bare hands. The Reliance painted him as a monster, a mixture of the genetic and the mystical: a monstrosity in the eyes of the Gods.

They somehow forgot to mention the fact that the soldiers the boy killed had only days before massacred his entire family.

"Was it true?" Finn asked, curiosity getting the better of her. "Did you see him start the fire?"

"No. But the executioner hanged him with steel boxes around his hands. Why would they do that if it wasn't true?" A good question; one Finn had no answer for. "They say all the half-breeds have dangerous abilities like that boy. They're a punishment from the Gods for the Disobedience waging war on the Reliance. They could destroy us all if we aren't careful," Nova informed her sagely.

Finn had a hard time imagining anything destroying the Reliance, let alone more half-breeds like that frightened little boy avenging his family.

"If their biggest sin is ridding the galaxy of a few platoons of soldiers, I can't say I'm too torn up about the 'half-breed plague.'" Finn scoffed, but as she met Nova's indignant stare, it quickly became a sigh. "You shouldn't believe everything you hear, Nova. Besides, there are only five, maybe six, alien races out of *thousands* that are even capable of breeding with humans. It's basic biology they would inherit some of the things that make them different from us and then some. Different doesn't mean dangerous."

At least, that's what Grim liked to say. Not that Nova understood biology any more than she understood anything else, which wasn't much. Finn wasn't all that keen on biology herself, but she did understand the basics, and she was a lot more prone to believe Grim's explanation of the science behind half-breeds than she was to buy into the Reliance's explanation of Gods and mysticism.

"It's wrong," Nova countered, "aliens and humans breeding. It's an abomination."

A direct quote from Reliance propaganda no doubt, considering *abomination* was not a word often tossed out in casual conversation on the Mud Pit.

In all their grand wisdom and foresight as they began to unionize the planets, the Arcturian forefathers never thought to account for cross-species breeding. It was rare, but it happened, and they'd been trying to remedy the oversight ever since.

Obviously dissatisfied with her silence, Nova continued.

"Well, I'm glad they're all dead. If I ever see one again, you can bet all your gold I'll be reporting him to the first Reliance soldier I can find. If I don't kill him myself, that is."

Finn turned her back on the bold proclamation and started walking. Nova wouldn't know how to kill a half-dead, three-legged dog if it limped right up to her, handed her a loaded gun, and rolled over.

After all, the woman prioritized Faze over a coat on a planet known for its acidic rain. Granted, Nova's Mudder parentage made her thick skin less likely to be affected by the chemicals constantly pouring down on the Mud Pit, but still.

The fact that she was foolish enough to buy into the Reliance garbage about half-breeds amused and irritated Finn in equal measure.

"Maybe the half-breeds just got better at hiding, Nova. Did you ever consider that?"

The conversation died on Nova's surprised, fearful squeak.

In the distance, the Dirty Molly's fluorescent green lights burned bright like a beacon; one of the only taverns on the Mud Pit where the criminal underbelly could conduct their business free from prying eyes. Reliance soldiers made a point to steer clear of it. Finn figured it was their way of fooling themselves into believing *they* controlled the Farthers.

They would never admit the truth of who really ran things here.

A chorus of yells and laughter coming from inside the tavern called to her, and they quickened their pace. Finn pushed her way through the wooden slatted doors, Nova hot on her heels, and the familiar scents of smoke, ale, and sweat immediately enveloped them. Most people wouldn't understand the comfort such smells brought Finn, but the Dirty Molly and all her unique scents and sounds became home the day she'd stumbled through the tavern's doors seven cycles ago, a filthy, half-crazed child on the brink of starvation who couldn't even remember her own name.

Grim showed her kindness that day, despite her feral attempts to sever his fingers from his hand with her teeth. He gave her a decent shot at survival: quite a magnanimous gesture considering what a huge undertaking caring for a borderline savage child had been for him. She certainly hadn't made it easy.

Several throats cleared and eyes shifted nervously when they caught sight of her. Finn grinned, waving to her onlookers.

"Thanks, Finn," Nova mumbled, tossing her new cape on the sticky, crud-covered floor of the bar before making her way to a table surrounded on all sides by freshly sodden Mudders. Finn sighed and gave her a half-hearted two-finger salute, weaving her way through the crowded tables.

"Finn No Last Name. Have a seat and a drink on me, my girl."

Doc, the Dirty Molly's co-owner and resident bartender, waved her over with a webbed hand and a toothless grin. Finn's lips quirked up in a smile at the use of the odd nickname she couldn't decide if she loved or hated.

Grim had taken the time to help her choose a name in their first few months together, growing tired of always calling her "*girl.*" It would seem, however, that he ran out of steam at first names and never got around to a last.

She slid into an empty stool in front of him just in time to catch the flaming red concoction he slid in her direction. Blowing out the flame, she arched a brow at the steam wafting up from the glass in front of her.

"Another one of your experiments, Doc?"

His yellow eyes lit up with excitement behind the spectacles he wore more for appearances than out of necessity.

"I call it 'Dragon's Breath.' A special drink for a special day. Go ahead and try it. I used real sunspot juice this time. None of that synthetic garbage for my girl."

He watched her with barely leashed anticipation, his scaled hands rubbing together in glee, and Finn smiled despite herself. She'd never been much for drinking, not that Grim would ever allow it. He claimed the dulling of one's senses to be the downfall of every great warrior, but Finn suspected a different motive. Though Grim was a man with few scruples when it came to Reliance law, he seemed to have several when it came to his underage ward.

Fortunately for them all, she was no longer underage.

Finn brought the glass to her lips and tilted her head back, letting the contents slip down her throat. True to its name, the sun-spot juice burned all the way down before settling into the pit of her stomach.

Despite her best efforts, Finn choked and looked up at him. "Delicious, Old Man."

He expelled a whoop of amusement and offered her a cheeky wink. Leaning in closer, he spoke softly so only she could hear.

"Happy Birthday, Finn."

He was gone before she could respond, moving down the bar to answer drink orders. She swiped the back of her hand over her mouth and grinned. The old man was a loon. None of them actually knew when her real birthday was, but exactly one cycle after the day she'd stumbled into their lives, Grim and Doc surprised her with a birthday party. Every cycle since, they'd been celebrating. She supposed life really did begin for her the day she found them, so she could never bring herself to fight the fuss overly much.

When he returned to her again, his yellow eyes glittered with mischief.

"Have you been watching the unionization ceremonies?"

"They're a bit hard to avoid these days." She glanced meaningfully at the holojectors mounted throughout the bar. "You?"

He smiled, pushing his spectacles up the bridge of his nose.

"About the same I'm afraid. Listening to all that Arcturian praise leaves a foul taste in my mouth, but I can't say it's bad for business. Puts everyone around here in the mood to get royally sozzled."

She choked back a laugh at that.

"Just once I wish we could get through a cycle without having to hear about how wonderful the Arcturians are." Finn complained. "If they're so wonderful, how come none of us have ever seen one?"

A few feet down the bar, a male who sounded like he was well on his way to sozzled sloshed a fair amount of foam over his pint as he locked eyes on Doc and piped up with enthusiasm. "I'll drink to that. They invade *our* planets sayin' they've been sent by the Gods, start a war with anyone foolish enough to argue, then we get shipped off to the filthy Farthers, and we're supposed to be *grateful* while they disappear in the lap of luxury? I say, screw the Reliance and screw the Arcturian forefathers."

At his yell, the rest of the bar chimed in loudly, raising their glasses and downing the contents. His version of events would earn him a whipping if the wrong person heard it, but Finn couldn't fault the man for his general attitude. Every cycle for the last century, Mudders and lower-castes alike were forced to pretend they enjoyed life in squalor.

At least here in the Dirty Molly they didn't have to pretend to enjoy it.

One of the aliens seated across from the bar, a Goslan with transparent skin and white eyes, stood on one of the tables, his skinny body swaying on his three-toed feet. Finding his bearings, he lifted a mug high into the air and drank heavily.

Once finished with that task, he turned his back to one of the many muted holojectors and dropped his pants, mooning the reporter still featured onscreen.

The entire tavern lit up with groans and catcalls. Finn looked away so fast she almost pulled a muscle. (Goslans were known for the abundant tentacles on their backsides, and she had no desire to feel Doc's sunspot juice coming back up her throat.)

Not quite finished, his high-pitched voice rang throughout the tavern.

"My ancestors fought alongside the Disobedience against the Reliance."

Several patrons grunted in approval.

"They understood the Arcturians were not harbingers of goodwill and prosperity. They understood unionization really meant tyranny. They foresaw this twisted caste system."

He hiccupped, and his entire body jolted before righting itself. When he continued, one long, translucent finger pointed to the red *X* tattooed beneath his eye.

"They put me in the criminal caste. I've never broken a law in my entire life. Upstanding citizen I am—"

A burly man next to him, obviously bored with his long-winded rant, tagged the back of the Goslan's shirt with a large mitt and pulled him back down into his seat.

Another round of cheers broke the newfound silence.

It was safe to say, lengthy speeches didn't sit well with the patrons of the Dirty Molly.

It didn't exactly help the Goslan's case that everyone knew him for his sleight of hand and skills as a gifted pickpocket. Not, as he'd called himself, an "upstanding citizen."

Doc shook his head at the display.

"I'll tell you one thing, my girl. It may pay the bills, but I'll be thanking the Gods when these celebrations are over."

His husky chuckle followed him down the bar as another thick-tongued patron called out for a refill. Finn moved to stand, hoping to track down Grim, but a voice in her ear stopped her before she could.

"You sure are a pretty little thing. What are you doing over here all by yourself?"

Finn turned to face the speaker, but the stench of liquor and various other body odors stopped her in her tracks. Unfortunately, as was the case with most Mudders, this man didn't see the importance in bathing, and his dark hair hung in an oily mess around his face.

Like the Goslan, a simple red *X* tattooed under his left eye marked him as a member of the criminal caste. According to the class system the Arcturians designed a century ago, both men sat a notch above Finn.

Clocking the knife sheathed at his hip, she stood, pushing her stool back and doing her best not to breathe through her nose.

"I guess that's what I get for using soap," she told him cheerfully. "Have you heard of it?"

The stinky man didn't appreciate her reply and moved to block her path, a sneer on his crusty face.

"What did you say?"

Finn smiled and eyeballed his body where it blocked her exit. Another man, one she recognized as a regular patron, called over from his table a few feet away.

"Go easy on him, Finn. He's new, he doesn't know the rules."

"You shut your mouth, Lucas," the mass of stench and oil spat at his friend. He turned his sneer on her again, his eyes slightly glossy from one too many of Doc's spirits. "Now that's no way to be, pretty. I just want to talk to you and maybe touch that hair of yours. I never seen anything quite like it. I bet men pay their weight in gold to run their fingers through hair like that."

He grinned and reached out a grimy hand to catch a few strands.

"Hey Lucas," Finn called, her eyes never leaving the man's hand as it inched closer, "did he just call me a doxie?"

Lucas's shoulders slumped on a sigh.

"Ah, c'mon, Finn."

The grimy hand near her head stalled just as Nova's head popped up amidst a crowd of splotchy-faced men.

"He did, Finn. I heard him."

"Thanks, Nova," Finn called. Her eyes returned to the man's, which now held a mixture of confusion and anger.

"It was a compliment," he mumbled through a thick tongue.

She'd grown accustomed to the attention her wild auburn waves garnered. She took care of herself and kept her hair and body clean, which meant the fiery locks adorning her head always had an extra spring to them, bouncing and falling in casual disarray around her shoulders. The skin on her face and body were also miraculously clear, free of the craterlike scars that dotted most Mudders' complexions, one positive to her arrival on the Mud Pit being that it took place after the crater-pox epidemic swept its way through the planet.

Most of the time, her reputation and Grim's protection were enough to keep drunks like this one from getting too close, but every once in a while someone would come along who hadn't heard of *Finn No Last Name*.

Finn's smile remained in place, her tone friendly.

"I'll make you a deal," she told the man. "Best me in a fight, and you can have a lock of my hair if you like it so much. I'll cut it off for you with my own knife."

The entire bar went silent, but the smelly man before her missed the electric shift in the air, his eyes shining with unveiled glee. Without bothering to respond, he closed the short distance between them with a drunken lurch.

With her hands gripping the bar behind her for leverage, Finn got her feet up in plenty of time, planting her muddy boots in the center of his chest and using her body weight to propel him backward. With the help of a few too many pints, and gravity doing the rest, her opponent flew to the ground.

He glanced around in shock before his glazed eyes met hers, fury reddening what little of his face she could see.

"You filthy doxie. I'll teach you a lesson."

The irony of him calling *her* filthy was not lost on Finn, nor was it lost on the rest of the bar if their groans of distaste were any indication. He got up from the ground and came for her again, this time using his hands to reach for her neck.

Finn easily dodged to the side and grabbed his left arm, twisting it behind his back as she slammed his face down on the bar. While he struggled in her hold, she casually twisted his arm up and back.

"Do you yield?" Finn asked him loudly to be heard over his grunts of pain.

"I'm going to kill you."

In his rage, spittle had begun to form at the corners of his mouth. Finn leaned in closer, flashing him a grin.

"Yielding would be a lot less painful," she advised.

She twisted an inch higher on his arm until she heard the *pop* of his shoulder dislocating, then released him. He fell to the floor with a scream.

"You broke my arm!"

"Relax, it's only out of the socket," she informed him. "Doc can put it back if you've covered your tab." Finn barely had a chance to turn around before the tavern once again fell into a loaded silence. She glanced sideways to see her opponent had pulled a long, serrated knife from his belt. He circled her and she moved with him, catching the worried look in Doc's eyes as she did. Seeing such a look on his sweet, scaled face, Finn decided to end things quickly, before they got out of hand.

However, she didn't get a chance to do much of anything. A bulky red arm shot out from behind her, grasping her attacker around his neck. The man's bloodshot eyes bulged in terror, his knife clattering to the floor.

Slowly, Finn turned to face the interruption.

"I appreciate the choke hold, but I had it covered, Grim."

Her words didn't seem to register with him, his furious bloodred gaze focused intently on the man squirming in his grip. He stood at seven-and-a-half feet tall and weighed over four-hundred and fifty pounds of solid muscle. With his leathery, dark-red skin and the glossy black horns curling back behind his ears, Grim surely looked like something straight out of a nightmare to the poor Mudder. That's what Finn thought when she'd first laid eyes on the behemoth. Fortunately for Finn, she'd been wrong. Unfortunately for the dangling man who looked an awful lot like a rag doll in Grim's tight hold, his nightmare was just beginning.

Khaleerians were known for their brute strength and short tempers, and Grim was no exception to his race. With a flick of his wrist, he sent the man flying across the tavern, upending a table near the doors.

"Get him out of my bar. If he dares come back here again, I will kill him myself."

A few patrons rushed to the fallen man's side and dragged his prone body out the door. Grim grunted, apparently satisfied as he scanned the room. When his eyes finally met Finn's, they softened a bit, returning to their natural black color.

"Come with me."

Nodding, she followed him past a few crowded tables and down a long corridor. When they reached his office in the back, he held the door open for her and she rolled her eyes, doing her best to mimic his gravelly voice.

"The smart ones will learn to avoid you. The others will have to be taught." Letting her speech return to its normal cadence she said, "How do you expect me to teach them if you keep butting in? If they start thinking I can't handle myself because of this, you'll only have yourself to blame."

The remaining tension left Grim's big body and he let out a low rumble of laughter.

"I pity the one who makes the mistake of thinking you cannot handle yourself, *Dhala.*"

My child. At his use of the Khaleerian endearment, Finn's smile softened.

"Besides," he growled, "the man dared to pull a knife on you in my presence after he'd been given the opportunity to yield. In *my* establishment. For that alone I should have killed him."

She couldn't fault him for his reasoning. Khaleerians possessed a strong code of honor, to be abided by at all costs.

Grim sat down behind his desk and motioned regally for her to take the seat across from him. She fought the laughter bubbling up at his high-handedness. Grim may have belonged to one of the lowest social castes in the Union, but one would have never known it by the way he carried himself.

Once seated, she studied him for a moment. She'd never been able to get him to reveal his true age (no matter how many of Doc's wicked brews she plied him with). Although Doc did let it slip once that Grim fought alongside the Disobedience in the war against the Arcturians, a war that took place more than a century before Finn's birth. However Doc also noted that Khaleerians aged slower than humans, which meant Grim was still a long way off from being considered an *elderly* citizen.

Finn stretched back in her seat and propped her boots on the edge of his desk, balancing on the back legs of her chair. He gave said boots a pointed look, but she ignored it. His black eyes grew serious as they studied her for a long moment. "You look tired."

"You always say that." Finn punctuated her statement with an eye roll, turning Grim's look of concern into exasperation.

"That is because it is always true. Why do you insist on living in that parasite-infested apartment? With the money you squirrel away, you should be living in comfort, not frozen on some stained mattress every night."

"You worry too much. It's giving you wrinkles. Besides, my mattress is spotless, thank you very much."

Finn hoped levity would shift the mood, but Grim's brow remained furrowed with concern. He was right. She had plenty of money saved up, more than any other young woman her age could ever hope to make. There was no reason for her to live on such meager means, but Finn liked her scrubby apartment. As much as she liked any place on the Mud Pit (with the exception of the Dirty Molly). Every time she thought about cashing in her gold and settling down someplace better, a little voice in her head whispered, *No.* Instead, she hid her earnings away like pack rats hid crumbs on the Mud Pit, saving it. For what, she didn't know. She only knew it was a compulsion she was at a loss to fight.

Finn's eyes shifted to the far corner of the office, where a new stack of peeling, leather-bound books was sealed within a glass case. The Reliance kept a tight lid on all literature, and those old books definitely looked black market.

Their presence wasn't surprising; half of Grim's office was filled to bursting with enough contraband to make an Arcturian swoon. He followed her gaze and his visage softened. Grim might have been a brute with a colossal body bred for war, but the man loved to read. A love he made a point to share with Finn, pouring over new books with her whenever they came in.

At first, she'd been content to look at pictures, nestling down in the corner of his office and listening for hours as he read to her. After a few months, though, her passive participation hadn't been enough for him, and he'd insisted on teaching her to read.

They'd painted quite the picture; the giant horned alien and his street rat, hunched over books for hours on end each day.

She eyed the new stack greedily.

"Those are new."

His dark eyes lit up with pleasure, and he stood, crossed to the case, opened it, and pulled out a small, forest-green book. He returned to his chair and slid the book with care to her across the desk.

"Happy birthday, *Dhala*."

A lump lodged itself in her throat, and Finn tried to force it back down as she ran trembling hands over the cracked leather. She traced the embossed title with her finger: *The Adventures of Huckleberry Finn*. Carefully, like Grim had shown her, she opened the book and leafed through the brittle, yellowed pages.

"You're giving it to me?"

She barely managed to choke out a whisper past the rapidly growing lump, but Grim heard her.

"You're twenty-one now. It's long past time you started your own collection."

She gaped at him. All the while, her hands clutched the book as though it might float away if she let go.

"Do you remember the first time we read it together?" he asked her, the ghost of a smile tugging at the corner of his full lips.

Of course she did. Finn remembered with all too vivid clarity how difficult those first few weeks on the Mud Pit had been. She'd been like a rabid dog, biting and scratching at anyone who got too close.

"You read it to me to calm me down," she whispered.

In the first few weeks she spent with him, she would curl up on a bed of blankets in the corner of the office, eyeing him like a caged animal as he sat at his desk and read.

Though she never spoke, it was obvious she had a particular fondness for the vagabond, Huck Finn, and his wild antics, offering her first smile by page twenty-two and becoming visibly distressed when Grim stopped reading for the day.

When the time came to select a name for herself, neither Grim nor Doc had been surprised by her choice.

"I don't know what to say, Grim."

He smiled and placed his hand near hers, close but not touching.

"That book is the only reason I still have all ten fingers."

She grinned sheepishly.

"Thank you, Grim."

He pulled his hand away and leaned back in his chair.

"But that is not the only reason I called you here. I have a job for you."

"Another one?"

"I always have jobs for you." He smirked, looping his thumbs through the straps of his black singlet. "You are in high demand, my talented little thief. But this job is of a more personal nature."

Finn sat up straighter in her chair.

"There is a courtesan on-planet entertaining Reliance officers. She has been seen wearing a gold locket with a true Khaleerian gemstone in the center of it. The necklace is of sentimental value to me. I had long since thought it lost. You are the only one I would entrust with the task of recovering it."

Finn's chest filled with pride. If this necklace was important to Grim, she'd have it back to him by nightfall.

She let a smile of anticipation spread across her face.

"Just tell me where to find this courtesan."

TWO

P er Grim's instructions, Finn made her way to the north sector of the city: the pile of dirt Reliance soldiers called home. Usually, the majority of soldiers stationed in the Farthers were new and untested rookies led by superiors who found themselves in the Farthers as the result of a disciplinary action. It made the courtesan's presence on-planet all the more surprising.

Courtesans were among the highest castes in the Union. The Reliance recruited them at a young age for their beauty and grace. The young men and women then underwent cycles of intensive training to learn how to best service the rich and powerful. They very rarely, if ever, took the time to journey out to the Farthers.

With her hood up and scarf covering the lower half of her face, Finn scanned the tents and billows of smoke dotting the garrison.

A line of children, alien and human alike, cowered together in the downpour next to the military outpost. A group of Reliance soldiers stood before them, calling each of them up one by one. One of the soldiers emerged from a tent carrying a gunmetal gray cube. It looked heavy, but still small enough for the one man to carry. Setting it on a rough-hewn table, he opened a panel and pressed a few buttons. The children jumped back in fear as the sides of the box fell away, revealing two shiny metal rings; some of them had never seen the Arcturian device used to permanently laser all Union members with the mark symbolizing their new caste. The device looked shockingly out of place in the otherwise squalid surroundings.

What would a unionization celebration be without a marking ceremony? Finn thought sarcastically.

As was the way since the war, when a member of the Union reached puberty, a ceremony took place to mark them with a tattoo design specific to their caste. For the lower castes it meant barcodes for vendors, *X*s for criminals and cast-offs, ornate collars for servants, a sun for Agrarians, and bands around the wrists for slaves. It served as a permanent reminder of their designated station and a painful method of forever sealing their fate. Most ended up with a tattoo identical to that of their parents, just as their parents belonged to the same caste as their ancestors before them.

They waited until puberty so the boys who showed potential as soldiers could be moved up, and girls who showed the beginnings of blossoming beauty could be placed into a more befitting caste or married off if need be.

A young boy at the front of the line stepped forward, drawing Finn's attention. The rags draping his body hung loose and limp around him. He didn't look a day over ten, but she knew he must be at least thirteen. Malnourishment played tricks on the mind when it came to age. One of the soldiers grabbed the boy roughly by the wrists and locked his forearms into the two chrome rings sitting on the table before him. Once the boy's arms were in place, the machine's halo of lights began to blink rapidly. Tension rippled through Finn's body at the sight. It seemed to catch on before her mind did.

The soldier's finger flicked the switch on the device, a low whine sounding as it started up. The boy's eyes squeezed shut in agony as the lasers' white-hot beams began marking his wrists all the way around with slave bands.

The pounding of the rain drowned out the sound of his screams.

Finn caught herself panting, frozen for a full minute, before she finally regained control. Rubbing the cuffs around her wrists, she shook her head forcefully. After a moment, her heartbeat slowed, and she turned away from the spectacle, continuing her search for the courtesan's travel pod.

Her feet squished through the mud, and she lost herself in the monotony of her steps. Before long, she caught sight of a pink-patterned parasol in her periphery. Finn turned to watch the back of a courtesan's hips sway in slow hypnotic movements as she made her way to the entrance of a sleek travel pod. Even in solitude, with no audience to take her measure, her body still performed as if for a crowd.

Crossing a path to the spherical pod entrance, Finn managed to make it to the alloy overhang without attracting the notice of any soldiers. Luck was on her side, and the marking ceremony on the opposite end of the courtyard seemed to be keeping them well occupied.

The pod itself was surprisingly large for a travel vessel, with a circumference of about twenty meters. Finn supposed the courtesan could comfortably entertain at least five officers at once. She clocked a newly renovated docking ramp, high-grade boosters, and a vacuum-sealed compartment near the ramp containing a pair of muddy high-heels.

Following the trail of pink, she climbed the incline of the short boarding ramp and reached the smooth metallic door, surprised and pleased to find the courtesan had left it open behind her. She took another cautious look around for any stray soldiers. There were none in sight. All she had to do now was sneak into the pod, steal the necklace out from under the courtesan's nose, and manage to do it all without the woman alerting any of the soldiers nearby that a thief was in their midst.

She almost grinned at the impending challenge but caught herself.

Finn slipped through the door, barely taking a moment to adjust to her surroundings before backing into the darkest corner of the pod. As expected, her entrance went unnoticed. The courtesan remained seated gracefully before the pod's controls, her slender shoulders ramrod straight as her fingers worked rapidly.

Her elegant up-do revealed a bare neck. *No necklace.* With a slow, practiced eye, Finn took in the interior of the pod for the first time.

It was nice, there was no question. Definitely nicer than anything Finn had ever known, but it seemed much too simple for a snooty courtesan and the elaborate tastes of her Reliance clientele.

Maybe she reserved fancier décor and setting for Inner Rings planets? Granted, she'd made it her own by adding crystal chandeliers and a giant four-poster bed with red silk sheets. Candles burned on a stylish chestnut bureau, and red and orange cloth draped the walls, giving the room a warm glow.

Finn's eyes landed on a chest of drawers next to the bureau, and the ornate, golden jewelry box that sat atop it. Sucking in a breath and plastering herself against the wall, she slowly sidestepped her way past the four-poster bed and over to the chest of drawers, all the while watching the courtesan for any sign that Finn's presence had been made.

When only a few inches separated her and the box, Finn reached out to tip the lid back and reveal its contents, hoping just a little to find Grim's necklace sitting at the bottom. Maybe then there would be something at least slightly challenging about this job.

"I'm sorry, I am no longer entertaining. Perhaps if you had knocked, I'd have been more inclined to extend my hours."

Finn's muscles locked, and her breath caught in her lungs. Slowly, she turned and found the courtesan still sitting with her back to Finn at the pod's controls. She couldn't help but be a little impressed at the woman's skills, not to mention the apparent nonchalance with which she had confronted an intruder who, for all she knew, might mean her bodily harm.

"What gave me away?" she asked, curiosity getting the better of her.

At her question, the courtesan finally turned from her controls and stood. Finn was wholly unprepared for the sight that greeted her. A knee-length amethyst gown hugged the woman's generous hourglass figure, further enhancing her already regal appearance. Glittering crystals embellished the off-the-shoulder sleeves where they rested on her suns-kissed skin. A jeweled comb secured thick chunks of her fiery red waves into graceful piles on top of her head. She was absolutely beautiful, breathtaking even.

A set of indigo eyes, almost the same shade as Finn's, watched her with an unreadable expression.

"The mud here has a . . . unique scent. You brought it in with you." Her gaze flicked meaningfully at Finn's boots.

Finn bit back a laugh. *She* of course knew that, but she hadn't bet on the courtesan's keen senses. Remembering the compartment for muddy shoes, she kicked herself for her overconfidence.

"Well, since we're here, I believe you have something that belongs to a friend of mine," Finn said. "He'd like it back."

At this casual mention of her reason for breaking into the courtesan's pod, those indigo eyes narrowed.

"And your friend wasn't brave enough to reclaim his possession himself?"

At the implied insult to Grim's character, Finn stiffened, the heat from the candles, combined with all her layers, making her break out into a sweat.

Suddenly the ground shifted beneath them. The walls of the pod shuddered, and Finn's legs wobbled beneath her from the force of their ascent into the morning air. She could tell from the panel's flashing light that the inertial dampener was working at full capacity. All at once, she realized what the courtesan had been doing at her pod's controls. She'd been entering coordinates. The pod was leaving the Mud Pit. Heart pounding, Finn pulled the scarf from her face and tore the hood free from her head; the cloying scent of the courtesan's candles combined with the heat of the pod making her light-headed. She pulled her pulse gun from its holster; she'd wanted a challenge, but this was more than she'd bargained for.

"I'm going to need you to turn this pod around."

The courtesan stopped breathing, her lovely countenance paling as her plump scarlet lips formed a small O of surprise. When her breath finally returned to her, her chest rose and fell with panicked breaths. The action drew Finn's gaze to the blue crescent moon tattooed on the inside of her left breast: the mark of a courtesan.

"Kyra?"

It took Finn a moment to realize the woman was actually speaking to her.

Kyra?

Had the sight of a weapon truly addled her brain? Finn kept the gun in her hand but brought her other free hand up in a placating gesture.

"Look, lady, I don't want to hurt you, I just need you to turn this thing around."

It was as if she hadn't spoken. Moisture began to gather behind the courtesan's eyes.

"Kyra? Is it really you?"

Finn didn't have time to respond. The floor beneath them shook again, causing the pod to tremble as the docking ramp connected with what must be a nearby orbiting ship.

Time was running out.

Taking deliberate strides, Finn moved to her, pushing the barrel of the gun into her side.

"Please," Finn pleaded, "turn this thing around."

The courtesan let out a small cry at the feel of the cold barrel, her expression shifting from hopeful shock to horror.

"What has happened to you, Kyra?"

She seemed genuinely confused, which only further fueled Finn's panic.

"Stop calling me that. My name is Finn."

The whooshing sound of the travel pod's automatic door where it now connected to a foreign craft spared the courtesan from having to formulate an answer.

"Welcome back, Iliana, I wanted to—"

The large man stopped mid-stride when he took in the scene before him. His mouth set in a grim line and his green eyes went cold as he regarded Finn and the gun she currently pressed into the courtesan's side. He loomed over her at six feet, his starched button-up shirt and fitted pants perfectly highlighting the lean muscles of his body. Everything about him screamed upper caste, from the clean cut of his clothes to the handsome cut of his jaw.

She'd really gone and done it this time. If this was a Reliance ship, Finn could find herself in a whole mess of trouble she'd had no intention of inviting. Her mind wandered to Grim and Doc. Would she ever see them again, or had she just guaranteed herself a life of imprisonment?

Shock replaced some of her fear when the man's expression morphed from cold anger to amusement. He arched a sardonic brow at Iliana.

"I was going to ask you if you were successful on Altara, but I suppose this answers my question." His gaze moved to Finn's revolver. "The only people allowed to carry weapons on my ship are me and mine. How about you hand over that gun and anything else you've got on you?"

His ship?

Well, it appeared as though Finn had just met the captain. He didn't bear the red-and-gold badge of a Reliance officer. Maybe she'd gotten lucky and this wasn't a Reliance ship.

Her lips lifted a fraction as she holstered the gun.

"If it's all the same to you, I think I'll keep my weapons. I just need a ride home, and then I'll be out of your hair."

Iliana, as he'd called her, looked up, her face suspiciously wet. Her beseeching eyes locked on Finn's. She seemed to forget the captain's presence in the room.

"Please, Kyra. I thought you were dead."

She wept openly now, hot tears flowing freely down her painfully beautiful face. Finn didn't know much about courtesans, but she did know that crying was forbidden in their ranks. The punishment for one who dared to express such an undesirable emotion usually involved a whip.

"Iliana, you want to tell me what the hell is going on here?"

The captain stepped forward, determination and concern furrowing his handsome brow. He'd probably never seen such a show of emotion from the stoic courtesan before.

"Shane, she's my sister."

At her proclamation, Finn let out a bark of humorless laughter.

"The hell I am, lady." She turned to the captain, voice lowered to a mock whisper. "Obviously there's something wrong with your courtesan . . . mentally speaking. Why don't you take me back to the Mud Pit so you can take care of *that*?" She nodded in the direction of said courtesan and waited for the captain to acquiesce.

Instead, he met Iliana's tearful but determined gaze.

"Are you sure she's your sister? Other than the eyes, she's nothing like you."

"Thank you," Finn said, grateful to hear someone finally say something sensible.

Her response seemed to shake something loose in the woman, and Iliana straightened her shoulders, the remorse and sadness erasing itself from her face as though someone had snapped their fingers and commanded it to do so. With quiet resolve she moved closer to Finn.

"You are my sister. I would not mistake my own flesh and blood. You are a part of me, Little One."

With her pronouncement hanging in the air between them, Iliana shot out a slender hand with lightning speed and caressed Finn's face. Finn recoiled from her touch, feeling only the barest whisper of her fingertips trailing a path down her cheek. The unwelcome contact, combined with that name she'd used, "*Little One,*" sent Finn's mind careening.

"Let's play space pirates, Li-Li."

The sun is warm on the girls' faces as they lay side by side on their stomachs under their favorite tree. Father is tilling the fields and the youngest is feeling restless. She knows Iliana likes to play space pirates, even though she claims to hate it.

Iliana groans and rolls over.

"Only if I can be the princess this time. I'm tired of always having to be an ugly space pirate."

The child giggles because Iliana could never, ever be ugly.

She marvels at how peaceful her big sister is doing nothing. She lies there, staring up at the clouds dotting the sky, lost in thought. If only she could be more like her big sister. Instead, the little girl is constantly fidgeting and tapping her toes. Father is always begging her to sit still, but she just can't. There's too much to do. Father would like to teach her to grow things. Iliana has already learned to work the fields. She has a way with the land, just like Father. For now, the child prefers running and chasing the animals, but maybe someday she will bring crops to life too.

"Maybe if you asked him, Father would let us go into town and ask some of the other kids to play. Then you could always be the princess."

The little girl's voice is hopeful, but she already knows what the answer will be. Father never lets them go into town.

"You know he won't let us do that. Besides, it isn't that bad. At least we have each other."

Iliana smiles, but her eyes are sad. She and her little sister are best friends, but they both wonder what it would be like to leave the farm, to make friends outside of one another. Iliana pulls her sister in for a hug, and they stay that way for a while, not feeling quite as restless as before.

"Love you, Li-Li," the little girl sighs.

"Love you too, Kyra."

Finn snapped into awareness, the room and its inhabitants coming back into focus. She found Iliana watching her cautiously, her face just as beautiful but years older than it had been in her mind only moments ago.

"What did you do to me?" Finn demanded, breathless.

"What do you mean? What happened?" She moved to come closer, but Finn's quick draw of her revolver punctuated by the cock of its hammer stopped her cold.

The specters of Finn's past had always been close but intangible, hanging on the fringes of her mind as though waiting for a chance to spring. When the courtesan touched her it was as though something shook loose. The vision of the two girls sprawled beneath the sun felt real, as though it really had happened to her once upon a time. But that was impossible. Finn didn't have a family, and she most certainly didn't have a sister from one of the highest social castes in the Union.

Being in orbit was messing with Finn's mind. She needed to get back home, back to Grim.

As they watched her and the gun trained on them with twin looks of strained vigilance, Finn backed up until she hit the pod's automatic doors.

For as long as she could remember, she'd always had a way with ships, buildings, terrain . . . anything that could be mapped; her mind seemed to function differently than most.

As Grim affectionately pointed out, *"While your memory for things of the past is atrocious,* Dhala, *it would seem that when it comes to memorizing maps you are somewhat of a prodigy."*

With one touch, Finn's brain became like a vacuum, sucking up the information and storing it away in separate compartments to be pulled out for later use. She never forgot a single layout. Finn could navigate any maze, building, or ship with the inventory of information stored inside.

Thanks to Grim's coaching, the seemingly useless quirk became one the many talents that meant her survival over the past cycles, and the reason she made for such a talented thief.

Running her free hand up the door, Finn stopped when her fingers grazed a raised serial number.

DGWD-88

The ship was an Ulta Dogwood, 88 class? It couldn't be Reliance issue; the 88 model cargo ships hadn't flown in a Reliance fleet in well over two decades. Absently, she wondered just what kind of crew she'd gotten herself mixed up with.

Quickly, Finn let her eyes slide shut as the Dogwood's layout filled her mind. Once she went out the automatic door, there would be an emergency travel pod down the hallway to the right. It should have more than enough fuel to get her back to the Mud Pit.

She glanced back at the captain and the mysterious courtesan one more time, her mind already focusing on the way to the travel pod. On a two-finger salute, Finn turned and bolted for the door. She slammed her hand on the blue button next to it and felt a gust of air as it *whooshed* open. She heard Iliana's gut-wrenching shout behind her, but didn't slow down. Without hesitation, Finn headed for the hallway to the right, sprinting for the emergency pod she knew would be at the end. It took her mere seconds to reach, but those brief moments felt like hours.

The door came into sight, and Finn's heart flared in hope. Before she even got the chance to slam her hand on the button to allow entry, two large mitts came down on her shoulders from behind.

Panic seized Finn with a will of its own. Lights flashed behind her eyes and, for a moment, she forgot where she was. Only two things registered in her mind: choking fear and the pounding of her pulse as it tried to leap from her veins.

Finn's elbow shot out behind her and connected with her attacker's hard stomach. She heard his grunt of surprise, but his hold only loosened minimally. It allowed her enough room to turn and face him, the heel of her gloved hand coming up to connect with his nose. His own hand caught her forearm in a bruising grip before she could inflict any real damage, forcing her to drop the gun she still clutched. Finn's mind cried out in alarm as she continued to fight, kicking her leg out to connect with his knee.

He let out a low growl, but continued to stand. Finn couldn't remember the last time she'd fought someone so strong. He snagged her other forearm and backed her against the wall, holding both arms above her head.

"Stop fighting me, woman. I'm not going to hurt you."

His gruffly spoken words brought Finn back to the present, and she found herself staring up into a pair of cerulean-blue eyes. He was bigger than the captain, a full head taller and even more heavily muscled. No wonder she couldn't bring him down with her frantic struggles. The tight black T-shirt he sported made it hard to miss the huge set of biceps and tightly corded abs she'd been working against.

He appeared to be in his early twenties. His five-o'clock shadow did nothing to hide the sharp blades of his cheekbones or the handsome cleft of his chin, but it was the icy blue eyes that would have made him the talk of the upper castes. They had a fetish for all things pretty, and Finn doubted if they'd ever seen anything so uniquely entrancing. She certainly hadn't. Those eyes provided a stark contrast to his ebony complexion and the blacker-than-night hair he wore in thick dreadlocks tied away from his face.

His full lips turned down in a frown, but he didn't seem too angry considering she'd just attempted to separate his kneecap from the rest of his body. Once she'd calmed, he released her from his grasp.

As soon as they were free, she rubbed her wrists, unconsciously reassuring herself the leather cuff she wore around each remained in place. He seemed to misunderstand her actions. Eyes on her wrists, his large hands moved toward hers, concern etching his dark brow. Finn flinched out of instinct more than anything else, and he stopped, that strange veneer of apathy slipping back into place.

"Everything okay here, Conrad?"

Finn looked up to find the captain and Iliana watching with tense expressions.

"I was looking for you and saw this one heading straight for the emergency pod. We didn't have any flight plans today, so I tried to stop her."

His gaze held Finn's as he answered, bending down to pick up her weapon and store it in the back of his pants. She couldn't quite stop the heat from flooding her cheeks at her savage reaction to his touch.

"Pulse gun, huh?" The large man's eyes glinted, seemingly impressed by her choice in sonic weapon. She gave her head a mental shake, effectively wiping away any remainders of panic, a mask of confidence taking its place as she addressed the captain.

"Your crew has a funny way of treating guests." She turned back to the brute in question, sidestepping around him to get closer to the emergency pod. "I was just leaving. The captain graciously gave me permission to use one of his travel pods to get home."

A breath away from the pod's door, Finn glanced over her shoulder to meet the captain's green gaze unwaveringly, daring him to contradict her. However, it was Iliana, the wretched courtesan, who spoke up.

"We aren't finished, Kyra."

Her voice was calm, quiet even, but the ferocity behind her eyes reminded Finn of a lost time long ago. Her vision went blurry, and her ears began to ring as another specter from the past broke through . . .

A little girl being scolded for sneaking away into the cornfields without telling anyone. Her father always slaughtered the pigs on a Friday, and she hated being near the barn when the time came to hear them meet their ends.

"You can't run off like that, Little One. I was so scared."

"I'm sorry, Li-Li. I won't do it again. I just didn't want to hear the pigs screaming."

"It's all right, Kyra. You have to stay close, though. I couldn't stand it if anything happened to you."

Disoriented, Finn's turned to face Iliana fully.

"Stop calling me Kyra."

The woman took another step forward.

"But it is your name."

Another memory came to Finn, this one more recent and certainly more welcome than the last two: Grim pouring over countless books with her, smiling as she learned to decipher word after word. The way his eyes shone proudly when she'd finished reading *The Adventures of Huckleberry Finn* all by herself for the first time. Her name was *not* Kyra; it was Finn, and this woman's interference was preventing her from returning home.

Without thinking, Finn lunged in the courtesan's direction, tugging at the ragged shirt she'd put on that morning.

"I'm not your sister, you cracked cow. Do you see any upper-caste marking on me?"

She didn't get far before two steel bands wrapped around her from behind and held her in place. Iliana regarded Finn with dawning horror, more unshed tears glittering behind her wide gaze.

"You're quite the little hellion, aren't you?"

Conrad breathed into her ear, his voice barely a whisper. She waited for her heart to pound in distress and the panic to cloud her vision, but it didn't come. Instead, her skin tingled where his arms held her, and Finn's mind slowly centered.

The captain seemed attuned to Iliana's distress. He reached out to touch her, but she shook him off. She still seemed horrified, but also determined as she approached Finn with firm steps.

"Show me your markings."

Everyone sucked in a breath at her command.

"You're cracked," Finn mocked. "Go float yourself."

Anger flashed in Iliana's eyes, and Finn found herself both surprised and supremely pleased to see it there.

"Dammit, Kyra, show me."

Finn went motionless, her body relaxing in the big man's hold. She could feel the heat in her own eyes as her lips lifted in a smile.

"Alright, courtesan, I'll make you a deal. Best me in a fair fight and you can see my markings."

Iliana's face looked aghast.

"I'm not going to fight you."

"Well then, there's your answer. No sister of mine would turn her nose up to a fair fight."

Instead of taking the appropriate offense, Iliana turned to the captain.

"Take off her gloves."

His eyebrows shot into his dark blond hairline but he obeyed, making his way over to Finn while the giant called Conrad held her steady. Finn pulled against his hold, kicking out her legs and cursing them all.

"You've all lost your minds!"

Finn bit and kicked to no avail. It took mere seconds for the captain to remove her gloves. Blessedly, he left her leather cuffs in place. Iliana's gaze searched her hands eagerly, her eyes shifting from confused to devastated.

"I—I don't understand. Where is the sun?"

Finn ceased her struggles.

"The Agrarian sun?" She couldn't help the cold laugh that escaped her. "Do I look like a farmer to you, lady?"

The courtesan's incredibly soft hands lifted to her mouth, and she let out a low keen of despair. Without warning, she collapsed to the ground.

"Oh Gods. Oh Gods. Oh Gods."

She repeated herself over and over. Dimly, Finn recognized the signs of a breakdown, but she couldn't wrap her mind around the why.

The captain rushed to Iliana's side and carefully gathered her in his arms. The courtesan barely seemed to register the movement. He turned to Conrad, tossing him Finn's gloves, and the brute released one of her arms to catch them. The captain's expression was a mixture of anguish and confusion as he commanded,

"Take her somewhere; just don't let her leave."

Finn's mind rebelled against his words, but the strange woman's most recent display left her too stunned to fight. With a will of its own, her body signed off and shut down, and it seemed to expect her brain to follow suit. Finn's eyes darted helplessly as Conrad released her fully to slide the gloves back over her hands and motioned for her to follow him down the hall.

As she trailed behind him with unsteady steps, she found it interesting that he didn't try to touch or restrain her in any way.

Finn didn't know how long they walked, the echo of Conrad's footsteps on the metal grille flooring and the erratic beat of her heart the only sounds that broke the tense silence. Any minute, she planned on coming up with a truly epic one-liner and making her grand escape: just as soon as the confusion in her mind cleared a little.

He slowed to keep pace near her side, walking so close, they almost touched. Finn inhaled his scent: a strange mixture of mint, oak, and just a hint of the neutral coolant used by older ships like the Dogwood model. The latter told her he spent a fair amount of time in the engine room, but she'd never met a mechanic quite like this one.

Something about him unsettled her, and she toyed with the idea of head-butting him and making a run for the travel pod again. She worked at making fists, but her hands and arms refused to cooperate, her heavy limbs hanging awkwardly at her sides.

"I can hear the wheels spinning in your head, hellion. Whatever it is you're thinking of doing, it would be in your best interest to unthink it."

The threat was clear, but Finn could also hear the amusement in the deep tenor of his voice and found it hard to muster up any real caution. If anything, his smug attitude began to penetrate the wall of numbness she'd been struggling to hold up since Iliana's breakdown.

He'd caught her off guard at their first encounter. That didn't mean she'd let it happen again. Her lips lifted in a genuine smile as she relished the image of knocking him and his overconfidence down a few pegs. He glanced in her direction, blue eyes shining with amusement.

"Now you're smiling? A lesser man would be terrified."

Finn looked up to deliver a withering glare, but his expression struck her momentarily dumb. A genuine smile lifted the giant's lips, and it was quite a sight to behold. She could just barely make out the shadow of a dimple beneath his coarse facial hair. Blinking, she forced herself to regain control of her thoughts.

"A *wiser* man would politely run away before I decided to show him just how terrifying I can really be."

His soft chuckle shook his chest.

Suddenly they stopped moving, and Finn watched a small, round light blink from red to blue above an automatic door as it opened before them. Conrad gently pushed her inside a faintly lit room before she had the chance to move. She took a moment to analyze her surroundings, letting him walk ahead.

She scanned the simply furnished room: a desk, a dresser, and a large bed the only furniture in the modest space. It reminded her of her apartment on the Mud Pit: small and simple. It was that reminder of home that finally shook some of the cobwebs free, recapping the injustice of the situation they had put her in. Finn felt a spark of indignation flare to life in her stomach, igniting and bringing strength back to her leaden limbs.

The door closed behind him, and, not wanting to waste another second, Finn sprang into action. Using his distraction to her advantage, she reclaimed the gun from where it rested in the waist-band of his pants. Diving out of reach, she landed in a crouch, her gun pointed at the juncture between his thighs.

He arched an eyebrow at her choice of aim, and they regarded each other silently for several tense moments. He gave no indication as to what he was thinking, carefully masking his features. It made him completely impossible to read, a fact that was as frustrating as it was impressive. Finally, Finn broke the silence.

"I've never been all that good at unthinking. I've always been a decent shot though."

She glanced meaningfully at his crotch. His hypnotic eyes widened at that, then hardened, and Gods, he made for a scary sight when riled.

Finn motioned with her head toward the opening they'd only just come through.

"Open the door and let me out. You've obviously got the wrong girl. I'm not related to that woman. This doesn't have to end badly for either of us."

He crossed his arms over his massive chest, his fists clenched as he continued to glare defiantly.

"And if I don't?"

She shrugged her shoulders.

"I thought the gun aimed at your dangly bits was pretty clear."

He didn't move to open the door or seem all too concerned with the possibility of being shot. Other than looking royally ticked off, he didn't give much away. Finn didn't relish the idea of trying to keep him in her line of sight and aim while making her way to the door. It would be too easy for him to ambush her, but she might have to take the chance. Keeping the gun trained on him, she sidestepped slowly in the direction of the door.

"The captain was pretty clear on you staying put," he pointed out. He continued to watch her calmly, his eyes following her with a predatory alertness.

"He's not my captain, and I didn't sign on for a kidnapping today."

Only a few more inches and she'd be at the door and that much closer to freedom. He still didn't make any move to come after her, which seemed a little too good to be true.

"I can't let you leave *Independence*."

"*Independence*?" Finn scoffed. "A little ironic for a crew with no qualms about taking prisoners, don't you think? Besides, I don't remember asking for your permission."

Finn shot him a triumphant glare as she hit the blue button next to the door hard with a palm to punctuate her statement. She tried not to panic when the door didn't automatically open, but when her heart began to pound furiously in her chest, she felt somewhat unsuccessful.

It could just be a fluke, she told herself.

She hit it again, harder this time, then twice more. The sting in her hand resonated seconds after the door still remained closed. All entry buttons on Ulta Dogwood 88 models blinked red when locked. This button clearly blinked blue. So why couldn't she get it to open?

Finn turned narrowed eyes on the only person in the room who didn't seem at all surprised by the anomaly. Conrad stood at ease, his arms still crossed casually over his chest. He watched her calmly with his token unreadable gaze.

"You can hit that button until your hand falls off, it still won't open the door."

Finn rolled her eyes in an attempt to hide her growing unease.

"Or I could save myself some time and just shoot you."

He didn't bat an eye at her threat or the gun still aimed squarely at his crotch.

"But we both know you won't."

His confidence irked, but as they mutually understood, shooting him would do nothing to help Finn. The sound would only draw more crew members to the room, leaving her outnumbered and outgunned. No, she wouldn't fire her gun unless it was absolutely necessary. Curse him for calling her bluff.

Finn pulled her arm back, putting her whole momentum into a punch, preparing to hit the button with so much force it would have no choice but to open.

She never got the chance.

Her body froze mid-action as though some unseen force had taken over the controls. Finn blinked once then twice, arm shaking as she strained to move it. No matter how hard she pulled, or how tightly her muscles tensed, her body remained frozen, feet planted firmly to the ground. Slowly, as though an invisible entity guided it, Finn's arm returned to its position at her side. When her fist gently unfurled of its own volition, she began to genuinely lose it. She struggled even harder, but the invisible force held her in place.

Finn's gaze lifted to Conrad. He regarded her calmly, too calmly, his hands held up in supplication as he approached slowly. Those eerie eyes of his seemed brighter than before, almost glowing in their brilliance. She'd first attributed their gleam to anger, but now she could see more lurked there: an intense focus behind their shine where they pinned her to the spot.

Something dark on his arm caught her eye as he approached. Finn discovered the edge of a blue tattoo creeping up his bicep and disappearing beneath his shirtsleeve, only to reappear again at the top of his shoulder and curl behind his neck. Its placement on his body marked him as a soldier, but she didn't recognize the intricate pattern. Something foreign and almost tribal about what little she could see of the design flashed warnings at her like a Reliance holojector. He caught her looking and adjusted his sleeve to cover the majority of the inking, anger and something else she couldn't name sparking in his eyes' glowing depths.

They continued to assess each other silently, and instinctual tendrils of alarm began to slowly unfurl deep within Finn's belly. Ever since Conrad had first touched her, she'd been having trouble controlling her actions. In his presence, her body refused to listen to her brain's commands. Judging by his knowing look, she'd venture to guess he knew exactly why that was. His strength, his strange marking, the door's timely malfunction; something didn't add up about the strange man.

As Finn watched his imposing form, mere inches from her now and holding her trapped in its icy gaze, she began to comprehend just how much danger she might be in.

All of the pieces snapped together with startling clarity, reminding her of the drunken tales she'd heard not long ago and Nova's story from just earlier that day. Could Conrad be a half-breed? Was that unnatural stare the reason she couldn't get her body to cooperate and commence with kicking his teeth in?

It was the only explanation that made any sense. Gods, how did he ever manage to make it into adulthood and escape the Reliance's notice? More importantly, did Iliana and the rest of the crew know what he was?

This man was a complete wild card. She didn't know much about half-breeds, but she knew enough to be wary. She'd already discovered him to be formidable if it came down to a fight.

Not to mention, if he could control her body and mechanical doors so easily, what else could he do?

Something akin to shock must have shown in Finn's expression and given her away, because the glow in Conrad's eyes began to dim as recognition took its place, the invisible hold releasing her from its grip.

Given his newly revealed abilities, Finn wasn't sure a sonic pulse would keep him down long, leaving only one other possible alternative. Sensing her opening, she took a chance and shot out her foot, landing a boot right between his legs in a crushing blow. She might not have known much about half-breeds, but eighty percent of the male races in the Union carried their family jewels between their legs. Apparently so did half-breeds if Conrad's savage *oomph* of pain was any indication. He immediately doubled over, and Finn took advantage.

If she could get out of this room, she could find a way off this ship. Odds were, Finn knew of hidden places on the Dogwood 88 its own captain didn't even know about. She just had to open the door.

She remembered most of these early model ships had a major flaw in their automatic systems. One sonic pulse to the door's control panel should be enough to short-circuit the system and cause it to retract. The newer models had fail-safes to prevent it. But "newer" hadn't applied to this ship since around the time Finn had been born.

Without hesitation, she shot a pulse in the control panel, the sonic boom ringing in her ears on impact and setting off sparks. The door opened in a rush. Finn darted through the opening and sped to the right, the walls around her fading away as different layouts flashed in her mind like a virtual map. The corridor ahead was empty, and she tore through it like a madwoman.

Conrad's heavy footfalls pounded down the metal grille flooring beneath them, spurring her on. She'd say this for the man: he recovered quickly. That was no love tap she'd given him.

Finn took a sharp left and then a right, navigating the ship with ease. Maintaining her sprint, she continued straight ahead, directly into a dead end. She heard Conrad's footsteps start to slow; the big man was probably assuming he'd won their round of cat and mouse. But Finn kept her pace, running straight for the wall. With about twenty feet to spare, she fired a pulse at the garbage-chute panel just above the floor to loosen it and holstered the gun, maintaining her speed. Using her momentum, Finn slid feet first through the chute.

Conrad's warning bellow echoed down the shaft behind her as she plummeted at an alarming rate.

THREE

F inn's stomach shot up into her throat as she continued to free-fall down the garbage chute. Hair blew around her in dark waves; one moment blocking and the next freeing her view in a twisted game of peek-a-boo. She pushed outward with her arms and legs and used their leverage against the walls around her to slow her descent. The rubber soles of her boots began to smell and her hands burned from the friction, but she didn't let up on the pressure.

After about twenty meters, Finn used all the strength in her arms and legs to stop her plummet. Carefully, she maneuvered her body so her back pressed hard against the far side of the chute. Her legs straightened as far as they could to push out against the opposite wall. Carefully shimmying lower, Finn moved her boots against the chute until she felt a section of metal grate to her right with some give. It had to be a vent.

Claustrophobia blackened her vision. Her heated breaths echoed off the metal around her as darkness shrouded the chute. She'd fallen too far to see much above or below and bit her lip, fighting the sensation of dread sitting in her belly like a weighted stone. Balancing her weight on one foot, Finn kicked out at the metal grate with her right leg, over and over, until it finally relented and she felt the mesh fold in on itself. With one more hard kick, the screws came loose and the entire vent cover fell from its place on the wall, tumbling down the chute. Finn did her best not to lose nerve when it took a solid thirty seconds before she heard the telltale thump signifying its landing.

Now came the hard part.

She took a deep breath and tried to mentally prepare herself for the tricky move she would need to pull off. Finn took a deep breath. As she released it, she also released the pressure of her legs on the wall, simultaneously throwing her upper body at the opening where the grate used to be. Finn hit the gap in the wall hard. The metal felt cool on her burning hands as the impact left her dangling above nothingness. She used the strength in her upper body to pull herself up as fast as she could, army crawling into the shaft the vent once covered.

Once she was inside, the shaft allowed her enough room to crawl comfortably without hitting her head or feeling too claustrophobic. She sat for a few moments on her heels, trying to get her bearings and catch her breath. She couldn't seem to get her hands to stop shaking, and she closed her eyes, focusing on slowing the pulse fluttering rapidly in her neck.

A kidnapping and a run-in with a fully grown half-breed all in the same day? And on her birthday no less?

Finn believed the more pious members of the Reliance called that *bad karma.*

She tried to calm herself by focusing on the familiar, imagining the Dogwood's layout in her mind's eye. This channel ran along a corridor mostly used for cargo storage. If all went according to plan, she should be able to drop down into the corridor without getting spotted and make her way back up to an escape pod.

If all went according to plan.

Finn moved forward on her hands and knees slowly, not daring to make more noise than necessary. She winced at every pop and wheeze of the metal around her. Eventually, she felt her way to an air vent below and drew one of her knives from its sheath on her thigh. Using the tip of the blade and the light sight on her pulse gun, she removed the screws holding it in place and carefully lifted.

Shining the light down, she saw stacked crates piled high to the ceiling and various other storage bins hanging from mesh netting filled the room below. Other than the clutter of objects, it appeared to be unoccupied. Finn sheathed her knife and swung down through the opening feet first. Landing in a crouch, she rolled to her side to take the sting of impact off her knees and ankles.

She hopped up fast, aiming her gun first to the left then the right, but she needn't have bothered. She was completely alone. Despite the adrenaline still pumping through her, Finn felt her first wave of relief since docking.

She made her way to the door slowly, the ship's motion sensor fluorescents illuminating her path as she went. The sounds of the Dogwood surrounded her like a living thing as she wove this way and that, past haphazardly stacked crates of extra supplies and parts.

Finn made her way to a tall metal door with a circular window. From the map in her mind, she knew it led to the docking bay, but her curiosity got the better of her and she shone the pulse gun's light through anyway. The door hid a huge room, the ceiling stretching high overhead. Massive machines used for transporting heavy cargo loomed above, secured to the thick walls. Other than that, it sat eerily empty, and tiny prickles of alarm began to spread throughout her body.

Why would a cargo ship be traveling without cargo?

She kept going, knowing the floor above would lead to her salvation. It mainly served as living quarters for crew, but it had the added bonus of three emergency escape pods waiting and ready for use. Finn followed the layout in her mind, letting her body guide her, instinctively knowing when and where to turn.

She reached a steel ladder, bolted to the floor. Her gaze followed it upward, seeing it disappear through a circular entryway in the ceiling. It led to the corridor of living quarters above. She knew there should be an elevator of some kind farther down the hall, but didn't want to risk running into anyone. Finn holstered her gun, needing both hands for the ascent. Instead, she pulled her knife from its sheath, placing it between her teeth as she climbed.

She climbed for several tense minutes before reaching the next floor. When she breeched the top, she stuck her head up only far enough to peer over the edge. All the doors—about ten on each side—appeared to be closed, and the hall was quiet aside from the constant hum and whirring of the ship.

Had they put the crew on lockdown for little old Finn? Feeling more comfortable with her chances of escape by the second, she inched the rest of the way up the ladder and stepped into the hall, knife in hand and back against the wall.

Heavy footsteps echoed from the end of the corridor, and Finn quickly darted around a corner, hiding from sight.

She recognized Conrad's voice first, laced with frustration.

"We haven't been able to locate her yet. We know she survived the fall down the garbage chute, but at this point she could be anywhere. You should have seen it, Shane. The way she navigated the ship, it's like she's been casing us for months."

Finn didn't need to look at him to decipher his feelings for her and her knowledge of their ship. The way he growled when he referred to *her* made his feelings perfectly clear. She couldn't say she blamed him: men tended to be a little prickly about their dangly bits. Unless he also happened to be a fast healer, he had to be more than a little sore right now. Finn stifled a small smile, waiting for whoever walked with him to respond.

Her body tensed when she heard the captain's voice.

"We know she wants off the ship. Wherever she is, she's going to come looking for a pod. I want someone guarding every corridor with an escape or travel pod. She's not getting off my ship until we have words." He paused, his sigh reaching Finn where she hid. "Was it really necessary to reveal yourself like that, Conrad?"

"I didn't think—she's difficult to control. I didn't have a choice."

Her heart sank. Escape wouldn't be as easy as she'd first thought, and it was all that dumb oaf's fault. His big, unavoidable half-breed reveal had sealed her fate. Now they were out to find her and safeguard their secret. Finn knew from experience that a person's silence could only be ensured one of two ways; neither of them looked particularly good for her right now.

"*Pssst.* Over here."

She turned toward the source of the whisper and saw a minia-ture purple hand sticking out of a doorway to the right, frantically waving her over. Her indecision didn't last very long. She'd take one tiny person over Conrad the half-breed and his captain any day. Finn rushed into the room and made sure the door closed behind her, turning to face her unknown savior.

The girl couldn't be much older than eight or nine, and even at that she looked small for her age. She gazed up at Finn with a pair of piercing green eyes, all the more striking in contrast with the unusual pale lavender hue of her skin. A voluminous fall of white-blond hair hung in ringlets around her elfin face. With her tiny stature and del-icate features, she reminded Finn of one of the mischievous fairy-tale sprites she'd seen pictures of in some of Grim's books.

She wore a pair of dark pants and a matching sleeveless shirt. Intricate vine-like markings, the same lush green as her eyes, wound their way up and around her arms and neck. Finn blinked, watching in shock as they seemed to sprout leaves and blossoms across every inch of skin they touched. She didn't think Arcturian laser guns were capable of such an elaborate design.

How did she get them?

"I was born with them."

The musical lilt to her high-pitched voice seemed to match her fairy-like appearance. Something about it soothed Finn, and she found herself relaxing a little in the strange child's presence. That is, until she stopped and thought about the girl's statement.

Finn hadn't spoken aloud.

The little girl giggled.

"No, you didn't. But I heard you anyway."

She heard her anyway? Finn didn't want to spare a millisecond pondering what that meant, because on this junker it couldn't mean anything good. Without a second thought, she turned her back on the kid and headed for the door.

"Wait, don't go. Please."

The desperation in her little voice stopped Finn cold, and despite her instincts telling her to run, she froze. Turning to face her, Finn found those wide green eyes watching her with such longing she couldn't help but pity the girl. She put the knife away and took inventory of her body, making sure the decision to stay was her own and no one else was pulling the strings. No, the guilt working its way up her throat definitely belonged to Finn. She locked eyes with the little imp.

"That's a neat trick, kid. Listen, I need a place to hide out until I can get to that escape pod down the hall. Will they come here looking for me?"

A hopeful expression lit up the girl's face as she shook her head vigorously.

"They won't look here, I promise. We're supposed to be on lockdown. And I can listen for them and tell you if they get close."

Finn had to hand it to her; she could definitely prove useful as a lookout. She gave the child her best intimidating glare, but knew it failed when she wasn't cowed in the slightest.

"Are you going to stay out of my head?" she asked the child.

"I'm sorry. I shouldn't have done that without asking. I'm not supposed to listen in on people's thoughts." Her brow furrowed as she thought about something, adding, "And anyway, I don't like poking around in your head."

A small part of Finn wanted to muster up some offense at her words, but mostly she just felt relieved. The idea of anyone but her being privy to her thoughts gave Finn chills. She'd heard of alien races capable of reading minds, but the Reliance kept most of them on lockdown. Gifts like that came in handy during the interrogations of suspected traitors and Disobedience.

Finn thought about her statement, mouth quirking up in a half smile.

"Why? Is it too messy inside there?"

The girl threw her hands up dramatically, earning her a wider smile from Finn.

"No, it's not messy enough. It's like all of your thoughts are locked behind doors, and you only unlock one at a time." Her face split into a wide grin. "Unless you're mad, then they all come bursting open."

Finn shook her head in confusion, regarding the child for a long moment.

"What *are* you?"

The imp giggled and rolled her eyes as if the answer should be obvious.

"I'm a girl, silly." She didn't wait for a response, moving forward to extend a dainty hand covered in those intriguing vine-like markings. "My name's Sotiri, but everyone just calls me Tiri."

Finn smiled down at her hand, but didn't reach out to take it.

"Nice to meet you, Tiri."

The child's smile faltered for a second as she considered Finn.

"Is it because of the way I look?"

Cycles of pain and rejection warbled her voice, tugging on something sharp in Finn's chest.

"It has nothing to do with you. I've just got a thing about being touched."

It was the best she could do by way of explanation, not quite sure how to articulate her aversion to one so young. Apparently it satisfied the girl. Her face broke out in a relieved smile and she opened her mouth to speak, but Finn cut her off before she could ask.

"A thing we will not be discussing."

Tiri's eyes glittered with mischief and curiosity, but she wisely changed the subject.

"Well, aren't you going to tell me your name?"

Finn tapped a finger to her temple.

"I figured you already knew that."

Tiri put her hands on her hips and gave Finn a frown.

Feisty little thing.

"I said I was sorry about that. Besides, it's polite for you to introduce yourself."

Finn arched a brow. The girl wanted to give *her* lessons on manners?

"You know, kid, at some point we should probably talk about the fact that you let a complete stranger—a complete stranger who is *armed,* I might add—into your room without any caution or reservation whatsoever."

Finn could give lessons too. The tiny sprite had the nerve to look annoyed.

"My name's not *Kid*, it's Tiri, and if you'd just introduce yourself, you wouldn't be a stranger."

Finn matched Tiri's frown with one of her own, struggling to follow her skewed logic.

"I think you're missing the point, *kid.*"

The girl didn't back down. In fact, she took a step forward, craning her neck to scowl up at Finn.

"No, I'm not. I know you won't hurt me, because I know you're not a bad person. I saw it." Finn stared at her, unsure what to make of the child's bold proclamation. "Besides, if you did try to hurt me, I wouldn't let you. I'm stronger than I look."

At the girl's boast, Finn grinned. She truly had no fear, even though she probably should. She had to give the kid credit; for such a teeny waif she had a backbone made of steel. Finn liked that.

"Fair enough. My name is Finn."

The girl's brow furrowed.

"Are you sure?"

Not again.

"Of course I'm sure," Finn growled.

Tiri's scowl transformed into a radiant smile, but Finn didn't give her the chance to ruin the moment by asking any more probing questions.

Stepping around her, Finn took a moment to explore as Tiri followed closely on her heels. They passed through a small entryway, and she found herself in a brightly lit bedroom. Out of all the quarters she'd seen so far, this one showed the most personality. A little four-poster bed covered in stuffed animals from multihued teddy bears to cats with tentacles sewn around the sides sat in the center. Next to it stood a small desk with all kinds of unusually shaped metal pieces organized on top.

She'd never been one for puzzles; the way her mind worked, they almost seemed too easy. But she could picture Tiri there, her little brows creased as she bent over one of the complicated metal objects, trying to figure out how to make it fit. She got so caught up in her imaginings it took a moment before she noticed the walls.

When she finally did, her heart did a double-tap.

Each wall of the room had been painted expertly and with astounding detail. Vivid greens, blues, purples, and pinks brought a mural of lush plant life and greenery—the likes of which Finn had never seen—to life. They seemed to have created a world for themselves on the four walls of the room, as though the markings on Tiri's body had sprung to life and taken on a spirit of their own.

Finn ran a hand over the mural, half expecting to feel the velvety soft petal of a flower on the pads of her fingers.

"Do you like it?"

Tiri's softly spoken words snapped Finn out of her reverie, and she stared down at the child in awe.

"It's beautiful."

Having lived on the Mud Pit for so many cycles, she didn't use the word *beautiful* often or at all, but she could think of no other way to describe what the child had created. She couldn't remember the last time she'd seen such vivid colors.

Tiri's eyes drifted lovingly over the trees and tall grass that seemed to blow this way and that as if pushed and pulled by some imaginary wind.

"I saw it in a dream."

"Must have been some dream," Finn murmured.

When Tiri didn't answer right away, she turned to find the girl staring off into the distance, her eyes glassy and unfocused.

Finn's skin prickled with alarm.

"Tiri, are you okay?"

She lifted a slender finger to silence Finn, her gaze never leaving some fixed point in the distance. When she spoke, her voice held a deeper monotone quality that seemed strange coming from her angelic face.

"They're talking about you."

Finn's muscles tensed. Every instinct she possessed told her to run, but as she watched Tiri's distracted gaze, she knew she couldn't. For whatever strange and inexplicable reason, she trusted the little girl.

"Who's talking about me?"

"Shane and Iliana."

Moving toward her, Finn bent down on her knees.

"What are they saying?"

She responded flatly in that same eerie tone.

"I need to know what we're dealing with, Iliana. Are you sure this woman is your sister?"

"I know my own flesh and blood. It's been eleven cycles, but that woman is Kyra. I knew it before I even touched her."

"Is she dangerous?"

"I don't know. I was seventeen the last time I saw her. I don't understand; she used to be so gentle. When we were little, she would spend all of her time with the animals on our father's farm. Birds, insects . . . any living thing she could find, they loved her. It was almost as though they were drawn to her goodness. I need to know what happened to her. Shane, do you think the Luminary knew who she was?"

The Luminary? Who or what was that? Finn's fists clenched and unclenched, aching for an outlet to the storm brewing inside. Why was this woman so intent on turning her world upside down? She hoped wherever Iliana's real sister was, she was well hidden and safe from the infuriatingly stubborn courtesan.

"Are you okay, Finn? You look kind of mad."

Tiri's voice had returned to its normal melodious quality. Her blonde brows wrinkled with a mature concern that appeared foreign on her young face.

Finn clenched her jaw, struggling to make her tone casual.

"I'm fine."

She could tell by Tiri's expression that the girl wouldn't have to read her mind to know she'd lied. Giving her a stern look, Finn dared the child to contradict her.

Tiri smiled, undeterred.

"Do you have any friends?"

Finn's head almost spun from how adept she was at changing the subject. Tiri blinked up, so wide-eyed and innocent Finn couldn't help but feel warmth in her presence.

"Of course I have friends. What kind of a question is that?"

Tiri scrunched up her nose, giving her face an adorably serious expression.

"You seem sad. Sad people need friends."

Finn had been called many things in her life—most hurtful, some disparaging, a few that made her proud—but no one had ever referred to her as *sad*.

"I'm not sad, I'm complicated," she pointed out defensively. "What about you, do *you* have friends?"

"Well, I've got you," Tiri pointed out in a cheery tone. "I can already tell we're going to be *very* good friends."

Finn's stomach flipped uncomfortably. How did she respond to that? Her experience with children was painfully limited, especially ones who wanted to be friends.

Tiri's strange reaction saved her from answering. Her eyes widened suddenly, and she whispered,

"Someone's coming."

Finn's heart hammered in her chest as adrenaline swiftly pushed her uneasiness into the shadows. Her mind flashed with possible escape routes before she stopped abruptly.

She met Tiri's wide, fearful gaze. Fear not for herself but for Finn, a stranger she barely knew, yet still considered a friend.

Planting her feet, Finn faced the doorway.

She never did care much for running.

FOUR

T he doors exhaled a menacing hiss, and Finn knew the moment someone entered the room. She drew her gun, ready for anything, but hoping for Tiri's sake that she wouldn't have to use it. The girl's eyes widened when she saw it, and Finn gave her what she hoped was a reassuring wink.

Conrad's deep voice echoed through the room before she got eyes on him. Great, the very last person she wanted to deal with. Although with Finn's tendency toward bad luck these days, she really shouldn't have been surprised.

"Tiri, I just came to check on you. The ship's still on lockdown—"

His gaze narrowed as he caught sight of them standing there together, eyes beginning to glow as he scanned back and forth between them. When he finally noticed the gun in her hand, they hardened. The raw anger on his face staggered her. She'd seen that look before, knew what followed. That look promised punishment. Would he take his anger out on her or would he hurt Tiri for her part in aiding Finn? He took a few rigid steps in their direction. Without thinking, Finn placed herself in front of the little girl, shielding her with her body.

He stopped immediately, his eyes widening with surprise and something else she couldn't quite decipher. She met them unflinchingly.

Tiri peered around her, frantically tugging on the sleeve of Finn's trench coat in a bid to gain her attention.

"It's okay, Finn. Conrad won't hurt me. He's my friend too."

Finn could see Conrad's brows rise in surprise at Tiri's casual use of her name. Keeping her eyes on him, she muttered to Tiri, "I'm starting to question your taste in friends, kid."

"Please, Finn. It's okay, I promise."

She finally turned from Conrad long enough to study the girl, trying to decipher the truth. Her round eyes were beseeching as she looked meaningfully at the gun Finn had aimed at the big man's chest. Both Tiri and Conrad watched her warily until she holstered it.

It took all her restraint to stand motionless as Tiri stepped around her body and ran into Conrad's big, open arms. She looked tiny wrapped up in them.

His whisper still managed to sound gruff as he held her tight.

"You okay, Lil' Bit?"

Finn observed them with a watchful gaze, never expecting him to be so gentle with her.

"Don't be mad at Finn, Conrad. I told her she could hide in here."

She leaned back in his embrace, regarding him with a somber expression, her tiny hands on his massive shoulders. His frown was stern, but not cruel like Finn had expected.

"What have I told you about strangers, Tiri?"

She dared to roll her eyes at him in vexation. Finn tensed, preparing to intervene if he tried to correct her for her insolence, but nothing happened. Tiri nodded her head in Finn's direction.

"*She* said the same thing. How come nobody trusts me?"

To Finn's shock, her petulance earned her a throaty chuckle and a tap of Conrad's forefinger on her pouting lower lip. Definitely not the response she would have expected. Further shocking her, he turned, his twinkling eyes holding Finn's as though they shared some kind of inside joke.

His expression turned more serious as he set Tiri gently down.

"Interesting stunt you pulled up there with that garbage chute. You seem to know your way around the ship. Have you spent a lot of time on Dogwoods?"

Thanks to her earlier eavesdropping, she knew his interest to be more than casual.

Finn shrugged her shoulders and gave him her most winning smile.

"Must have been beginner's luck."

His jaw clenched in annoyance, and his eyes flared a deeper shade of blue.

"Regardless, the captain would like a word."

Finn held her ground, unmoving, and his answering sigh was heavy. "That wasn't a request; you can come with me on your own or I can carry you. It's your choice."

Before Finn got the chance to kick his teeth in, which happened to be her inclination at that moment, Tiri shocked them both by placing herself between them.

The ferocious look on her face stopped them cold. She leveled Conrad with her glare, backing away slowly until she stood next to Finn. She latched on to the pocket of her trench coat once again, this time showing Conrad whom she sided with in the matter.

Finn couldn't decide what touched her more; the fact that the little girl was actually trying to protect her or that she took extra care not to touch her in deference to her previously stated aversion. Finn also couldn't tell who appeared to be more surprised by her show of solidarity, herself or Conrad. Judging by the stunned look on his face, her guess would be Conrad. He ran a hand through his dark hair in frustration.

"I'm not going to hurt her, Tiri. We just want to talk to her."

He met Finn's gaze while he spoke, as if willing her to believe him. He looked tired, and she couldn't help but feel an involuntary twinge of pity for him.

"If I come with you willingly, can I go home?"

He watched her carefully.

"The captain is open to that discussion."

Finn gave him a curt nod. She certainly didn't trust him, but she wanted to go home. If that meant talking to the captain, then so be it. There was still hope she could get out of this mess. Finn reminded herself of all the jobs and all the paydays these last cycles; all the lessons from Grim about how to deal with the enemy. She'd have to stop being stubborn and try for a little diplomacy if she ever hoped to make it back to him and the Mud Pit. Finn turned to Tiri and crouched down beside her.

"I'll be fine. I'm stronger than I look. Just ask Conrad." Finn shot a glance at his lower half, earning her a hard glare from the big half-breed. Tiri grinned at hearing her earlier words turned back on her, and Finn hit her with an answering smile. "Take care of yourself, *kid*."

Tiri beamed, releasing her hold on Finn's pocket and watching her follow Conrad out the door. He called back to the little girl before leaving.

"Under no circumstances are you to leave this room. You got me, Lil' Bit?"

She growled in response, followed by a cheeky salute, and Finn bit back another smile at her temerity. It felt strange to admit, but she would miss the girl's firecracker personality.

They stepped out into the corridor, and Finn felt his gaze on her. Sure enough, when she looked up, she found him watching her intently. Seeing as she held his full attention, now seemed as good a time as any to lay down some ground rules.

"Let's get something straight. I have nothing against half-breeds, but if you so much as hint at using your abilities on me again, let's just say any hope you had of progeny will disappear out the window and I'll make that love tap I gave you earlier seem like foreplay."

"That's a bit dark for someone with nothing against half-breeds," he remarked, not at all concerned by her threat.

"I was taught to fight fair. I may not have a problem with *what* you are, but the second you use your abilities on me, all bets are off."

Just like before, Finn couldn't read the expression on his face, and found it more than just a touch disconcerting. She raised her eyebrows, willing him to speak.

"You and Tiri seem to have made fast allies. She doesn't usually become attached so quickly."

Finn somehow doubted that. The girl exhibited many qualities, but *timidity* didn't come close to making the list. She shrugged her shoulders in response, hoping he'd take the silence as an invitation to end the conversation.

He didn't catch on.

"Are you always so talkative?"

Looking up, she found his blue eyes sparkling and that perplexing dimple back in place. He smiled. Finn stared at it, transfixed.

"No," she muttered, still staring.

His quiet laugh echoed down the halls around them, but he didn't comment further.

An uneasy feeling began to shadow her, her skin tingling. Less than an hour ago, she'd kicked this man in the balls. How could he act so easygoing?

As they passed the emergency pod at the end of the corridor, Finn felt a surge of longing, a deep instinctual part of her urging her to make a run for it. She fought the impulse and ignored the knowing glance Conrad shot her way.

She followed him down a passageway dotted with bright artificial lights, and he ushered her through the steel gray doors of an elevator. Finn leaned back against the farthest wall, choking down a rush of claustrophobia when the doors closed.

Her stomach dropped with the ascent. She forced herself to focus on breathing, hazily noticing that Conrad still watched her. Gods, didn't he have anything better to do?

The elevator continued to rise, and Finn filled with a sick feeling of dread. She chose to look down and concentrate, else risk losing the battle with her stomach.

"Nice bracelets."

Finn's eyes shot up to find him staring pensively at the leather cuffs covering her wrists. It made her feel exposed in a way she didn't like; as though he could see through the material, straight to the destroyed flesh beneath. Taking into account his half-breed genetics, maybe he could. Finn crossed her arms like a petulant child, glancing meaningfully at the markings on his neck.

"Nice ink."

His gaze narrowed, flaring a lighter blue, and she smiled inwardly at the telling action. His eyes glowed brighter when he experienced anger, something that seemed to happen a lot around Finn.

The elevator shook slightly before stopping altogether.

The doors opened to reveal the captain waiting for them in what appeared to be an expansive dining room. He sat comfortably at a long table, his booted feet propped up on a nearby chair and his hands rested at ease behind his dark blond head. His sharp gaze assessed them, contradicting his calm demeanor.

He looked Finn up and down before speaking.

"You gave us quite the runaround today."

She didn't bother answering, taking a moment to center her thoughts and stare at the homey-looking space instead. With the exception of Tiri's room and its walls of wonder, everything else on the ship felt cold and disconnected.

This room was different.

This room radiated intimacy. It spoke of a place where people gathered to laugh and maybe even discuss their day. In a way, it reminded Finn of a much cleaner version of the Dirty Molly, from the warm amber and muted sage hues of the walls, to the metal flooring covered by a vibrantly patterned area rug.

She eyed the rectangular table surrounded by at least twenty chairs of differing sizes and styles. The mixture of colors and hodgepodge of items felt right together, and she decided that under different circumstances she might like this room.

She might like it a lot.

Finn looked up to see the captain studying her curiously, and she quickly guarded her expression. She'd expected Conrad to go over and stand beside him in a show of unity, but he surprised her by staying close to her side.

When the silence dragged on, Conrad answered for her.

"It turns out Tiri was hiding her in her room."

The captain frowned at that, but his tone remained light, too cheerful for the setting or the circumstances.

"That girl is too trusting for her own good."

He continued to watch Finn as though he had all the time in the worlds, making her fingers twitch for the comfort of a gun in her hand. Instead, she straightened her shoulders and managed a casual tone.

"Do you mind if we get this over with, Captain? I'd like to get off this ship."

He sat up, letting his feet drop to the floor and resting his hands on the table.

"Really? I couldn't tell." A wry smile lit across his face, making him appear younger. A few years older than Conrad perhaps? "I think we should properly introduce ourselves, don't you? I'm Captain Shane Montgomery."

He extended a large, tanned hand, and Finn sighed inwardly.

More handshakes?

She'd never met a crew so caught up in pleasantries. She didn't move to take it.

"I'm Finn."

He pulled his hand back, unaffected by the rejection.

"Last name?"

"No," she answered.

His body tensed in a way that told her she'd surprised him.

"No?"

"I don't have one."

His forehead creased in confusion.

"I just assumed it was Terrandon, like your sister."

She ran the name around her mind a few times, trying to see how it felt. Nothing. It didn't sound familiar at all.

"Are we still on this, Captain? I thought that little breakdown outside the travel pod earlier made it pretty clear I'm not your courtesan's sister, and she knows it."

Shane frowned but didn't answer. Instead, he changed the subject.

"Conrad has informed me that he was a little careless with his abilities earlier. I'm sure you've also noticed that Tiri is far from the average little girl. The . . . *blended* on my ship have found a sanctuary of sorts here, a place they can call home. I'd be more than a little put out if anyone tried to change that. When you leave here, I trust you'll keep that in mind. We don't want any trouble, but if you do anything to compromise their safety, that's exactly what you'll find."

Blended. That was a new one. Nicer than half-breed, she had to admit.

His manner remained friendly, his undertone not so much. She admired his casual subtlety. The fierce protectiveness of his crew reminded her of Grim, and she started to feel a small amount of respect for the man. The confirmation of Tiri's *blended* status didn't alarm Finn. She'd already arrived at the same conclusion herself. She wondered if more people like Shane Montgomery existed out there in secret, protecting half-breeds from the Reliance. It was an interesting thought, and one that would shake the Arcturians to their core if they knew about it. The idea gave Finn a twisted sense of satisfaction.

"Like I told Conrad earlier, I don't care what he is. I just want to go home."

He shared a brief look with Conrad before returning his gaze to her, his smile back in place.

"Good, that's settled then."

Finn offered him a barely perceptible nod, fighting the need to shake from relief. Home seemed so close she could almost taste it.

"Fine," she agreed, "then our business here is done."

Her body moved for the elevator doors, but Conrad's imposing form already blocked her path. She glanced back to find the captain watching her.

"Not quite yet. Unfortunately, Conrad discovered earlier that all of our travel and escape pods are in need of some serious repairs. They won't get you where you need to go until we can get new parts."

Finn felt the exact moment her blood turned to fire. Every cell within her veins ignited, burning a pathway to the center of her chest where her pulse pounded.

They meant to keep her here.

She should have seen it coming, but like a fool she'd assumed they would let her go. She'd gotten comfortable with her freedom on the Mud Pit these past cycles. With Grim's protection, she'd grown to think of herself as untouchable. Today, that overconfidence had done her a disservice. A strange ringing in Finn's ears began to sound, panic washing over her body in a deluge of sensation.

She reached for her gun, needing to feel its weight in her hand. Before she could grasp it, Conrad's arm grabbed hers, twisting it behind her back. Finn's stomach turned at the sensation, heartbeat hammering in her temples.

These people have no honor.

She felt the uncontrollable surge of tears fighting their way up her throat as she let her eyes slide shut, watching her future disintegrate behind their lids like the ashes of a dying flame. What would Grim say if he could see her now?

Finn forced her eyes to snap back open and scowled when she found the captain watching her with a mixture of pity and concern. She couldn't lose it in front of these two, couldn't show them any sign of weakness.

"You expect me to believe that all of your pods suddenly stopped working? Do I look stupid to you?"

Finn fought Conrad's hold, using her anger as added leverage, squirming and twisting like a madwoman. Still she gained no ground. Curse him for being so strong.

Shane eyed her warily.

"No, but you do look a bit crazed."

Finn thrust her head backward and winced when it connected with Conrad's face. He grunted, but still refused to release her. She felt the weight of her gun being removed from its holster, followed by each of her knives. The loss made her fight even harder, yelling as she did.

"Get your hands off me, *mutt*!"

She heard his sharp intake of breath at the derogatory slur, but she existed now solely for self-preservation. It allowed no room for caring.

He didn't let go, his grip tightening.

"What do you want from me?" she demanded.

Shane approached her carefully, like one would an animal caught in a trap.

"We have a job on Cartan in a few days. If you like, you can charter a hover pod back to Altara from there."

Finn slowed her struggles, trying to understand. How did he expect her to swing that? Cartan sat smack dab in the middle of the Inner Rings.

"You actually think I'm going to charter a hover in the center of the Reliance?"

His eyes narrowed.

"The only people who run into trouble with the Reliance are fugitives and criminals. You got something you want to tell me?"

Finn ground her teeth and glared at him.

One look was all it would take for any one of the upper-caste elitists to see *criminal* written all over her; from the way she navigated a ship to the way she dressed, and he knew it. Neither Finn nor the captain seemed willing to speak the truth aloud, so she stared at him instead.

He sighed, rubbing his neck.

"You haven't seen your sister in eleven cycles. Would it kill you to spend a few days getting to know her again?"

Finn stilled in Conrad's arms, too stunned to move.

"*That's* what this is about? You want to keep me here for *her?*"

His eyes held hers. They were unapologetic.

"As I said before, our pods are in need of repairs. If your stay on my ship has the added bonus of you and your sister reconnecting, then so be it."

Reconnecting? Blind fool. The sincerity in his eyes said it all. He really believed keeping Finn on his ship served some kind of benevolent purpose; as though Finn had any intention of reconnecting with a perfect stranger.

"This is insane. You know that, don't you?" Finn leaned in as far as Conrad's hold would allow, willing Shane to hear her and understand. "If you're so convinced she's telling the truth, answer me this: How come she's up here sitting pretty and I'm down on the Mud

Pit cleaning shit off my boots?" She scoffed when he didn't answer. "Exactly. That woman is not my sister."

His eyes moved past her, as though he'd lost patience, and Finn raised her voice to regain his attention.

"But Captain?" When she had his eyes, she continued. "Even if she was my blood, that woman is not my family. She's a glorified doxie. The only difference is, a doxie at least tries to make an honest living, while I'll bet every coin your courtesan has earned reeks of Reliance."

"That's enough, Finn."

Conrad's soft command startled her out her rant. He surprised her by releasing his hold, letting her go.

After a beat, Shane scrubbed a hand down his face. When he next spoke, his voice was gruff.

"Conrad will get you set up with some quarters. I know you won't believe this, but you are not a prisoner here. However, whether you like it or not you're stuck with us until Cartan." He fixed her with a hard stare. "Until then, you are not to physically harm a single member of my crew. That includes your *sister*. Do we have an understanding?"

Finn nodded, too exhausted to muster up any more offense at his assumption she would hurt his crew.

"Good, because if you break my rules, I will float you myself."

Finn gritted her teeth at the threat and smiled.

"I have a few rules of my own. No one touches me again." She glanced pointedly at Conrad. "And no more half-breed body control. If any one of you breaks *my* rules, all bets are off. Understood?"

Both Shane and Conrad regarded her stonily.

"Fair enough," they agreed in unison.

FIVE

To call the ride down in the elevator *tense* would have been a massive understatement. Finn struggled with the sensation that the walls closed in on her, Conrad's angry silence doing nothing to ease her agitation. His rigid stance and clenched fists served only to punctuate his ire.

Despite all of her internal justifications, calling him a *mutt* still didn't sit right. Even a thief of Finn's ilk maintained standards for behavior, and the way she'd acted had been nothing short of shameful.

She hated that she felt guilty. For the Gods' sake, Conrad had played a major role in keeping her on this ship against her will. She felt shame for her words, but what did they expect from someone they held captive?

"Thank you, sir, will you show me to my cell?"

Not going to happen.

Finn shook her head, trying to expel the unwanted feelings with it. At the movement, Conrad finally looked her way. She almost wished he hadn't when she glimpsed the harsh glow of his eyes. Crossing her arms, she tried to swallow the lump in her throat.

Gods, the guilt was unbearable. She did her best to compel it away, but none of her usual tricks seemed to be working. Sighing, Finn cleared her throat and tried not to shrink from the anger in his gaze.

"Look, I—"

Just the sound of her hoarse voice seemed to light the powder keg of his temper, and he turned on her, backing her farther into the corner of the elevator with his size. He trapped her there, with his arms against the wall, one on either side of her head. She had no choice but to crane her neck up to meet his gaze.

Finn could almost feel the heat from the fire in his eyes, but it didn't escape her notice that even in his wrath he took care not to touch her. Whether for her comfort or because of her rules, she couldn't be sure.

"Let's get one thing straight. You don't know me."

"I—"

He cut her off before she could form her thought.

"I want you to stay away from Tiri while you're here. The girl's got tender feelings, and the last thing she needs is some bigot stomping all over them."

His chest heaved with heavy breaths as he ran a frustrated hand over the back of his neck. They watched each other for a long moment. If possible, the elevator began to feel even smaller.

Finally, he backed away.

Finn ignored the gut instinct to punch him outright for calling her a bigot. She couldn't fault him for his assumption: she'd behaved like one. Her cheeks heated, and she knew they must be as red as a Reliance soldier's badge.

Stubborn pride urged her to remain silent, but a more foreign part of her actually wanted to make things right, at least in some small way. Truthfully, she didn't want his opinion of her colored by some panic-induced words.

She spoke quietly, voice rough.

"I would never say anything like that to Tiri. I shouldn't have said it to you either. I—I'm . . . sorry that I did."

Conrad stood silent for so long, she began to wonder if he'd even heard her feeble effort. She chanced a look up and found him watching her with an intense expression she didn't even bother trying to interpret. The way his eyes pierced hers made Finn's skin prickle with awareness and her throat go dry. Another silent moment passed between them before the ground shook and the doors opened.

Tiri stood just outside the elevator, arms stretched wide and eyes wild with excitement.

"You're staying!"

Finn exited into the hallway, grateful for the interruption as Conrad followed close behind. She didn't bother to look at him. He may have forbidden her from seeing Tiri, but she should at least get a chance to say goodbye. Her stomach flipped in an unfamiliar sensation, taking her by surprise.

"Just for a few days," she corrected, bending down. "Listen, Tiri, we won't really be able to see—"

Finn didn't get a chance to finish before Conrad cut her off again.

"Tiri, since you've already been busy eavesdropping, why don't you help me pick out a room for Finn?"

Conrad's subtle reminder of the rules on mind-snooping didn't escape Tiri's notice, and she had the decency to look contrite.

"Sorry, Conrad."

She turned back to Finn, contrition quickly replaced by a broad grin, and Conrad rolled his eyes. She clearly harbored no fear of the big man. How had Finn ever worried that he would hurt her?

"Come on, Finn. You can stay next door to me. We're going to have so much fun."

"Go on ahead, Lil' Bit. She'll catch up."

Conrad's response left Finn too busy snaring mud flies with her wide-open mouth to formulate a reply, and she rounded on him as soon as Tiri was out of earshot.

"What gives? I thought you didn't want me around her."

He crossed his arms and leaned against the wall, regarding her languidly. All traces of his former anger seemed to have disappeared.

"I changed my mind."

Over the last sixty seconds he had transformed from a man on the razor's edge of rage to the picture of relaxation. She'd been wracking herself with guilt for upsetting him, this man who played an integral part in holding her prisoner. The same man who now looked completely at ease watching confusion darken her face.

"You changed your mind," she repeated. Her voice was deceptively calm, and he offered her a lazy smirk in response, his dimple firmly in place.

"Yeah, I've been known to do that from time to time."

So the mercurial half-breed liked to play games, did he?

"Okay, big guy," she whispered, her eyes smiling. "Game on."

She took off after Tiri, leaving him delightfully confused and alone by the elevator. She didn't know how she planned on messing with the big half-breed, but apparently she had plenty of time being imprisoned to figure it out.

Before long, Finn found the girl in a room just next door to hers, as promised. The space's sheer size instantly overwhelmed her, more expansive than anything she'd ever known.

The bed in the center of the room looked decadently plush, at least two times bigger than her tiny mattress on the Mud Pit, with soft white pillows and matching sheets. A small circular window on the far wall displayed a spectacular view of glittering stars, made all the more brilliant by their contrast with the black abyss surrounding them.

Taking in the lack of holojectors on the white walls, Finn found herself face-to-face with the first bright side to being stuck on *Independence*: at least she wouldn't have to suffer through any more unionization celebrations.

"You even have your own desk. Do you like to draw?"

Tiri pointed over to a solid-looking metal desk attached to the wall beneath the window. Antique paper and colored pencils were stacked neatly in a tray on top. Finn walked over in a trance. She'd never seen drawing paper and pencils before, let alone held them.

When the Arcturians invaded, bringing with them advanced tech, pen and paper became a thing of the past. The Reliance opted to trade them in for more practical electronic holopads, holojectors, and comm devices. Art, and the tools associated with it, remained reserved for the highest castes; those who could better appreciate it. The contents of that desk alone were worth more than Finn's last three jobs combined.

Finn ran a hand over the paper reverently.

"I've never drawn before."

She looked up to find Tiri watching her with a dopey grin.

"I can teach you."

Finn picked up a pencil the same light blue as Conrad's eyes and smoothed her fingers over its glossy surface.

Where did they get their hands on these?

A slightly accented voice turned their attention to the front of the room.

"You also have your own bathroom and shower."

Tiri squealed and ran over to the mysterious voice.

"Hi, Isis!"

Finn almost forgot to breathe when she caught sight of the regal-looking, long-limbed female standing across the room. She was at least six-feet tall; Tiri's head barely reached her waist. Dark purple robes cloaked her willowy body from neck to feet. The skin visible on her hands, neck, and face was a glossy, deep sky-blue with glittering diamond patterns interspersed throughout.

From what Finn could tell, her body appeared to be completely hairless. Even her head was smooth, with only those twinkling diamond configurations to add dimension. She lasered Finn with a pair of breathtaking silver eyes that didn't seem to miss a beat.

An Aquariian. In the flesh. This day just kept getting better and better.

Finn didn't know much about the all-female race of aliens. No one did. They remained as mysterious as their ability to procreate despite the lack of males in their race. She'd love to know how they managed that.

Most of them lived isolated lives since being forced off their home planet of Aquarii. It had gone down in history as one of the quickest Reliance victories.

One thing the Aquariians *were* widely known for: being the most peaceable and pacifistic of all the races in the Union.

Tiri interlaced her small hand with the Aquariian's slender blue fingers and smiled up at Finn.

"This is Isis. She's my friend too."

Finn almost snorted but caught herself. The kid had certainly put together an eclectic circle of acquaintances, Finn included. Isis offered her a warm smile, taking a few steps in her direction. She moved so gracefully, she almost seemed to glide.

"You, my dear, are not nearly as terrifying as you were made out to be."

Finn arched a brow, surprise pulling a genuine smile from her lips.

"Just wait until you get to know me better," she advised.

Isis gave a soft laugh and motioned toward a bundle of clothing she held under her arm.

"Shane mentioned you would be staying with us for a few days. I thought you might like some clothing to wear. You should find any other things you may require in the bathroom."

She set the clothes down on the bed, and Finn nodded distractedly. Tiri immediately began to rifle through them with the kind of efficiency and enthusiasm that would do a Mud Pit urchin proud. Finn looked back up at Isis. She'd never expected such polite hospitality and accommodations.

"Did he also happen to mention I'm your prisoner?"

The Aquariian had the audacity to stifle a chuckle.

"He mentioned you had some reservations, but I assure you, once you get to know the crew a bit better, you'll fit right in. Now, is there anything else you need?"

She shook her head. She'd gotten by with a lot less for a lot longer. However, her curiosity for this ship and the strange mix of people on it grew.

"What are you, the maid?"

Tiri burst into a fit of giggles. Isis continued to regard her politely, but her silver eyes sparkled with amusement.

"Heavens no, child. Actually, I am a healer. I take care of all the crew's medical needs. However, today I am your welcoming committee."

And what an interesting welcoming committee they'd chosen. Maybe Finn could get some information out of her.

"There is one other thing you can do for me. You can tell me about this job on Cartan."

The Aquariian fixed her face with a practiced smile, alerting Finn that the next words out of her mouth would be a lie. She'd spent enough time around good liars to recognize when one was staring her in the face.

"I have no idea what you mean."

Finn's patience waned.

"Look, I just want to know what I'm mixed up in here. What kind of work does the captain do?"

Another blank smile.

"Oh, this and that," she returned.

Finn narrowed her eyes; this Aquariian would have to do a lot better than dodgy answers if she intended to deter the Mud Pit's top thief and prodigy.

Isis seemed to read exactly that in Finn's expression and gave her a long, pointed look before continuing.

"Come along, Tiri. Let us leave Finn to herself for a time. I am sure she would like to wash the grime of the day off and change. It was very nice to meet you, my dear."

Tiri offered her a helpless backward glance before Isis ushered her out of the room, leaving Finn alone with her thoughts. *Dismissed* might have been more accurate.

Three days.

She had three days to play the perfect prisoner and find a way home to Grim. Then she could forget all about this heap and the strange crew who seemed so desperate to keep her here. Finn decided to follow Isis's advice. A shower sounded like an excellent idea.

The bathroom was small but still plenty spacious for her needs. Finn bypassed the sink and toilet and headed straight for the rectangular stall in the corner of the room. It took up the most space in the area, but she didn't mind. On the contrary, she let out a sigh of pure joy at the sight of it.

Finn didn't often find herself looking for the silver lining, but as she regarded the shower stall longingly, she knew she'd found it.

Caught up in anticipation, she undressed quickly, barely grimacing when she removed her gloves and leather cuffs.

The stall's sensors registered Finn's body heat as soon as she stepped inside, and sprays of water set to the ideal temperature to soothe aching muscles hit her on all four sides. She groaned at the sensation, body going limp. After several bliss-filled minutes, Finn ran a hand under another sensor below the spray, watching as a puff of white foam spilled out onto her palm. The stall immediately filled with the scent of lilacs, and her eyes drifted shut in relaxed pleasure.

She washed thoroughly, trying out three more sensors with varying flowery scents before she decided she'd used more than her fair share of the hot water. By the time she finished, Finn imagined she must smell like a walking, talking synthetic flower cart. She wrapped herself in a large fluffy towel and ran a hand over the steam on the mirror.

Her eyes caught the edge of a jagged scar running from the top of her left shoulder down her back, and she fought the wave of nausea that arose at the sight. She turned around, craning her neck to see her upper back in the mirror.

Raised, puckered scars, angry and red against the porcelain white of her skin, crisscrossed a haphazard pathway down her back. They stacked one on top of the other, so thick she could barely see any spots of unblemished flesh beneath them.

Sometimes, when Finn first awoke from her nightmares, she could still hear the inexplicable crack of a whip chased by the echo of screams, the sounds inescapable inside her head.

Slamming the cuffs on her wrists, she slipped on her gloves and exited the bathroom in a rush. She rummaged through the clothes Isis had left on the bed, hoping to find something with long sleeves and a high collar.

She settled on a pair of stretchy black pants that fit a little loose on the hips, and a long-sleeved grey shirt. She paced the floor for a full minute, staring down each bare, white wall of the room before she lost fortitude.

Patience had never really been one of her strengths.

Besides, no one said she couldn't leave the room, only the ship.

She reached for a pair of socks, softer than anything sold on the Mud Pit, and dragged them over her feet. She was about to pull on her boots when she realized how utterly filthy they were. They probably could have tracked her through the ship just by following the trail of mud. Finn went back into the bathroom and cleaned her boots until she could see the black rubber soles for the first time since Grim had given them to her eight cycles ago. Slipping them on felt like wrapping up in a familiar blanket. By the time Finn got them laced up and ready to go, she'd started to feel more like her old self.

She slipped out the automatic doors without any problems. Apparently, she really did have free rein of the ship.

Taking full advantage of it, she headed down the hall in the direction of one of the escape pods. Finn didn't know what she expected to find there, but she needed to see for herself the condition of the pods that had left them in *such great need of repair*. The hallways still sat strangely unoccupied, and she didn't run into anyone on the way.

Finn placed a hand on the button outside the door and almost laughed nervously when it easily opened in front of her. Would escape really be this effortless? She realized her clothes were still in the room down the hall, but quickly trampled that thought. Everything could be replaced.

She stepped inside and took inventory. The pod was a smaller model, built to accommodate only three. A domed window covered half that space floor to ceiling, revealing the vast spacescape outside the ship. Three high-backed chairs were bolted to the floor facing the window, an impressively scaled control panel set up in front of them.

Finn went over to the panel, finding an intact comm screen ready and waiting for use.

Someone had definitely messed with the panel, but rather than harm it, they'd made some extraordinary improvements. Finn could never claim to be a tech expert. She might have been able to navigate any ship she got thrown on, but she had no way of knowing how they put the things together. However, even she could see that the out-dated Dogwood model's technology had been enhanced by a skilled hand. They'd chosen to add three additional flightscreen monitors above the console, as well as several complicated-looking keypads on the board Finn didn't recognize, enhancing the pod's usability.

She powered up the control panel and tried entering some coordinates with the touch screen. Almost immediately, a flashing red error signal stating INVALID ENTRY greeted her. She let out a breath she didn't realize she'd been holding and scanned the panel, thinking hard.

Getting down on hands and knees, she checked beneath the console. Finn didn't know exactly what she was looking for, her eyes searching through the usual rainbow of wires that made her head spin.

Minutes later and on the verge of giving up, she did a double take as she noticed something very important missing from the console's underbelly. Several cut wires rested right where the navigation hub should have been. Finn would have bet all the gold she owned that they had removed the navigation hubs on every single pod on the ship.

"I'll say this about you. You're persistent."

The self-satisfied tone in Conrad's voice made her forget to be embarrassed that he currently had a choice view of her backside where she hunched on all fours beneath the console.

Finn turned to find him leaning in the doorway, eyes shamelessly focused on her rear, arms crossed, and lips turned up in a smug grin. She jumped to her feet with lightning-quick speed, ignoring the flush rising in her cheeks. For the first time since meeting him, she actually felt happy to see him. The outrage currently rising with each breath she took needed an outlet, and Conrad seemed like the perfect man for the job.

"Repairs, my ass. You removed the navigation hubs, you bastard."

He made a disappointed noise in the back of his throat, eyes twinkling.

"And what an ass it is. Tell me, are you always this vulgar?" He didn't bother trying to hide how thoroughly he was enjoying himself at her expense. "My parents were married, by the way."

The random statement, so casually delivered, deflated some of Finn's anger. She found herself suddenly less interested in maiming him and more interested in what the devil he was talking about.

"What?"

"You called me a bastard. My parents were married, so you'll have to dip back into that colorful vocabulary of yours for a more suitable insult next time."

As seemed to be his habit, he left her speechless. Half the time, he seemed to hate her, alternating between intense silences and varying degrees of anger. The other half of the time, their interactions went like this: eyes shining with humor and that ridiculous dimple so out of place on his handsome warrior's face.

Finn realized she'd been staring and gave herself a mental slap.

"Marriage between races is illegal."

He smiled, but it didn't reach his eyes.

"Maybe by Reliance law."

He watched her closely, as though her response held some kind of importance to him.

"How come everywhere I go, you seem to pop up?" she asked, crossing her arms protectively.

He pulled away from the door frame and stalked over to her with slow, calculated steps. The way he moved was pure lethal grace, his tightly corded muscles flexing with each step. He stopped just a breath away, towering over her. Eventually, she'd get a crick in her neck from having to stare up at him.

"If I had to make an educated guess, hellion, I'd say *you* were following *me*."

His deep voice rumbled and his massive frame took up all the space around her, completely surrounding her with his presence. When she breathed, she inhaled his unique scent.

"Then your education must be as lacking as the rest of you."

The heat from his powerful body enveloped her, making her head spin as though she'd had one too many of Doc's special Dragon's Breath shots. She'd never had this reaction to someone before. She felt weightless and heavy at the same time, breaths coming in short pants as if some unknown force had sucked all the oxygen from the room.

Her eyes darted up to find his. There was no mistaking the hunger she saw there. Finn's stomach flipped and she licked her lips nervously. His eyes followed the movement and returned to hers. Their bodies stood so close, only a few more inches and they'd be touching.

What would it feel like?

Between her aversion to skin-to-skin contact, her reputation, and an overprotective mentor to send potential suitors running, Finn's experience in the matters of seduction was painfully lacking. Besides, on the Mud Pit, physical encounters were less about companionship and more about economy, and Finn was more than happy to leave such business to the doxies.

For the most part she was satisfied with her solitary existence, but something about the way Conrad's presence left her pleasantly light-headed told her she'd been missing out on something all these years.

Finn's heart pounded at his nearness, but not out of the usual fear. She began to panic, terrified by how *not* terrified she seemed to be at the prospect of touching Conrad.

Shaking herself free from the trance he held her under, she cleared her throat and backed away so forcefully, she hit the wall of the pod with a loud *thunk*.

Conrad, as though nothing had happened, returned to leaning against the doorframe. She watched as his face quickly morphed into a blank expression.

It took a little longer for Finn to compose herself, her stomach fluttering like a thousand tiny moths had been set loose inside. Everything felt so confusing. Why did she have so little control when it came to Conrad? Something about this ship seemed to lower her guard. Had they been on the Mud Pit, she felt certain she would have sent him to the ground with a swiftly delivered blow to the jaw for his audacity. Had he used his powers on her again without her even realizing it?

Finn forced herself to stand away from the wall and eyed him warily. He ran a hand through his dark hair; the only indication he gave that he might be at all affected by their strange moment.

"Shane asked me to bring you to the rec room. He'd like to introduce you to the rest of the crew. Are you going to behave yourself?"

Finn's hands moved to her hips, and she shot him a peevish look.

"I could ask you the same thing."

He didn't like that one bit, his eyes starting to glow in that eerie way they did. His next words came out as a growl.

"Just remember your promise to the captain."

She took an involuntary step toward him.

"Maybe you should focus on keeping your own promises. I'm sure *Shane* would love to hear how his half-breed muscle was using his powers to seduce the prisoner."

His jaw clenched so tight, she began to worry it might break. Forever seemed to be housed in the next silent, tense seconds that passed between them. If possible, his eyes glowed even brighter.

"Believe what you want, hellion, but you and I both know I don't need my powers to seduce you."

Her heart pounded at his words.

He had to be lying; the alternative didn't bear thinking about. Granted, she'd never been properly seduced before, so she had no real experience to draw from. Still, his casual dismissal echoed in her ears.

Believe what you want, hellion, but you and I both know I don't need my powers to seduce you.

Wait a minute. Hellion? That was the fourth time he'd called her that.

Finn's spine straightened as she realized she'd earned herself another nickname.

"Just keep your hands to yourself," she demanded.

His body remained equally rigid, but he gave her a barely perceptible nod and turned to leave. His control astounded her.

Finn shook her head and left the pod a moment later, walking at a brisk pace until she caught up with him. She followed at a safe distance—a few feet behind—already knowing how to get to the ship's recreation room located on the same floor as the crew's living quarters.

Finn fought against her racing thoughts and unfamiliar feelings, digging deep for some blessed feeling of numbness to wash over her. All she ended up with was a nagging tug of guilt for her most recent interaction with Conrad. She knew what it felt like when he used his powers on her. This had been different.

She heard the hum of voices just before reaching the open doors and felt a flutter of unease. What would she be walking into? Conrad stood just outside, waiting for her to catch up.

Finn straightened her shoulders, forcing her body to relax into her casual, confident pose. Doc liked to call it her *force field of badassery*, saying it radiated off of her whenever she walked into a room. The corner of her mouth pulled up into a half-smile, the memory of Doc giving her the last push she needed to stand tall as she walked through the doors of the rec room.

Everyone immediately fell silent when she stepped inside, followed closely by Conrad. She let her eyes flit around the space with casual disinterest, a somewhat difficult undertaking considering all there was to see.

A small-scale bar to the left included several bottles of varying sizes, shapes, and colors lined up on a multileveled glass case. It stood tall behind a bright neon countertop flashing back and forth between greens, blues, purples, and pinks. The intensity of the colors almost made Finn's eyes tear. Three downy-soft couches and more than a few hollowed out egg-shaped chairs spread throughout the room, all in differing shades of beiges and browns.

Movement caught her eye, and she noticed two holojectors with the sound turned down mounted on the walls, displaying flashing images of the Union of the Planets news and entertainment.

Finn looked away long enough to land her gaze on the most impressive object in the room, a green, felt table with numbered multicolored balls spread out over the top: an honest-to-Gods Earth pool table. Grim once tried to replicate one for the Dirty Molly using synthetic materials. It turned out nice, but nothing—she realized—compared to what stood in the center of the rec room The genuine felt on this one looked fuzzy and soft to the touch, and Finn's palms itched with the urge to run her fingers over it.

She forced herself to stop staring when Shane stepped into her line of sight. He gave Conrad a quick once-over, and she couldn't help but notice the slight frown at whatever he saw there. Finn threw Conrad a sideways glance of her own and saw the storm clouds brewing behind his eyes. There seemed to be a moment of silent communication between the two men that ended with Conrad's curt nod.

Shane turned, smiling brightly.

"I thought it would be best if you met the rest of the crew. Tiri and Isis you already know. They're on cooking duty tonight, so you'll see them at dinner."

He motioned to a man and woman standing by one of the couches. They appeared to be Finn's age, maybe a little older, both of them with matching, smooth dusky skin and striking amber eyes.

"Meet the twins, the best damn pilots this side of the Union. They keep us flying straight."

The woman's petite frame sported a tight, white T-shirt and a pair of brown suspenders a shade darker than her skin. She eyed Finn mischievously while sucking on some kind of hard candy attached to a green stick. Her bright pink hair was pulled tight into high pigtails, and as she turned to elbow the man next to her, Finn noticed an elaborate marking in the shape of two fish forming a circle just above her cheekbone.

Finn had no idea what caste the marking signified. Like Tiri's and Conrad's markings, they appeared completely foreign. Her twin wore an identical one above his cheek.

Two more half-breeds?

Her stomach roiled uncomfortably at the thought of how vastly outnumbered she was.

The young man was at least two heads taller than his sister, lean but still muscular in his matching sleeveless shirt and suspenders. His hair, short and spiky, had been dyed a bright neon yellow. He offered Finn a slow, seductive smile and sauntered forward, his pink-haired sister close behind.

"So this is our sexy stowaway. Trust me when I say it's *very* nice to meet you. I'm Jax. This is my sister, Lex."

Finn almost laughed at his impudence, forgetting her discomfort, but managed to stop herself. She thought she heard Conrad growl behind her but figured it must have been her imagination. When she glanced back at him, he appeared impassive as ever.

As her twin continued to eye Finn lecherously, Lex stepped forward, practically buzzing with energy.

"Ignore my brother; he's a total slut. Guys, girls, he'll go for anything with a pulse." Her eyes lit up as she got even closer, invading Finn's personal space to an alarming degree. "You *have* to show me how you did that trick with the garbage chute. I'm dying to try it. Will you show me?"

Her smile was infectious, and Finn found herself returning it easily, all the while trying to keep up with the rapid way the woman's mouth moved. She watched expectantly, her amber eyes radiant with unbridled excitement, and Finn offered a nod. Her answering joyful shriek left everyone's ears ringing.

Shane came up and wrapped an arm around Lex's dainty shoulder, placing a chaste kiss on her forehead.

"Over my dead body, Lexie girl."

"Oh come on, Shane. Don't be such a baby."

She rolled her eyes, but the obvious admiration in her gaze said she would do anything her captain said. The easy affection between them was completely unheard of. Most crews stayed together out of necessity, but these people seemed to actually like one another. Did they act this way for Finn's benefit or was the trust she glimpsed genuine?

Finn looked back at Conrad, curious to see his reaction to the crew's odd introductions, and found him staring across the room at the other side of the bar. She followed his gaze to see the last person she'd yet to meet, a teenage boy probably no older than fourteen, standing by himself and glowering at the group.

He looked like something straight off a Reliance holopad screen. It genuinely surprised Finn to see him on a ship like this, surprised her that the Reliance hadn't snatched him up the second he hit puberty. So attractive he was almost pretty, the boy boasted brooding good looks. He possessed a face rife with hard angles and smooth skin, as though it had been sculpted from stone by an artist's hands. His long, dark hair fell into upturned eyes so obscure, they seemed to be as black as the spacescape outside.

Right now those eyes were fixed on Finn, seething in unmistakable hatred.

She winked, letting him know it would take more than a look to intimidate her. His alabaster hands formed fists at his sides.

"AJ, get your ass over here."

The kid took his time responding to Conrad's barked order, never once taking his gaze from Finn's. The room fell silent again as he made his way over to the rest of them, stopping a few feet away.

Shane placed a hand on the boy's shoulder and squeezed gently.

"This is AJ."

AJ jarred his body out from under Shane's hand, his pale face pulling into an ugly sneer.

"All of you are crazy if you think I'm going to make nice with her."

Finn offered him a smirk of her own, rounding on Shane.

"See, this kid gets it." She turned back to the boy. "And what is it you do on the ship, AJ?"

He crossed his arms at his chest, the picture of arrogance.

"I'm in charge of special projects."

She smiled in feigned ignorance. He was making this too easy.

"Is that code for janitorial services?"

Finn heard Conrad's long-suffering sigh right before AJ's fists clenched even tighter, his face morphing into an angry dark red. This short fuse of his could prove to be problematic.

He turned toward Shane, so furious he almost looked apoplectic.

"Why are we even letting her stay on the ship? She could be a Farthers spy for all we know." His head shot back to Finn, his black eyes spitting fire. Ebbs of color began to spark in their depths, and Finn wondered if her imagination might be playing tricks. "Or she could be one of their whores. Is that what you do? Lie on your back for Reliance coin?"

Finn forgot about his odd eyes. Keeping her smile in place, she turned to the rest of the room.

"Did he just call me a doxie?"

The only person who bothered to give her an answer was AJ himself.

"You're damn right I did."

"All right, then. Fair is fair. I'm going to punch you now," she warned him.

The anger left his face, surprise and confusion swiftly replacing it as his eyes went wide. Finn squared up and punched him in the jaw, making good on her promise. He didn't even try to block her. She heard Shane's shout just as the hit knocked the boy on his rear end, his lip splitting at the contact.

Lex let out a whoop of laughter and high-fived Jax.

"New girl rocks!"

Finn felt Conrad's hot breath growling in her ear a moment later.

"Was I hallucinating or did you not promise you wouldn't hurt a single crew member on this ship?"

Finn nodded over at the teen holding his face and shooting daggers at her with his strange eyes.

"He's fine. Besides, I gave him fair warning. He could've blocked me." Before Conrad could light into her, she turned to face him, expression serious. "You should be thanking me. I just taught him a valuable lesson. He'll get a lot worse if he says something like that to the wrong person in the Farthers."

Conrad rolled his eyes and muttered under his breath, "I happen to be in full agreement with you this time. The boy needs to be taught a lesson." Finn watched him send a dark glare toward AJ, whom Shane was helping to his feet. "Next time, maybe try a little impulse control, Hellion."

Conrad gave her one last look of exasperation before stalking over to AJ and roughly tagging the back of his shirt. No one else in the room seemed particularly fazed when Conrad practically dragged him out the door.

Lex sidled up beside her, whispering conspiratorially.

"Okay, forget the garbage chute. You have to teach me how to do *that*."

She shot her fist out in a fake jab, followed by the sloppiest upper-cut Finn had ever seen. Lex's eyes narrowed in a mock glare, her voice deepening in imitation.

"*'I'm going to punch you now.'* Gods, that was amazing."

Finn found herself returning the hyperactive woman's smile. Jax grinned and gave her what she translated to be a nod of approval, while Shane eyed them all warily, obviously less than thrilled with her most recent behavior.

He released his stare to turn fully on the twins.

"Don't you two have some work to get back to?"

Lex stuck her tongue out at him, quickly popping her candy back in her mouth and skipping toward the door. Jax's eyes widened in feigned horror, his hand coming up to clutch at the left side of his chest.

"Oh my Gods, Captain. Who's flying the ship?" He grabbed his giggling sister by the shoulders, shaking her as he called out to no one in particular, "We're all going to die!"

Then, as if nothing had happened, he wrapped an arm around his twin and calmly grinned back at Finn.

"Later, sexy stowaway."

When her eyebrows shot up, Shane shook his head and offered her a helpless shrug.

"I've tried to get Isis to medicate them, but she refuses." A few awkward moments passed with nothing but the hum of the ship to break the silence before he spoke again. "I'd appreciate it if you'd stop attacking my crew." Finn opened her mouth to argue, but he held up a hand to silence her. "I'm not saying AJ didn't deserve it, but we take care of our own here, with our own set of rules. He won't disrespect you again, I can promise you that. But I need you to keep those fists of fury to yourself, impressive though they may be."

He shot her a wry smile. It softened his face, adding a hint of yellow to his eyes. She found herself smiling back.

"I won't make you a promise I can't keep, but as long as your crew respects my rules, I'll respect yours."

He nodded, lines of worry beginning to crease his brow.

"That brings me to my next order of business. Iliana is a member of my crew—"

Finn didn't let him finish, the smile already falling from her face.

"I think it's best if you keep that woman out of my way."

He ran an agitated hand over the back of his neck.

"I had a feeling you were going to say that. Look, Iliana's a grown woman. She doesn't listen to me as it is. Where you're concerned, I might as well be talking to a brick wall. She's a lot like you in that way." He had the audacity to grin. "She's determined to find out where you've been all this time."

"I've been on the Mud Pit for the last seven cycles."

His grin morphed into an expectant stare.

"And the four cycles before that? Where were you then?"

Finn masked her expression, giving nothing away.

"I don't know, and even if I did, I'm not sure I'd be inclined to share with a glorified doxie and her crew of kidnappers."

He watched her for a long moment, his eyes laced with disappointment and just a touch of sadness. Curse it all if she didn't feel that strange tug of guilt again. Finn could see the wheels spinning in his head as he tried to unravel whatever mystery she'd presented him with. She'd caught the same look on Grim's face many a time when he didn't think she was watching.

"I can't even begin to imagine what you've been through, Finn. I'd just hoped that whatever it was hadn't taken your humanity from you. I guess now I have my answer."

Those words, so softly spoken and laced with pity, unraveled something inside of her. Finn barely choked back the strangled gasp as a piece of her deep within the confines of her chest collapsed. *Humanity.* Truthfully, she didn't even know what that word meant anymore. She told herself it shouldn't matter. She was surviving the best way she knew how, but the rationalization sounded empty even to her.

Shane cleared his throat and started to walk away. He took one last backward glance at her before delivering his final punch.

"When we reach Cartan, we can part ways and you can pretend like this was all just a bad dream."

Finn frowned at his retreating back, feeling sick inside.

What did he know of bad dreams?

SIX

Finn spent the next few hours counting holes in the ceiling, contemplating skipping dinner altogether. She was no stranger to hunger, and Shane's earlier words in the rec room still stung, making her less than eager to see him again.

She hated admitting it, but something about what he'd said had resonated within her, echoing off the hollow confines of her chest. It seemed the mysterious captain of *Independence* had no trouble seeing the darkness lurking inside of Finn. The empty void of her past dripped from her like poison, pumping through her veins and tainting the very air she breathed. She didn't know if she could ever purge it.

Every night she awakened terrified from nightmares, and every day the fatigue grew as she struggled to hide from the elusive specters that refused to release her.

She sat on the bed in her temporary room for a long time, unable to appreciate its downy softness. She stared out the window into nothingness, mood as black as the endless chasm outside.

Finn became so wrapped up in her thoughts she barely registered the sound of her door opening from the outside. She glanced back and saw Tiri walk in, her clothes and face streaked with the remainders of whatever she'd been busy cooking.

As if sensing Finn's disquiet, she didn't say anything, her normally vibrant presence somber. She merely walked over to the bed and took a seat a few inches away from Finn, close but not touching. They sat together like that for a long time in companionable stillness, staring out the window into the abyss.

Finally, the child broke the silence.

"Are you coming to dinner? Isis and I made something special for you."

She waited patiently for Finn to answer, her eyes earnest. Finn couldn't imagine what they'd made.

As much as Finn wanted to hide away in isolation for the next three days until they reached Cartan, claustrophobia and excess restless energy would never allow it. She might as well kick things off with an awkward dinner. If she were being honest with herself, she didn't have it in her to deny her only friend on the ship. Finn stood up from the bed and gave Tiri a wary smile.

"What are we waiting for?"

The girl answered Finn with a megawatt grin of her own, and they both made their way out the door and down the hall to the elevator. Finn's stomach lurched at the sight of its metallic doors. She braced herself and stepped in beside Tiri, closing her eyes and attempting to prepare herself for the stomach-dropping sensation about to hit when they began to ascend. Her efforts were somewhat thwarted by Tiri as she began a chorus of constant chatter, ranging from the dinner she'd prepared to her favorite things to do on the ship.

Finn opened her mouth to cut her off, needing silence to deal with her rising anxiety, but was shocked out of her thoughts with a question.

"I know you don't like touching, but what about kissing? Because if kissing is okay, I think you should kiss Conrad."

Finn's eyes shot open at her casual suggestion.

Where did that *come from?*

She gave the girl the best frown she could manage and put her hands on her hips.

"First of all, that is none of your business. Secondly, I do *not* want to kiss Conrad. Ever. Got it?"

The little imp didn't bother answering. The elevator doors opened in front of them, revealing the dining room, where the rest of the crew waited. Finn looked down in shock. Tiri had managed to distract her yet again. She didn't even remember feeling the jar of the elevator as it climbed. Tiri looked back at her with a sly grin, and Finn knew diversion had been her intention all along.

She stepped out of the elevator and onto the metal flooring of the dining room, still looking dumbstruck. Tiri disappeared around a corner, no doubt heading to the kitchens to serve, leaving Finn exposed and uncomfortable without her presence.

Shane sat at the head of the table in a tall-backed chair so ornate it could have passed for a throne. His eyes met Finn's, and he gave her a subtle nod of greeting that she didn't return.

To his right, Lex and Jax sat in matching chairs smaller than Shane's, upholstered in a colorful paisley pattern. Lex practically vibrated in hers when she caught sight of Finn.

"Finn, we saved you a seat."

She motioned to the chair directly across from her, a stocky wooden thing that looked to have seen better days. Finn pulled it out and plopped down, surprised to find it quite comfortable despite its boxy appearance.

The elevator doors opened again, but she didn't have to turn around to know who stepped out of them. Conrad's presence seemed to fill the room with tense energy, making her arms tingle from the sensation. She could almost feel his eyes burning a hole in the back of her head. She winced as his large hand pulled out the tall, black chair to her right and he sat down next to her.

Shane glanced up at him.

"Where's AJ?"

Finn kept her eyes on the table and waited for Conrad's gruff response.

"He's skipping dinner tonight."

His off-the-cuff response sent her mind spinning in all kinds of unwanted directions she felt helpless to control. Sure, he'd acted like a brat, but she'd already given him a beating for it once today. How badly did Conrad punish him afterward? So badly that he couldn't make it to dinner? Finn thought back to Conrad's face when he'd dragged AJ from the rec room: seething anger and raw aggression.

Her stomach flipped as she thought about the strangely beautiful boy, lying broken and bloodied on his bedroom floor.

Casually, so as not to draw attention, Finn searched Conrad's knuckles for cuts or blood. They looked clean and unmarred. Slowly, the tight coils of tension in her stomach eased a little, and she exhaled the breath she'd been holding.

Finn thought she'd been subtle in her inspection but knew she'd thought wrong when Conrad leaned close, speaking in an irritated voice only she could hear.

"Quit looking at me like that. I didn't beat him."

Finn breathed a sigh of relief, even as she realized she'd misjudged him yet again.

Their side conversation caught the attention of the rest of the table. Jax and Lex grinned back and forth at one another like a couple of idiots, while Shane regarded the pair pensively. Finn didn't like the look in his eye, so she decided to change the subject.

"How long have all of you been flying together?"

Shane grabbed the steel cup next to his place setting and took a long swig before answering.

"Conrad and I have been together since we were kids. The twins joined us about three cycles ago."

Interesting. Conrad and Shane grew up together? She stored that information away for later use.

"This is a merchant ship, right?" she asked, forcing a casual tone.

The twins' smiles disappeared from their faces. The table remained quiet for a moment before Shane answered.

"Yes, it is."

Finn remembered the vast cargo hold she'd seen several floors below; the one that currently sat empty.

"I noticed you don't have any cargo. And you've got an awfully small crew for such a big ship."

Granted, their basic needs were covered, but they still scraped by with the bare bones of a skeleton crew. Finn found the abnormality more than just a touch peculiar. Shane regarded her cautiously, and she knew his shuttered expression guarded something. They were all acting pretty squirrelly for the innocent crew of a merchant ship.

"We like to keep things tight. We'll be picking up some more crew on Cartan, as well as cargo."

Everything about his cadence seemed polite and straightforward. Everything except the cunning light in his eyes that told her he was lying. Finn leaned forward in her chair and matched his serious expression.

"What kind of cargo?"

She chanced a look at everyone else at the table. Jax and Lex remained uncharacteristically quiet, deferring to Shane's leadership. Conrad watched Finn, his serious eyes thoughtful. The tense silence lasted so long she figured Shane wouldn't answer, but he surprised her by leaning forward in his chair and cocking a brow.

"For someone who can't wait to get off my ship, you're awfully interested in it. In fact, you seem to know a lot about Ulta Dogwood 88s. What is it you do for a living, Finn?"

I know a lot about all kinds of ships, she thought to herself smugly.

He didn't intend to give her any information, that much was clear. Remembering Isis's dodgy answers back in her room, Finn decided to return the favor, smiling and leaning back in her chair.

"Oh, this and that."

Shane's eyes narrowed as he took another sip of whatever filled that steel cup.

"And what exactly does *this and that* entail?"

She knew how childish it seemed, but if she could get at least some small amount of enjoyment from her stay on his ship, she planned to take advantage. Finn took a deep breath and pretended to think about it.

"Well, I'd say it's mostly a little of *this* and a lot of *that*."

She heard Conrad heave a trademark sigh next to her, but Shane didn't have a chance to respond. Isis and Tiri appeared around the corner with trays of food. Finn noted that the dainty purple chair to the captain's left remained noticeably vacant and realized (with relief) that Iliana would not be joining them.

Thank the Gods for small miracles.

Tiri appeared next to her, all smiles as she placed a steaming bowl of red stew on Finn's place setting. The bowl brimmed with large hunks of meat, vegetables, and spices. Nothing in her life had ever smelled so mouthwateringly delicious.

The first bite felt like a taste of the heavens, the savory flavors hitting Finn's tongue and sliding down her throat. She ate so quickly, the stew burned going down, but she didn't care. She still choked back a moan with every bite.

Dinner seemed to pass by in a blur as everyone hurriedly talked over one another, telling jokes and regaling the group with boisterous stories. No one seemed concerned by the fact that Finn listened in while they openly discussed their day. She didn't learn anything useful, but she had to admit she liked being a part of the atmosphere. If she closed her eyes, she could almost pretend to be sitting on a stool at the Dirty Molly. Their smiles came so easily, their laughter filling the table with warmth and an undeniable sense of companionship.

Too soon, it seemed, Tiri brought out dessert, setting a delicious-looking pastry on the plate before Finn. On it lay a round piece of soft, spongy cake drizzled with a mixture of honey, sugar, and fresh berries.

The girl sat down in a plush green seat to Finn's left and watched her intently. When Tiri smiled from ear to ear as Finn took her first bite, Finn knew this had to be the *something special* she'd mentioned earlier. Finn closed her eyes in bliss as the explosion of flavors hit her tongue: the spice of the cake, the sugary sweetness of the honey, the tart pop of fresh berries as they exploded in her mouth. She couldn't bring herself to question where they'd gotten their hands on fresh fruit, too lost in the foreign sensations of joy dancing on her tongue. The cake was decadence in its purest form.

Finn opened her eyes to find everyone at the table watching her, their facial expressions varying from rapt attention to silly smiles. Her gaze sought out Conrad of its own accord. She found him watching her with a warm glint in his eyes.

She grinned at him through a mouth full of crumbs.

After another few bites, everyone resumed their excited chatter, and she chanced a glance up at Tiri. Leaning over, she whispered in the girl's ear so only she could hear.

"Thank you. This is the best cake I've ever tasted."

Tiri's answering grin was radiant as she leaned in to whisper back, "Happy Birthday, Finn."

Finn shook her head, just barely containing a surprised bark of laughter as she took one last bite of cake. She could still feel Conrad's stare like a physical touch and turned to find him watching her, a look of baffled curiosity on his face. When his azure gaze fell to her mouth, Finn realized she was still smiling.

SEVEN

A pair of lifeless eyes, one blue and one milky white, stare back at her. They're pleading for her to save them.

Finn woke up, throat raw from her screams, heart pounding a mad rhythm. Her sheets lay in chaotic disarray around her. She took in a few rasping breaths, letting her eyes adjust to the darkness.

Safe.

The word didn't soothe her like it usually did.

Those eyes, so innocent and full of fear: one blue and one opaque. Finn felt tears burning a pathway up her throat and choked them back, panic threatening to send her into darkness.

A new panic gripped her chest as she remembered where she slept, remembered the other crew mere feet from her room. Finn's solitude on the Mud Pit meant she never worried about her nightmares disturbing others. Here on *Independence*, sensitive ears surrounded her on all sides.

Maybe no one heard.

Her hope died a sure, quick death when the floor creaked. She glanced up to see Conrad leaning against the open doorway, looking rugged and disheveled from sleep. The glow from his eyes illuminated a pair of very broad shoulders, thickly corded arms, and the hard planes of an exceptionally naked chest. Those markings of his stood out in full view, winding a magnificent trail up his biceps and around his neck before finally coming to rest in intricate geometric patterns above his pectorals. The runes blended together seamlessly. From there, a light dusting of dark, curly hair led down to a flat stomach, where a pair of black pants slung low on the blades of his hips.

She pulled the sheets up to her chest with shaking hands.

"How long have you been standing there?"

He watched her cautiously, but his eyes also held something akin to sympathy. Seeing it there, Finn wanted to get mad, to rail at him for daring to look at her in such a way. She much preferred his anger to his sympathy, needed it to keep the chill deep within her from spreading. She wanted to provoke him but feared if she opened her mouth, her teeth might start chattering. It took all of her concentration to hold her body still when it wanted so desperately to tremble.

"Not long. I heard screaming," he said, his eyes roving over her intently. "Is everything okay?"

Finn tightened her muscles, refusing to let them shake.

"Everything's peachy. Except for the pervy half-breed breaking into my room in the middle of the night."

Out of the corner of her eye, she saw him make his way slowly to stand by the side of the bed. Not exactly the reaction she'd been hoping for.

"Nightmares are nothing to be ashamed of, Finn."

"Thanks, but the only nightmare I seem to be having is the one where I'm stuck on a ship with a half-breed who won't leave me alone."

She turned to glower up at him and promptly lost all train of thought as he took a seat on the edge of the bed, next to her knees. Not touching her, but so very, very close.

Finn tried to swallow, throat suddenly dry at the hungry look he was giving her.

Every type of lascivious male seemed to find his way to the Mud Pit. Finn had been on the wrong end of more than one lustful gaze. But there was something different about the way Conrad looked at her. Something almost reverent in the way his eyes held hers. It did strange things to her, things she'd never felt before.

"Why do you look at me like that?"

His brows furrowed in confusion.

"Like what?"

More footsteps shattered the moment, and they both turned. Tiri stood just inside the doorway, dressed in a long pink nightgown, clutching an oversized pillow. She looked painfully young as she wiped the sleep from her eyes with a little fist.

Conrad instantly crossed the room to her side.

"What are you doing up, Lil' Bit? Are you okay?"

"Finn needs me."

Eyes half closed from sleep, she marched over to the bed, and grabbed as many pillows as she could carry. Ignoring both of them, she lined the cushions up and down the middle of the mattress from the headboard to Finn's feet. When she finished, they became a fluffy little barrier, dividing the bed into two halves. Finn offered Conrad a helpless look of confusion, but he didn't seem to have a clue either.

Tiri climbed into the bed on the opposite side of the pillows from Finn, snuggling deep into the covers.

Finn figured it out before Conrad.

The little girl fully intended to spend the night in her bed. Knowing Finn's aversion to being touched, she'd created a solution to the problem the way only a child could. A strange sensation of warmth she was wholly unprepared for began to spread throughout Finn's chest.

Tiri blinked up at Conrad, dismissing him with a yawn.

"Good night, Conrad."

The poor man looked back and forth between them a few times before shaking his head in defeat.

"Good night then."

He gave them one last backward glance before leaving, the door shutting gently behind him. No longer comfortable with the darkness, Finn set the room's lights to a low dim.

Tiri turned her head to look up and whispered softly, her round eyes solemn. Liquid began to pool in their depths. Finn could see the wetness spilling down her cheeks onto the pillow between them.

"I didn't mean to listen in on your thoughts, but you were screaming so loud. Screaming her name. I'll keep the nightmares away, Finn," Tiri whimpered. "I promise."

Finn shushed her gently and got into bed.

"It's okay, little one," she soothed.

Finn felt tears of her own burning the backs of her eyes, threatening to fall. No one had ever offered her comfort so selflessly. The desire to reach out and wipe the tears from Tiri's cheeks, to hold her in her arms until the world was right again, nearly overwhelmed her.

This child was changing things inside of her.

Finn's fingers tingled with the urge to run them through Tiri's hair. Instead, she placed her hand on the pillow by the girl's head, just close enough to feel her warm breaths fanning out across her fingers. They fell asleep that way, side by side. Only a wall of pillows separated them, bridged by Finn's hand reaching for her.

As promised, Tiri kept the nightmares at bay.

EIGHT

Finn became aware of her body slowly the next morning, her limbs coming to life languidly as her eyes fluttered open with an alien sense of laziness. She couldn't remember the last time she'd slept so well. She stretched both arms above her head and let herself enjoy the moment.

All at once, she remembered she hadn't slept alone, and Finn's eyes snapped open as they searched out Tiri. To her surprise, she found the other side of the bed empty, the line of pillows between them still in place.

How late had she slept?

Finn threw the covers off and climbed out of bed, heading to the desk chair where she'd unceremoniously piled the extra clothes Isis had given her last night. She'd just started digging through the array of pants and tops when something on the desk caught her eye. The colors drew her attention first, but as she looked closer and the images began to take shape in her mind, she felt her chest squeeze and the air leave her lungs.

Somehow, the child had managed to capture Finn perfectly: the lines of her face (all at once sharp and soft), the deep indigo of her round eyes, the wild and untamed curl of her dark hair. However, the expression on her face seemed wrong. In the picture, Finn's lids looked heavy and her lips curled slightly upward. For once, the skin of her forehead was smooth and relaxed in a mixture of bliss and tranquility. Finn had never seen that look on her own face before.

Tiri had drawn her leaning against a tall tree with lush, green foliage. Something about it seemed so familiar. Finn scanned her memories and realized Tiri had managed to replicate the oak from Finn's mind. The one she'd seen yesterday as a young Iliana and the small child she'd called Kyra discussed space pirates and venturing into town.

She'd drawn every crevice, every chip in the bark exactly as Finn remembered it. Together, all of the colors ebbed and flowed in a kaleidoscope of beauty.

She'd even managed to make Finn beautiful.

Before she could put a name to the strange emotions swirling in her gut, she noticed the small, careful script just underneath the tree's thick trunk.

Important meeting today in the cargo hold. You're not supposed to be there.
Don't be late!
—Tiri

Finn laughed, loud and boisterous. Grabbing the first pair of pants and shirt she saw, she nearly sprinted to the bathroom and took a quick shower. She dressed and ran her gloved fingers through her hair, letting it fall down past her shoulders. Moving over to the desk, Finn picked up Tiri's drawing, folding it carefully and placing it inside her right boot.

She had no idea how late she'd slept or what time it was, but there was no way she intended on missing a super-secret meeting in the cargo hold. An opportunity had presented itself, and Finn planned on finding out as much about the tight-lipped Shane and his crew as she could.

She sped out the door and headed down the hallway away from the elevator, pausing to take a couple of long, lingering looks down the corridor. As quietly as possible, she maneuvered herself down the ladder protruding from the hole in the metal-grate flooring.

Her impatience to get to the cargo hold urged her to descend as rapidly as possible, but she forced herself to practice stealth, stopping every few steps to listen for voices. When nothing but the drone and purr of the ship's inner mechanics greeted her, Finn continued downward.

After what felt like an eternity, her boots met the floor. She immediately crouched low, backing into the shadows of the farthest wall.

The doors to the hold stood open, and Finn could just barely make out the sound of muffled voices from where she stood. Slowly, she crept closer, placing herself just outside the door while still safely hidden in the shadowed corner formed by two walls.

From around the bend, she could see Shane's back as he ran a hand through his hair in frustration. Conrad stood rigid next to him. He was dressed head to toe in black, a pair of dark shades, considered stylish by upper-caste standards, covering his peculiar eyes. Even his markings were hidden by the clothes he wore.

Could this be the meeting? Just the two of them in the cargo hold?

Then Shane shifted a little, and Finn's jaw dropped in shock as his movement revealed familiar faces casually seated around the hold.

It was a well-known fact that Grim served as the most renowned and talented middle-man in the farthest reaches of the Farthers. Anyone who wanted a job done and wanted it done right went to him.

Everyone else went to see the Toad.

Granted, no one actually called him that to his face, lest they end up in pieces scattered across the fiery rings of Solidar. Much like "Finn No Last Name," it just happened to be a very accurate moniker that had stuck over time.

He did in fact look like a toad. His body stretched as wide as he was tall, with a bumpy amphibian-like complexion, a pair of beady black eyes, and a tongue that refused to stay inside his mouth.

Business was business, however, and certain relationships had to be maintained no matter how disgusting the other party. Finn herself took meetings with the Toad on occasion, when Grim found himself too busy.

Nevertheless, even if she'd never met the man, she could still testify to his toadlike appearance because he currently sat on a metal box in the hold in front of her, his short legs crossed regally while he glared at Shane as though he found the very sight of him offensive.

With a webbed hand, he adjusted the cravat on his three-piece suit. Despite his appearance and the often violent nature of his dealings, the Toad liked to maintain a cultured and dignified persona.

One never glimpsed the man without a three-piece suit and his gold cufflinks firmly in place.

"I only made the trip out here, Montgomery, because you came so highly recommended. However, I don't know what my associate was thinking. There's no way you and your tiny crew can pull off a job of this magnitude."

Finn's eyes drifted over to the hired muscle standing on either side of him, arms crossed and prepared for a showdown. Her pulse jumped at the sight. The Toad didn't mess around when it came to the bodyguards who protected him. The two brutes accompanied him everywhere, and thanks to the insane amount of Yellow Faze they dosed with, they were dangerous in a way that had even Finn on her best behavior.

Shane's crew took a job on Cartan for the Toad? Finn couldn't decide whether she wanted to laugh, cry, or keel over from shock. She really had gotten herself involved in a veritable catastrophe. That thought led to Iliana, the reason she'd ended up on board in the first place. What part did the courtesan play in all of this?

Shane's voice interrupted her thoughts.

"I assure you, we are more than equipped to complete this job. My contact led me to believe this was already a done deal. You knew our numbers before you set foot on our ship, so you'll have to forgive my confusion with your change of heart."

The Toad's beady eyes blinked then narrowed.

"I don't think I like your tone, boy." His glance shifted over to Conrad. "And I don't like the looks of that big one. A man who wears shades to a business meeting is a man with something to hide."

Conrad's shoulders stiffened, his fists clenching infinitesimally. Finn found her own body tensing in time with his. They would get themselves killed if they didn't tread carefully. The Toad didn't handle slights well.

The Toad began to move in a circle around Shane and Conrad, his doped-up muscle close on his heels, and Finn's palms began to sweat. Conrad's body remained strung tight, ready to pounce.

Don't do something stupid, Conrad, she urged with her mind.

The thought suddenly occurred to her that she could intercede in this situation. A smart person would just stay put and let the chips fall where they may, maybe even take a chance at escape when all was said and done. But as had been her habit of late, Finn wasn't exactly thinking like a *smart* person.

The prospect of escape didn't appeal to her nearly as much as the prospect of showing her captors just exactly whom they'd chosen to mess with. Shane and Conrad wanted something from the Toad, something they couldn't get without Finn's help. The shift in power energized her in a way nothing else had in cycles.

Finn walked with an extra spring in her step as she made her way into the hold, her shoulders back, her spine straight, and her head held high. She sauntered over to the group, stopping just behind Conrad. The tension in the room immediately shifted as all eyes turned at once, finally registering her entrance.

Conrad's and Shane's expressions went from comically stupefied to furious when they registered her presence. After a moment of hesitation, they both moved in her direction, getting ready to remove the rude intrusion, no doubt.

The Toad stopped them short, his voice higher and much chipper than they'd surely ever heard it as he called out, "Finn No Last Name. What in the Gods' names are you doing on this heap, my girl?"

Finn almost laughed watching Shane and Conrad exchange a glance, back to looking stupefied again. Instead of answering the Toad, she gave the two men a long, hard look and arched her brow.

She could see Shane's pride warring with his desperation as he regarded her stonily, his jaw clenched tight.

Finally, it seemed, desperation won out and he mouthed out a silent *"Please."*

An overwhelming glow of satisfaction filled her as she strolled over to the Toad, fake smile firmly in place. Reminding herself to use his given name, she called out, "I wouldn't say it's a complete heap, Julian. The showers here are heaven."

He liked that, and a wide, toothless smile broke out on his face, causing his tongue to slip out the side of his mouth even farther.

"Had I known you were going to be here, I would have flown out sooner. You look lovely as always."

The Toad had been smitten ever since their first encounter, something Finn took full advantage of when it suited her. Now that she glimpsed an ample view of the hold, she could see their Lantus ship docked in the massive space. It was the newest model (only the best for the Toad), and she paused for a moment, longing filling her as she imagined flying off for the Mud Pit in it. She shook the thought free. The Toad was a necessary evil, but Finn knew it best to keep her distance.

"It's been awhile, Julian. How's business treating you these days?"

"Not as well as it's been treating you. You're becoming quite the legend. When are you going to leave Grim and come to work for me?"

Finn let her fake smile broaden.

"When you pay as well as he does."

The Toad knew where her loyalties lay, but he chuckled anyway.

"We both know he'll never let you go." He paused a moment to look her over. "I know Grim didn't send you out here. This job is all mine, and it's going to make everyone involved very rich. I was considering giving it to these two, but there's no way they could pull it off." He leaned in conspiratorially. "Plus, I don't like the looks of that big one. He won't take off those shades."

Conrad's big body radiated aggression, massive arms crossed tightly at his chest. Finn gave him a stern look to back off, and turned fully to the Toad. In a voice so low only he could hear, she leaned in as close as she dared and whispered to him. Taking her time, she explained to the Toad exactly why the big man couldn't remove his shades.

Her gaze never left Conrad's, and the wary glare he leveled her with was clearly visible behind his dark shades. She imagined his eyes glowing bright with his fury, and some twisted part of her reveled in it. When she finished, the Toad regarded Conrad for a long, tense minute.

Suddenly he burst into a fit of the loudest laughter she'd ever heard from him.

"Poor bastard, that explains it then."

Finn grinned right along with him, offering Conrad a pitying glance and ignoring the glowering coming from Shane's direction. When his laughter finally subsided, the Toad regarded Shane seriously.

"All right, boy, you can have the job on one condition."

Shane's green eyes grew intense as he answered. If he was at all surprised by the Toad's turnaround, he hid it well.

"Name it."

"Finn goes with you. She's the only one skilled enough to see this through. I trust her with it, or no one."

Shane's glance shifted to Finn, and she thought about everything that had transpired in the last day. So many feelings and desires warred with one another. She wanted off this ship, but its crew had presented her with a mystery she wasn't ready to leave behind.

Besides, a few more days with Iliana gave her ample opportunity to steal back Grim's necklace. Finn had never failed a job . . . *ever*. She wasn't about to start now.

She broke Shane's gaze and turned back to the Toad.

"You've got a deal."

He gave his webbed hands a clap and nodded at his muscle, giving them the okay to relax.

"Good. You'll need to be on Cartan tomorrow night for Senator Califax's Annual Reliance Victory Ball." He pulled a large envelope from the inside pocket of his suit jacket. "Here are your invitations and a map of the senator's estate, including security measures that have been added for the event."

Finn took the package from him with numb fingers and shot a questioning glance at Shane. He planned on taking a job at a ball celebrating the unionization?

The Toad continued, undeterred, directing his comments to Shane now.

"I've also included pictures of the artifact. Don't screw this up, Montgomery." His face softened as he regarded Finn one last time. "I look forward to seeing you again, my sweet."

He gave her a parting bow and a wink, heading off in the direction of his ship with his two guard dogs close behind. She didn't think he'd bother with any further parting words for Shane or Conrad, but he surprised them all by stopping just before stepping into his ship. Offering Conrad an amused smirk, he yelled, "Good luck with those ocular worms, my boy. You can never be too careful with doxies these days!"

With that, the Toad disappeared into the interior of the Lantus. Finn's mouth twitched, but she forced herself to remain indifferent as she felt Conrad's eyes burning a hole into the back of her head. She walked briskly out of the hold, followed by Shane and Conrad. The door sealed behind them; then the ship's outer doors opened, and the Toad departed.

Finn took a step back toward her quarters when Conrad's large forearm hit the wall in front of her, blocking her path. He pulled the dark shades from his face, and the harsh glow of his eyes illuminated the shadows around them. He leaned his head in close to Finn's, a muscle ticking in his jaw.

"Ocular worms?"

Finn bit her lip, fighting the smile tugging there. She gave him the most innocent gaze she could muster.

"It was the best I could come up with at the time."

His eyes narrowed, lasering in on her mouth, where she'd begun to lose the fight with her amusement.

"You think this is funny?"

"A little." Finn couldn't hold back the snort of laughter any longer, he looked so affronted. "Come on, Conrad. You were going to lose the job, and I saved the day. Just say thank you like a big boy."

Shane rolled his eyes, regarding them both like a couple of unruly teenagers before spearing her with a stern gaze.

"Finn No Last Name?"

She took a breath, recovering from her laughter.

"I told you I didn't have one."

He shook his blond head in vexation.

"And how exactly do you know the Toad?"

Finn felt the smile drop from her face, a serious expression matching Shane's taking its place.

"I meet all kinds of people in my line of work."

"What line of work might that be?"

"I think you already know the answer to that, otherwise I wouldn't be standing here. I also think it's time you both told me what's going on."

Shane tensed at the impatience in her tone.

"Look, I appreciate you helping us out with the Toad. You have no idea how much. But I need to fill the rest of the crew in on what's going on. Conrad can brief you on the details of the job for now. I'm trusting you to understand how important this is to all of us. We land on Cartan tomorrow."

His casual dismissal pricked her temper, and as she watched him disappear around a corner, she turned it on the only person left in the hall.

"What was that all about? Why are you all so secretive?"

Conrad leaned against the wall in a casual pose, his otherworldly eyes watchful. Most of his earlier anger seemed to have dissipated.

"Don't ask me. I'm just here for the doxies."

His mouth set in a hard line, but his eyes sparkled with just a touch of humor. Finn supposed she was forgiven then.

"How is the courtesan involved in all of this?"

"Ask her yourself."

She'd say this for the big half-breed, at least he had the temerity to look her in the eyes when he gave her crooked answers.

"Fine, let's get this briefing over with. I'm not going into this job blind."

Conrad motioned for her to follow him, leading her down the hall and into one of the storage rooms she'd passed yesterday. He took the large envelope from her grip and sat down on a wooden crate, nodding for her to do the same. She did, feeling at ease for the first time during her stay as her instincts took over. Prepping for a job was something familiar, something Finn excelled at.

Conrad dragged another crate between them and removed a map from the envelope, spreading it across the top of the make-shift table. Out of habit, Finn ran her hands over its surface, scanning the interior of the manor depicted there with the pads of her fingers.

The senator's home was a massive three-story estate, the entire property spanning across four acres of sprawling hills. She let her eyes roam over every nook and cranny, committing them to memory. Her palms began to tingle over the map as the images took shape in her mind.

It came as easily to her as breathing, a part of her so ingrained, she never worried it might one day fail her. She often wondered if her talent was some kind of consolation prize for her memory loss. It was as though the Gods had felt so sorry for the girl with no memories, they'd gifted her with the ability to memorize whatever she wanted whenever she wanted with a simple touch. She figured at this point, life owed her an advantage or two.

Once she felt comfortable that all the information had been committed to memory, she leaned back and looked at Conrad. His stare held a mixture of brooding curiosity and intense concentration. He pulled the rest of the papers from the envelope and spread them out, his eyes never leaving hers.

"You just memorized that map, didn't you?"

It was a statement, not a question, and she didn't bother insulting him by denying it.

"I'm pretty amazing, aren't I?"

His brows arched at her casual jest, and he leaned back.

"You're definitely full of surprises."

That strange electricity began to charge the air between them as his gaze held hers. Finn found it difficult to look away, hypnotized by the gentle look of affection and amusement on his face as he watched her. Being alone with him like this was dangerous in a way she'd never experienced. Her whole body flushed with heat, and her lungs seemed to have difficulty getting enough air.

Finn cleared her throat, forcing her head downward at the papers scattered in front of them.

"Tell me about the job."

She didn't bring her eyes up to his again, instead focusing on the detailed surveillance the Toad had managed to gather on the senator and his security.

"Tell me how you know the Toad. He seems rather fond of you."

He sounded like he might be gritting his teeth. Curiosity won out, and she looked up to find he was indeed clenching his jaw.

"Everyone knows the Toad, including you, so why are you looking at me like I've done something wrong?"

Darkness clouded his features as he regarded her sullenly.

"I don't like him."

Finn laughed; she couldn't help herself.

"Join the club. No one likes him. The only reason he gets as much business as he does is because of those two meteorheads he pays to follow him around. You saw how big they are. He doses them with Faze to keep them nice and strong. I once saw them tear a man in half with their bare hands. It was gruesome."

Conrad grimaced.

"How did you end up on a hellhole like Altara?"

The temptation to answer him was surprisingly strong. He seemed genuinely interested, and Gods knew he was easy to talk to. But for all she knew, he could be gathering information for Shane, or even worse, Iliana.

"I'm a thief, Conrad. There's no better place for someone like me. Now tell me about the job."

The subject change didn't deter him. In fact, he smiled.

"Senator Califax and his wife are hosting a Reliance Victory Ball at their home tomorrow night. The place is going to be swarming with Reliance soldiers and government officials. We'll be attending as invited guests."

Conrad held up four invitations with large red and gold Reliance insignia seals and fancy cursive lettering dancing back and forth across the front. The red and gold Arcturian eye that had long ago become the symbol of the Union blinked from the upper corner. Finn frowned up at him.

"*We?*"

"The job was meant for four people. Shane, Iliana, AJ, and myself. You'll be taking AJ's place."

Finn almost laughed, but when his expression remained serious her jaw fell open.

"There are so many things wrong with what you just said, I don't know where to begin."

Finn was beginning to think the only mystery this crew presented might be the mystery of their missing sanity. AJ, the adolescent hothead, brought no assets whatsoever to a team of thieves. Conrad was a half-breed, the very last being in the galaxy who should be walking into a den of Reliance soldiers and aristocrats. If his eyes glowed even once, outing him for what he was, he'd be as good as dead. Finn didn't know much about Shane's skills as a thief, but she was definitely starting to question his judgment as the ringleader of these haphazard fools.

The only person in the group that made any sense at all was Iliana. She retained the training and caste level the group needed. As a courtesan, she could blend effortlessly into a crowd of Reliance well-to-dos and officials. Without her, they would be outed immediately.

"Care to share what's got you all riled now, Hellion?"

"You mean aside from the fact that this is the worst plan I've ever heard?"

At her outburst, he chuckled.

"You're not giving us much credit. We have done this before, you know."

Finn jumped up from her seat on the box and began pacing. Her agitation proved too much to keep her still as she railed at him, thinking things through.

"Well, I haven't. My specialty is stealth, not fancy parties. I'm made for the sidelines, not the center of the Reliance's attention. While we're on the subject, do you know how dangerous it is for you to go there, to the Inner Rings, parading around in all your half-breed glory? For that matter, what were you thinking today with the Toad? Do you have a death wish or something?"

Finn paused mid-rant when she realized Conrad wasn't responding, and turned to face him. She gasped, finally noticing he'd stood up sometime during her tirade, planting himself directly in front of her.

His full lips twitched with amusement, causing her brows to furrow in confusion.

"Do you find the prospect of death funny?"

He took another step toward her, placing himself just a breath away.

"Not at all. I just didn't realize you cared so much."

Finn scoffed.

"I care about the fact that I seem to be prisoner to the galaxy's most irrational, ill-prepared criminals."

"I think you're starting to care about us more than you're letting on. Why else help us when you could've used the Toad to escape?" he asked.

Finn took a clumsy step back, her vision clouding as his powerful presence overwhelmed her.

"And end up on today's lunch menu for those bodyguards of his? I don't think so."

He followed as she backed up. Placing both hands on the wall behind either side of her head, he caged her with his body and his heat. Bending down, he levelled her with an intense scrutiny.

"Would it be so terrible to admit you're starting to like it here?"

Her heart pounded in her chest, face flushing at his nearness.

"To admit I like being a prisoner? Yes."

Conrad scanned her face for a moment, lips quirking in amusement.

"You're not a prisoner, and you know it." He leaned in closer, putting his mouth at her ear. "If you want me to respect your rules, you're going to have to start respecting mine."

Finn swallowed hard, her heart pounding through her body.

"What rule?"

His hot breath washed over her in a low whisper.

"Don't lie to me."

It took a moment for his words to register, the feel of his body heat making her mind foggy.

This had to be payback for her ocular worms story; at least that's what Finn was telling herself. Conrad was messing with her, he had to be. The air got trapped in her lungs as he ran his nose along her hair, breathing her in. The muscles in his arms bulged and strained where he pressed them hard into the wall on either side of her head. Finn felt heat pool in her belly at the sight of his barely restrained strength. Finally, he pulled away just enough to let his eyes meet hers again, and she sucked in a breath.

Their depths were back to glowing, only this time their luminescence was so powerful, Finn felt caught by the sheer beauty of it.

Her lips parted in confusion. She had thought they only glowed in anger.

Noticing the direction of her puzzled gaze, he jerked away from her, scrubbing a hand over his eyes. When he next looked back, the bright light within them had been extinguished, replaced by a cold, indifferent stare.

Her stomach felt hollow and her skin instantly cooled at the quick turnaround in his demeanor.

"There's not much more you need to know about the job," he said, his tone cold and professional. "Your part is simple. Get me to the senator's office in the manor's west wing and I'll take care of the rest."

Finn's mind scrambled to keep up with his rapid about-face.

"You're really going?"

"Yes, I'm really going. Despite being a good-for-nothing half-breed with terrifying glowing eyes, I can still get things done from time to time."

His words hit Finn like a slap. He still thought she judged him for being a half-breed. It almost seemed as though he judged himself. As the realization sank in, a different kind of heat spread throughout her body, coloring her cheeks with anger and embarrassment. Her hands shook; she couldn't decide whether she wanted to punch him or shake him.

Foregoing either option, Finn watched him for a long moment, finally noticing the vulnerability lurking just beneath the surface of his anger. His muscles were tensed; he looked ready for a fight and was probably relishing the idea of unleashing some of that self-hatred.

She shook her head, suddenly exhausted. She didn't know what possessed her to do it, but she felt herself approaching him slowly, waiting for him to meet her gaze. When he did, she searched his eyes, trying by sheer force to make him see all the things she couldn't express with words.

When their blue depths simply narrowed further in confusion, she sighed.

"You're an idiot."

With those parting words, Finn left him alone in the storage room.

NINE

Finn urged herself to forget Conrad and concentrate on tomorrow's job. As she made her way up the metal ladder, she mulled over just exactly how they might pull off such an unfeasible task. She'd never been to a ball before, didn't even know what to expect from one. The thought had her stomach tied up in knots.

Finn stepped off the ladder and onto the metal-grate flooring leading to her bedroom. The thought of heading back there to let her thoughts eat at her filled Finn with dread, but she couldn't think of anywhere else to go.

She decided to let herself wander, shifting her brain onto autopilot. Her body turned this way and that in conjunction with the ship's layout as it appeared in her mind.

She didn't pay much attention to where she went, hardly surprised when she didn't run into another soul on her walkabout. She struggled to block out thoughts of Conrad as her feet carried her deeper into the ship. Why did her body react so strongly to his presence? It seemed to operate on its own volition whenever he held her in that hypnotizing stare of his.

The sound of gentle humming distracted Finn from her thoughts, and she took a moment to examine where she'd ended up. She'd headed north, deep into the center of the ship. To her left sat the engine room, the heart of the Dogwood. Glancing over her shoulder toward the sound of the humming, she found herself staring at a door where a wall should have been. She supposed she shouldn't have been surprised to discover such an anomaly on the already strange ship.

Finn pressed her palm against its sensor, watching it flash blue before opening. A gust of sweet, moist air hit her in the face, and her eyes widened as she scanned the interior of the room. Calling it a room didn't really seem to do it justice.

Someone had transformed it into *paradise*.

Lush greenery, flowers, and plant life completely covered the walls and floors. Everywhere Finn looked, her senses were assaulted by sweet, cloying scents and colors so bright she didn't understand how they could be real. The ceiling arced into a vast dome, some of the tallest trees and ivy reaching almost as high as the apex of the circular glass. She found herself surrounded on all sides by blossoms and flowers in the most brilliant purples, reds, blues, and pinks she'd ever seen.

Finn reached out her hand to gently caress the deep crimson petals of a flower the size of a fist. They felt just as soft as she'd imagined they would, filling her chest with a sense of peace.

"It is quite a sight to behold, is it not?"

Finn spun on her heel, almost tripping in her haste, to see Isis standing tall next to a bush bursting with ripe, purple berries. She wore a robe that at times seemed silvery and at others the palest blue. The way it shimmered and transformed left Finn so distracted, she forgot to answer.

Isis smiled warmly, breaking Finn from her trance.

"I'm sorry. I didn't know anyone was here."

"Do not fret, my dear. You are most welcome in my sanctuary. The blood of a grower runs through your veins, does it not?"

Finn's brow puckered in confusion.

"Nothing much grows on the Mud Pit."

She watched as Isis bent her elevated frame to kneel on one knee, cradling the blossom of a flower between her palms. She found something oddly familiar and comforting about the woman's presence.

"I was told your father was of the Agrarian caste," she informed Finn absently. "The gift of life is a most beautiful thing."

As Finn watched in a daze, the blossom began to grow in the woman's hands, its light pink petals unfurling as though stretching after a long nap. Isis gave the flower a coo and a loving pet before standing to her full height, her silver eyes regarding Finn kindly.

Before Finn could think better of it, she asked,

"How did you do that?"

"It is the balance of life. I am a healer by nature. My very essence depends on my ability to sustain life in the beings around me. I bring life to the flower, and in turn the flower gives life to me."

Finn thought about the lush plant life Grim had told her existed on Aquarii, and realized it must have been entirely sustained by the Aquariians and their unique gifts.

"Come. Sit with me, won't you?"

Finn looked around helplessly, unsure of where to step, not wanting to disturb even the smallest bud. Isis's smile widened.

"Take off those boots. How long has it been since you felt the grass caress your toes?"

With shaking hands she unlaced her boots, removing one then the other carefully so as not to disturb Tiri's sketch and setting them down. Finished, she pulled off the gray socks she'd put on that morning and tucked them inside her boots.

When Finn's bare feet touched the soft blades, she sighed, a smile breaking out on her face. All at once pliable and prickly, the grasses tickled the bottoms of her feet and snuck in between the spaces of her toes. She looked up at Isis, and the woman beckoned her over with an elegant wave of her blue hand.

Every step sent a foreign pulse of elation straight to Finn's chest, and her hands tingled from the overwhelming sensation of it all. Something tugged at the back of her brain, a strange sense of recognition, as though the grass under her feet were an old friend welcoming her home after a long separation. She followed Isis's tall form to the base of a wide tree bursting with ripe orange and green fruit. She couldn't name the tree, but just looking at the fruit told Finn it would be delicious and sweet.

The oasis made her think of Tiri and the girl's strange markings, as well as the mural in her room. Finn bet she loved it here.

"How long did it take you to create all of this?"

Isis laughed at the question, a merry, tinkling sound just as bright and graceful as the rest of her.

"My child, you make me sound like one of the Gods. I cultivate, I do not create. Not yet, anyway." She offered Finn a secret smile. One that made her feel as though she might be missing something important. "As with all living things, there is an ebb and flow to my garden. I merely maintain the balance of that rhythm."

Finn nodded her head and tried not to look as confused as she felt. The woman spoke in riddles.

"So, Aquariians believe in the Gods?"

"I myself believe in a great many things. For example, I believe you have vast potential, Finn No Last Name. I believe you have come to us for a reason. In time, if you open yourself up to it, your purpose will be revealed."

Finn sat down, unable to hide her disappointment as she ran her hand through the blades of grass beneath her.

"Damn, I was really hoping you weren't crazy like the rest of them. You know I'm a thief, right?"

Although, considering the crew Isis ran with, Finn's admission probably didn't mean as much as she'd once thought.

The woman's peals of answering laughter filled the space around them. Every plant, flower, and leaf seemed to sigh with pleasure in response.

"My child, what a delight you are. *What* we are is not nearly as important as *who* we are."

Finn bit out a humorless laugh. The very sentiment went against everything she knew to be true. Every member of the Union *was* their marking, from the first moment laser singed flesh.

"Who, what, it's all the same to the Reliance. That kind of talk gets you killed where I come from."

Isis gave Finn's leather cuffs a long look, and she clenched her fists under the scrutiny.

"Perhaps the worlds are ready for a change. *Perhaps* it is time for you to remove your chains."

Blood pounded in Finn's ears.

"I have no chains."

Isis barely flinched at the fire in Finn's voice.

"They are chains of your own making, but they are chains nevertheless."

Finn's hands balled into fists, her rage sucking the oxygen from the room until every blossom seemed to shrink from her. Screams echoed in her head, threatening to send her spiraling into a black pit of despair.

"You don't know the first the thing about me."

Isis's answering smile was benevolent.

"I know more than you think. My little Sotiri is quite fond of you, and she is an excellent judge of character."

Isis reached out, dreamily stroking a bundle of creeping ivy.

Finn scowled.

"I'm starting to question that."

"Tiri is so much more than you think." Isis relinquished the vine and turned to face her fully. "She is unlike anything else in the worlds." Her silver eyes penetrated Finn's with their intensity. "Much like you, Finn. I see a light in you, even if you don't. I am trying to discern how far you would go to protect something so precious, because as surely as I see your light, I see that a time will come when Tiri will need you."

"Isis? Isis, are you in here?"

Finn recognized Iliana's pleasant call the moment it sliced through the garden sanctuary, interrupting their perplexing conversation. What had Isis been trying to say? Protect Tiri from what?

As though nothing were out of sorts, Isis leaned away, her beautiful blue face the picture of serenity.

"We are over here, Iliana. Come and join us."

Finn snatched up her boots, her gut still churning from shock and confusion.

"I was just leaving."

She didn't wait for a response; the need to get out of the same room as the courtesan and the strange ethereal alien who saw too much compelled her to move. She held her boots in front of her like a shield, keeping her eyes focused on the ground bursting with life below.

She made it all the way to the door only to find Iliana's smooth bare feet blocking her path. Her toenails were painted a dark crimson, reminding Finn of blood and the Reliance. The scent of her perfume wafted over to her, intermingling with the scents of the different buds and blossoms.

Lavender and honey. It smelled expensive.

"Get out of my way, Iliana."

"You can't even look at me?"

Hearing the courtesan's indignant tone, Finn tried to remember why she'd promised Shane she wouldn't commit violence on his ship, coming up empty. Her eyes traveled up Iliana's body.

Today, her curves spilled over a slinky deep-blue number. Two triangle cutouts at her hips exposed the gold-dusted skin underneath. A pair of long, lace sleeves wound their way down to her hands. Her flaming red waves hung in a single braid down the left side of her shoulder, little tendrils escaping here and there. Three sapphire orchids embellished the braid, their jewels sparkling in the oasis's artificial light.

Gods, everything she owned would be enough for Finn to retire on alone, without her haul on the Mud Pit. She made a mental note to sneak into her room later and snatch those hairpieces.

Iliana's indigo eyes flashed with determination as they held Finn's.

"We need to talk."

Finn scoffed.

"I have nothing to say to you."

She moved to the left, but the soft pressure of Iliana's fingers as they brushed hers stopped her.

Something about the touch undid her, and Finn found herself lost in the midst of another vision.

The sound of muffled crying wakes the girl in the night. It's dark and it takes a moment for her eyes to adjust. When they do, she sees him. *He is standing over Iliana's bed and she is crying.*

The child clutches her dolly tighter to her chest.

"Li-Li?" She manages to choke out.

His head shoots up and he glares at her. He is swaying more than usual and his eyes can't seem to focus. He takes a stumbling step forward. The girl can't help the squeak of fear that escapes her as she scrambles back against her headboard, her dolly falling limply to the bed. Before he can reach her, he trips over his feet and falls to the ground in a heap, grumbling and growling incoherently.

A few seconds pass in tense silence before she hears him snoring. The child releases the breath she is holding and whispers as loudly as she dares.

"Li-Li?"

Iliana gets out of bed slowly and makes her way to her sister's, crawling in beside her. Her cheeks are wet with the tears still flowing freely down her face, and her eyes look far away. She rarely cries, even when she's hurt.

The girl reaches out and strokes Iliana's hair. It feels strange to be comforting her big sister instead of the other way around, but she does it anyway.

"Li-Li, why are you crying?"

She doesn't answer for so long, the girl starts to worry. She just sits there with her knees pressed up against her chest, and her arms wrapped around herself. Finally, her head moves as if she's just registered her little sister's touch, and she turns to her. Her eyes are wide and full of fear. The little girl has never seen them like that before, not even when Father died.

Suddenly Iliana's arms latch on to her, and she's wrapping her sister in a hug. Her whole body is shaking, and the girl squeezes her back with everything she has.

Iliana pulls away and holds the child's face in her hands.

"I'm going to get us away from here, Kyra. I'm going to keep you safe."

Her eyes are so desperate, so full of fear. The girl doesn't know what else to say. They lie down in bed together, wrapped in each other's arms as Iliana continues to sob quietly.

Eventually, her cries subside and she falls asleep. Kyra stays awake, her eyes heavy, listening to their uncle snore on the floor.

Iliana's concerned voice snapped Finn out of the memory.

"Kyra? What just happened?"

What happened indeed? She was reliving moments that couldn't belong to her. Yet the more she had them, the more they started to feel like they were hers. Finn looked at the woman standing before her, an older, colder version of the weeping teenager she'd glimpsed in her mind.

"Talk to me, Kyra," Iliana demanded.

She brought a crimson-nailed hand from behind her back, and Finn finally noticed the object she'd been holding there. The blackened head looked as though it had been scorched from fire, the blond yarn hair completely singed off save for a single strand on the left side. There was no mistaking the cloth hands and feet, or the tattered remains of a cornflowerblue dress. It was the little girl's dolly Finn had seen not moments ago.

A sad, ashy, burned-up version of it, at least.

Finn reached for it, pulling it away from Iliana and clutching it to her chest as though reuniting with a long-lost treasure. As she cradled the doll, she felt her knees go weak, her vision blurring in and out of focus. Somewhere, far away, she heard Iliana call out for her. Then there was nothing but black.

TEN

S unlight shines brightly through the window, burning the backs of her eyelids and waking her before she is ready. Birds chirp cheerfully outside, and for a moment she feels happy. Then she remembers: Father is dead. A tiny whimper claws its way up her throat and she turns to wrap herself in Iliana's arms. Lately, her big sister has been sleeping in Kyra's bed. She reaches out, but Iliana is not there. Wiping the sleep from her eyes, Kyra looks around. Something is wrong. Iliana never leaves her alone.

"Li-Li?"

"She's gone."

She looks up and sees him standing in the doorway. He looks so much like Father it makes her chest ache, but he is not her father. There is no kindness in his bloodshot eyes.

He sways over to her bed and she pulls the covers up to her chin, suddenly nervous to be alone with him. He sits down and runs his fingers through her hair. His words come out slow and clumsy.

"Your sister left you, Kyra. She burned down my barn and left you all alone to pay off her debt."

Her stomach drops, but she doesn't believe him. Iliana would never leave. He leans in close and she can smell the alcohol on his breath. She crinkles her nose.

"Your sister was going to be my ticket out. I owe a lot of money to a lot of people, Kyra."

He grasps her chin hard, and tears sting at her eyes.

"Luckily for me, I found someone whose tastes run a little younger than most, and he's willing to pay top dollar for you."

Kyra doesn't understand what he means, only knows the sour taste of fear and bile, her breaths coming fast and hard. Footsteps sound from the hall, and she sees three Reliance soldiers walking into the room. How did they get in the house? Where is Iliana? She tries to burrow further under the covers, but Uncle Henry pulls her up.

One of the soldiers is carrying a strange box. Her heart drops.

She begins to scream.

"Don't let them kill me, Uncle Henry! Please."

He backhands her, and she tastes the coppery tang of blood.

"Shut up, you stupid girl. They're not going to kill you. They're here to mark you."

Kyra holds her stinging face. She's too young to be marked, not yet eleven, and this isn't even a proper marking ceremony.

One of the soldiers steps forward and pulls her to her feet. He turns her roughly around, grabbing her arms and holding them out from behind as the one carrying the box sets it down on her bed. The one holding her pushes his knee into the back of her leg and she falls to a kneeling position in front of the box. The other with the box pulls her arms forward, into the locking rings as the one holding her leans forward and presses a button on the device, powering it up. Kyra is too shocked to struggle. The lasers bite into her pale skin, burning with an intensity that leaves her crying and nauseous with pain. She struggles in their hold, flailing through the grueling pain. Finally, it is over. The device releases her. She pulls her hands free. She is expecting the mark of her caste, the Agrarian sun, to be placed on the outside of her hand. Instead, she sees the bands of a slave burned into the flesh of her wrists in full circles.

Kyra screams. She screams until her uncle backhands her again and the world goes dark.

"Talk to me, Little One."

Iliana's concerned voice ripped Finn from her memory. She found herself flat on her back, the grass of the oasis cradling her prone body as Iliana and Isis leaned over her with twin looks of apprehension. The doll lay at Finn's side, button eyes staring lifeless at the domed ceiling above. Finn wiped at her face, surprised to feel wetness on her hands. Had she been crying?

"Please, Kyra. Tell me what's going on."

Finn gritted her teeth and glared at the woman standing before her. The pieces once strewn about the void of her mind had finally fallen into place, the specters of her past irreversibly catching up to her with a finality that would have left her reeling were it not for the powerful fury spreading like wildfire within the confines of her chest.

She didn't like what they had revealed.

"You must have been thanking the Gods when you realized I didn't remember you."

Iliana leaned back at the vitriol in Finn's harsh whisper.

"What?"

Finn sat up, climbing to her feet.

"When you finally convinced me I was your sister, what lie were you going to feed me, I wonder? Were you going to say we were tragically separated by a flood or some such other disaster? Given enough time, I might've actually believed you."

Iliana began to look sick, her hands fisting in her pretty gown. Finn ignored her growing unease, turning to Isis. The woman watched her with a cautious gaze.

"In reality," she told the Aquariian, "My sister left me. She left me in the care of a drunken uncle so I could be sold off to pay his debts. Debts she was set to pay. Now, my memory is still a little fuzzy, so you'll have to forgive me if I get the details wrong, but I believe that means my sister sent a little girl to the slaughter, so she could run away like a coward." Finn turned back to the sister in question. "Does that sound about right, *Li-Li*?"

At the use of her old nickname, Iliana fell back, her hand coming up to her mouth to stifle a choked sob.

"Please Kyra."

"Kyra is dead," she told her coldly. "My name is Finn."

Shouldering past her, Finn pushed her way to the door and out into the hallway, where she could finally breathe again. Fresh tears wet her cheeks, but she forced herself not to think about them.

All this time. All these cycles never knowing where she came from or why she ended up on the Mud Pit all alone to fend for herself. This was the answer the Gods had in store for her? A selfish viper for a sister and a drunken uncle who sold his family off like chattel. What was the good in remembering if this was the end result?

Finn swiped angrily at the tears falling down her chin. Forcing one foot in front of the other, she began to march down the hall, slowly making her way back to her room, seeking the comfort of the familiar. She'd only made a few turns, winding her way past the engine room and another docking bay for smaller pods, when she heard the sound of footsteps behind her.

At that moment wearier than she ever thought possible, Finn turned, ready to tell Iliana off. She ended up surprised and only slightly relieved to see it wasn't her sister who had followed her.

"You have *got* to be kidding me. Do you people take turns or something?"

AJ stood a few feet away, his legs spread wide like a gunslinger. He looked as magnificent as yesterday, dressed head to toe in black, his dark hair falling into his eyes.

"I owe you an apology."

Everything from the tense line of his body to the clench of his fists undermined his words. He left no room for doubt. The boy had come looking for a fight, even seemed eager for it.

Finn eyed him carefully, checking to see if he carried any weapons. He didn't look to be packing, but it didn't do much to ease her discomfort. Something disquieting in the way he looked at her sounded little alarm bells in her head. Yesterday he'd barely been able to contain his rage, acting very much like the hormonal teenager he was. Today he looked confident, lethal even. What did he have planned?

"You'll have to excuse me if I find that a little hard to believe."

Finn glanced meaningfully at his fists. He grinned cruelly in response. Curse Conrad and Shane for leaving her weaponless on a ship with a clearly deranged adolescent.

"I guess there's no point in keeping up the ruse then," he sneered. "You stole that job from me. I finally had a chance to prove my worth on this ship, and you danced in here, entrancing everyone into thinking you're good for something other than Mudder whoring. But I know the truth."

As soon as the words left his mouth Finn came at him.

She should have been concerned with the pleased look in his eyes, but the thought of kicking his teeth in commanded her full attention.

When she reached spitting distance, his eyes began to change, their spacescape-black color whirling into a glimmering mixture of reds, greens, and purples. Finn froze in place without even thinking about it.

Those were Anunnaki eyes.

Her hands fell flaccid at her sides, and she felt a smile forming on her face. Those eyes, they were just so . . . beautiful. *He* was beautiful.

"We're going to talk, you and I," he stated calmly. "Then, when we're done, you're going to get into that loading dock and I'm going to float you."

Float her? Finn didn't want to die, did she? Her brows furrowed as she tried to think about it, but then she found herself staring into those magnificent eyes of his with all their swirling colors. Every time she blinked she found a new pattern. She would do anything he said to keep seeing them.

"Okay," she breathed.

He took a step toward her, and Finn reached out her hand. A warning tugged at her mind, something about not being touched, but she wanted to feel those colors on her hands. As soon as she reached for him, he backed away.

"Tell me who you work for in the Reliance. Are you a spy? Tell me why you're here. Answer honestly."

Finn thought about her answer, wanting to make sure she got it just right. She wanted to make him happy.

"I don't work for the Reliance." Her smile broadened to a grin. "I steal things from them. I came because Grim told me a courtesan was wearing a necklace that belonged to him. I want to get Grim's necklace for him."

He glared at Finn, his angelic face menacing. The colors in his eyes deepened in their intensity, and she almost staggered back from the beauty.

"I told you not to lie to me."

His body thrummed with anger, so much so that he shook from the force of it. Her bottom lip began to quiver. Finn didn't want him to be angry with her. He might take the colors away. She searched her mind for a way to fix things, to put a smile on his glorious face. When the idea hit her she grinned, tearing off the leather cuffs around her wrists.

Why had she been wearing them in the first place? Finn held up her wrists for him to see.

"See? I'm not lying. The Reliance made me a slave. I'll never serve them again."

The colors in his eyes dulled for a moment as he staggered back, gaze locked on her scarred, crudely banded wrists. He shook his head, the colors quickly returning to their full vibrancy. Again, he returned to her.

"That proves nothing. I've seen men with those marks do terrible things in the name of those they serve. This is pointless; you're clearly of no use to me." He motioned with his hand to the door that led to the small docking bay. "Now, do you see that door?" Finn nodded her head, eager to meet his gaze again. "That's not a docking bay. That's the door to a haven unlike any you've ever known. Think of the one place you've been longing to go. Can you see it behind that door?"

Oh Gods. As he spoke, Finn began to see it. Behind the window of the door lay Grim's office. Finn could see his messy, haphazard stack of maps and papers, his glass display of prized books, her blanket in the corner near his desk. Her heart ached with yearning at the sight. Finn's hungry eyes returned to his, awaiting instruction.

"All you have to do is open that door. Once you're inside, I'll press the button to release you to your haven."

She nodded eagerly, already imagining herself curled up in her corner, safe and warm. Through the window she saw Grim, hunched over a book at his desk, his dark brow furrowed in concentration.

Grim.

He noticed her and looked up, a small smile forming on his lips as he waved. Tears began to warble her vision. Had it really been this easy all along? Finn turned back to AJ one last time, following the circular patterns of the reds, greens, and purples. A fat drop fell down her cheek as she whispered,

"Thank you."

She ran to the door, clumsy in her eagerness, and pressed her hand down hard on the blue button. It opened, and the scent of old leather and dust assailed her senses.

Home. Finn was going home.

ELEVEN

Finn closed her eyes in bliss, eager to hear the sound of Grim's gruff voice. She waited for it to hit her, but it never did. Nor did the raucous sounds of the Dirty Molly and her inhabitants.

Finn opened her eyes, confusion taking hold as she took in the small room around her. One domed window that also served as a docking door, metal-grate flooring, and steel walls greeted her. Just like the rest of the ship.

The ship.

Oh Gods, he was going to float her.

Unable to think about what had just transpired, her survival instincts kicked in. Finn turned and ran for the door leading out of the pod as fast as she could. As soon as her face reached the window, he was there, his eyes back to their normal black color and smug as she'd ever seen them. Finn made a move for the button, but it blinked an angry red. He'd locked her in.

Her hands slammed on the window as she pleaded with him.

"AJ, let me out."

The scars and markings on her wrist drew her gaze, and her stomach lurched. She'd removed her cuffs. Finally, the panic she'd been choking back surged to the forefront. He'd been so powerful; it had taken mere seconds to fall under his thrall. He watched her for a long moment, hatred and something else seething in his gaze.

Indecision?

Her breaths heaved in her chest as hope bloomed. Finn could work with that.

"AJ don't do this. You're not a killer."

Rage flared to life on his face, his pale skin reddening.

"You have no idea what I am, no idea what *they* made me."

"Who? Shane and Conrad?"

His hot breath fogged up the window as he leaned in close, seething.

"The *Reliance*."

Without giving her a chance to formulate a response, he tore his shirt off and tossed it aside. In the short time she'd known him, Finn had come to think of his face as the epitome of beauty. The body he'd revealed beneath his shirt, however, was the antithesis. While his pale chest heaved, Finn's eyes roved over the gruesome scars and burns that riddled its sculpted length from neck to abdomen, the most appalling of which was a brand just above his navel in the shape of the Arcturian eye.

Finn wanted to vomit at the sight; she could only imagine how *he* felt every time he looked in the mirror. He watched her with barely leashed fury.

"Get your eyeful. It's the last thing you'll ever see."

Her body tensed as the boy raised his hand. If Finn hadn't been watching so closely (seeing as how her fate rested on it), she might have missed the way it shook.

AJ was having second thoughts.

Abrupt movement behind him caught Finn's eye before she could act on his indecision. As she watched, AJ flew backward through the air like a shred of paper caught in a gust of wind. She pressed her face against the glass for a better look, her heart pounding.

Conrad stood tall and furious in the hall, his chest heaving. He looked like one of the Gods, a mighty force to be reckoned with. He held AJ against the wall with the power of his mind, the boy's feet dangling above the floor as his arms flailed.

He turned glowing eyes to the glass window and met her gaze. If possible, he looked even further enraged. With a wave of his arm, he sent AJ crashing headfirst into the ground, knocking the little psychopath unconscious. Steady strides carried him to Finn, where he slammed his hand on the wall by the door. The button above her turned blue seconds before the door blessedly opened.

His heavy breaths filled the air around her, enveloping her in his scent. Finn put her hands behind her back and glanced up at him, feeling exposed without her cuffs. They stared at each other for what felt like an eternity, neither one of them speaking.

Finally, she broke the silence.

"It would've been nice to know there was an Anunnaki on board gunning for me."

"*Half*-Anunnaki." Conrad remained disturbingly still, leveling her with an intense glower. "He's half-Anunnaki, Hellion, and right now it's taking all my restraint not to beat some sense into the little shit."

Half? She'd been taken down by a *half*-Anunnaki?

Finn smirked as the rest of his sentence sank in. She was more than a little tempted to head out and do some damage to the kid herself. Then her mind drifted to the look on his face when AJ had removed his shirt. As he'd watched her take in every grisly marring of his flesh, finally landing on the brand above his navel, he'd looked . . . broken.

She glanced up at Conrad, the glow in his eyes dimming, but his face still furious on her behalf. She took a step toward him, offering a weak smile.

"How's this for a distraction? It turns out Iliana really is my sister, and she's a pretty rotten one at that."

A look of surprise crossed his face, replacing the pure aggression. He stepped toward her until mere inches separated them.

"You're having quite the day, aren't you?" His eyes gentled as they searched hers. "Are you sure you're all right?"

Finn nodded and inhaled deeply, savoring the feel of his body heat—

"What the hell is going on?"

At the sound of Shane's angry yell, both of their bodies immediately went rigid, thrumming once again with anxiety. Finn's stolen moment of calm was over. Shane stormed over to AJ's still form, checking his pulse before turning his angry gaze to her.

"What did you do?"

Now that the shock had worn off, Finn felt the first tiny lick of anger beginning to uncoil within her, quickly burning into a flame. She took a step forward, getting ready to light into him, but Conrad stepped in front of her before she could.

"Wipe that look off your face, Shane. AJ just tried to kill Finn."

Shane looked dumbfounded, and Finn felt a slight twinge of compassion for the man. Ever since she'd first set foot on his ship, his world had been flipped on its head. He looked from Conrad to her, then down at AJ.

"That's impossible. Why would he do that?"

Conrad crossed his arms, the picture of impenetrable force. In this, he served as her staunch ally.

"I saw it myself. He mesmerized her into walking into the docking bay and had his hand on the opening valve before I got to him."

Shane shook his head, his eyes still disbelieving.

"It doesn't make sense. Why would he hurt her?"

Finn stepped around Conrad. "I think I can help with that. *Special Projects* over there is more than a little piqued that I'm replacing him on the senator heist. And I'm pretty sure he's still convinced I'm a Reliance spy. Also, your boy is severely disturbed, mentally speaking."

Shane had the nerve to glower at her, his tone borderline hostile.

"You don't know what you're talking about."

Bending down, Finn snatched the leather cuffs and gloves lying at Shane's feet, not bothering to hide her ruined wrists. She knew they saw the scars and markings when they both hissed in a breath. She slammed the cuffs down into place and regarded Shane coolly.

"I know a lot more than you give me credit for. I'm also not the one running around this ship trying to off people, which if I remember correctly is against your precious rules."

Shane regarded her pensively for a long moment, but she didn't give him a chance to say anything. Ignoring them both, she stomped away, waiting until she rounded the corner out of view before sprinting to her room at full speed.

When Finn got there, Iliana and Tiri waited for her, their faces ranging from worried to terrified, respectively. Her head pounded with the force of an oncoming headache, but she tried her best to compartmentalize.

Finn ignored Iliana, meeting Tiri's wide gaze.

"Tiri, I need you to do something for me. Can you tell me what Conrad and Shane are saying?"

She didn't even hesitate.

Sweetest child, Finn thought, *I'm going to steal you something extra shiny for that.*

She closed her eyes. When she next reopened them, they appeared blank, staring off into the distance. Speaking in that creepy monotone voice Finn found so unsettling, she said:

"He's gone too far this time, Shane. I think it's time you accepted that the boy isn't right. We didn't get to him in time."

"He's our brother, Conrad. He just needs more time to heal."

"No, he's your brother, and your guilt in this has blinded you. He's had three cycles of healing. Three cycles of coddling. He's dangerous, Shane, why can't you see that? He almost killed someone today, do you understand? You're putting everyone at risk with this stubbornness."

"The day I took you in, you became my brother, Conrad. The day AJ was born he became your brother as well. He's mine by blood, but he's yours by choice. Or have you forgotten the oath you made?"

"I will never forget. But that doesn't change the fact that his mind is twisted. Warped by what the Reliance did to him. Don't let your sentiment cloud your judgment."

"I find it ironic you would talk to me about sentiment clouding judgement. He stays on my ship where he belongs, Conrad. You will act as Finn's guard until we arrive on Cartan tomorrow. His abilities don't work on you; I can't think of a better man for the job. That is my final decision. You don't have to like it, but you will follow it."

Tiri shook her little head, her eyes clearing.

Finn offered her a smile.

"Thanks."

Her brow furrowed.

"Are you sure you're okay, Finn?"

Finn knelt down in front of her, putting her at eye level. The little girl looked more serious than she'd ever seen her. Finn couldn't imagine how frightening all this must be for her. Had she been watching? Had she been the one to alert Conrad? Before Finn could reassure her, her already large eyes widened even further and she whispered, "Uh-oh."

It served as the only warning Finn got. A huge bang sounded behind them, and they both turned to see Iliana slamming her foot against the wall.

"Gods curse him. Stubborn, mule-headed excuse for a man."

Her growl ended with two more kicks, and Finn raised her brows involuntarily. A few moments later, Iliana seemed to remember her audience and turned to Tiri.

"Why don't you take Kyr—Finn to your room, Tiri? You two can start those drawing lessons you were telling me about."

The child nodded solemnly, glancing back at them one last time before disappearing around the corner. When Iliana turned to face her, Finn ignored the dent in the side of her elaborate shiny blue heel and cut her off.

"I'm not going anywhere."

She might as well not have spoken. Iliana glared, her normally pristine eyeliner smudged just a touch, and the color on her high cheekbones as red as her hair.

"If you want to be called Finn, I'll call you Finn. If you want to hate me, then so be it. I can take any of it so long as you're here and you're alive and well. What I cannot take is losing you again, so you'll excuse me if I'm not interested in listening to your stubborn defiance. Now quit being a brat and go to your room so I can throttle Shane for this."

She spun, and the train of her dress swayed as she made her way down the hall like a woman on a mission. Finn stared after her, mouth agape, until her figure disappeared. Blinking several times, Finn shook her head and made her way inside her room.

Tiri turned from her seat at the desk when she heard her entrance. Dropping the colored pencil in her hand, she hopped down to walk over to where Finn stood and studied her face. Finn couldn't decide if the girl was trying to determine her well-being or if the little imp had invaded her thoughts again.

Finn narrowed her eyes, but instead of looking guilty, Tiri grinned. "You could lie down and I could draw you a picture," she suggested.

She wore her perfect little ringlets up in pigtails dangling just above her shoulders. A pale green dress draped her tiny frame, with matching green bows above each pigtail. The color emphasized the vinelike markings weaving their way across her skin.

Finn sighed. How could she deny her? She made her way over to the lush bed, tossed her boots on the floor, and stretched out, sighing for a completely different reason when her body sank into the downy softness.

How did a little girl always seem to know what she needed? Finn heard the sound of metal against metal as Tiri pulled the chair out once again, settling herself behind the desk.

Closing her eyes, Finn found herself lulled into a state of relaxation by the sound of pencils scraping paper as Tiri shaded, sketched, colored, and created. It was the last thing she heard before falling into a blissful, dreamless sleep.

Minutes (or more likely hours) later, Finn awoke to darkness, save for the artificial glow of the lamp perched on the desk. She shot up in bed, finding Tiri's side empty. Still sensing she wasn't alone, her eyes flew to the desk where the lamp's glimmer illuminated Conrad's broad back.

Someone took his guard duty *very* seriously.

Where was Tiri when Finn needed her? She lay back down as quickly as she dared, trying to make as little noise as possible. What kept him so preoccupied over there? His head bent low under the light, and he appeared to be studying something on the desk. Maybe he was preparing for the job tomorrow, exactly what Finn should have been doing. Instead, she'd been caught napping.

She fingered her cuffs, remembering with vivid clarity his sharp intake of breath at the sight of her scars and markings. She felt color rush to her cheeks in a hot wave. Whether in embarrassment or anger, she could no longer tell. Her heart raced, her stomach churned, and her head ached from the burden of trying to bear it all at once.

Had AJ really tried to kill her only just today? She thought about his hand, and the way it shook as it hovered over the opening valve. Would he really have opened that door and floated her? Throwing a hand over her eyes, Finn groaned inwardly. *Yes. No. No. Yes.* The internal debate could go on for hours.

Finn longed for the comfort only Tiri's presence could bring her. She harbored a sneaking suspicion that Conrad was to blame for the girl's absence. The thought had her grinding her teeth in annoyance. She'd much rather be sharing the room with her little friend than a giant half-breed who constantly frayed her nerves.

A thought struck her. If Tiri could read thoughts, maybe she could she hear Finn's now. Could they communicate this way from different rooms? Feeling ridiculous, Finn closed her eyes and concentrated.

"Tiri? Are you there?"

She almost laughed at herself when she got no response. Obviously her sanity had suffered from the day's events. The idea only further propelled her restless energy, and she was just preparing to thrust herself out of bed when a strange buzzing filled her ears.

"Finn? We're breaking the rules, but I like it."

Tiri's melodic voice filled her head like an internal comm device, and it took every inch of her restraint not to shout out in surprise.

"Tiri? I can't believe this actually worked! Why aren't you here? Did Conrad kick you out?"

"He says it's not safe right now. I'm staying in Isis's room." Finn glared at the half-breed's back before Tiri continued. *"It's okay, Finn. Conrad can keep the bad dreams away too. You'll see."*

Finn wanted to ask her what she meant by that, but another more important question plagued her mind.

"Tiri, I need to ask you a question about AJ."

"Wouldn't you rather ask me about Iliana? You were thinking about your farm in your sleep."

Finn bit back a growl of frustration.

"I definitely do not want to talk about Iliana. Listen to me Tiri, was AJ going to float me today? Would he have pushed the button?" The child hesitated for a long moment, making Finn think they'd somehow lost the connection. *"Tiri?"*

"I don't know. He doesn't know either. He screams a lot in his dreams, like you. But his mind scares me, Finn. It's not quiet, like yours."

Her voice quivered at the end with her fear, and it sparked something inside Finn, something protective.

"It's okay, Dhala. *You don't have to go inside his mind. I shouldn't have asked. Go to sleep, we'll talk tomorrow."*

"What does Dhala *mean?"*

"It means, 'quit asking questions and go to bed.'"

Her answering giggle soothed Finn.

"Good night, Finn."

"Good night, Tiri."

"Are you done pretending you're asleep, Hellion?"

Conrad's deep voice cut across the silence, startling her so much she shot up in bed before remembering he still sat in the room. He watched her from the chair, his massive arms folded at his chest, the ghost of a smile on his handsome face. Finn clutched her pounding chest. How long had he been watching?

"Was that really necessary? I almost died once today—are you trying to finish the job?"

A shadow passed across his dark features and his eyes hardened, making her regret her choice of words. She decided to change the subject quickly.

"What do you have over there?"

His eyes softened infinitesimally.

"Come and see for yourself."

Her curiosity outweighed her nervousness at his nearness, and she found herself padding across the cold floor to the side of the desk.

Finn stopped when her eyes fell on the pieces of paper strewn about before him.

She looked down and noticed her boots at his feet: definitely not where she'd left them. Her picture, the one Tiri had drawn for her earlier that morning, the same one that used to sit safely inside her boot, now lay in front of Conrad. The colors on the sides looked smudged, as though he'd run his fingers across them over and over again.

Had he seen the note? She didn't want Tiri to get into trouble.

"For all the grief you give Tiri about snooping," she groused, "you don't have any problem invading *my* privacy, do you?"

He surprised her by smiling, his cerulean gaze glancing between the drawing and Finn.

"Can you blame me? She captured you perfectly. It's beautiful. *You're* beautiful."

Her face flushed with heat at his praise. Had anyone ever called her beautiful before? If they had, it had never felt like *this*. Everything from the curve of his lips to the sincerity in the glow of those eyes told Finn he meant what he said. Her muscles tightened with discomfort.

"What are you talking about? That looks nothing like me. And stop being so nice. It's weird."

He shook his head at her and pulled out another page.

"However, I think this one is my favorite."

Finn nearly gasped. In the picture, she couldn't have been more than five cycles. Her wild auburn curls barely reached her ears, and her large indigo eyes seemed to swallow her face. Tiri had drawn her with a giant, dopey grin on her face, her front teeth longer and wider than the rest.

"Good Gods, I look like a mule," she lamented.

In the drawing, smudges of mud dotted her cheeks and clothes as she cuddled a pink piglet on a throne of hay. Another memory tugged free, coming easier and more swiftly now, as though she'd disturbed a nest of long-resting birds. They now flew around in such a flutter, she merely had to reach out and one would easily land within her grasp.

She'd named the pig Nerelius, too young to understand how dangerous her attachment to the farm animals could be. When the time came for Father to slaughter him with the rest, she'd been heartbroken.

She never named the piglets after that.

Conrad watched her, his face thoughtful. He seemed as entranced by the drawings as she was. He chuckled as his hand traced the outline of her buckteeth.

"You had fangs even back then."

His tone dripped with affection, and she found herself laughing right along with him. As she watched, he pulled out one last piece of paper.

"What does this one mean?"

From corner to corner, the majority of the page had been shaded black with heavy-handed, angry strokes. In the center, Tiri had drawn two large eyes filled with pooling tears; one blue and one white.

The blood drained from Finn's face. Without thinking, she grabbed the paper from him and tore it in two, throwing it to the ground. Hands trembling, she crossed over to the bed and sat down, the image like a stain on her mind.

Conrad immediately came to her.

"Finn?"

She cleared her throat and clasped her hands tightly together so he wouldn't see them shake.

"Tell me about AJ. Why do you think his mind is warped?"

He sat down beside her, his lips pressed together and his eyes tight. It was the only indication he gave that the subject change upset him.

"I should've assumed you'd have Tiri listen in."

"I won't apologize for looking out for my safety."

He exhaled, a deep and heavy thing, before turning his gaze to hers. The stubble on his square jaw seemed shorter than yesterday, making the hard lines and edges easier to see.

"I would never ask you to. What AJ has done betrays our very way of life."

Finn crossed her legs and leaned a little closer. His eyes glowed in response.

"Tell me about him."

Conrad scrubbed a hand over his face. He looked as tired as Finn felt.

"I'll tell you the parts I can. Most of it is not my story to share." She couldn't fault him for that. Rather, she respected him for it. "Shane's father was a colonel for the Reliance."

Finn sat up straighter. Her first assessment of Shane had proved correct. He did, in fact, have Reliance written all over him. So how did he end up the thieving captain of a bunch of half-breeds?

"Let me finish this before those wheels in your head start spinning again. Shane and I crossed paths when we were both children. I was seven cycles, Shane twelve. By that time, Shane had grown to see his father for the monster that he was. He was cruel and vicious, the kind of man who took pleasure in what he did for the Reliance."

The hardness in his gaze when he spoke of the man told Finn he'd witnessed firsthand just how horrifying Shane's father could be. Anger flared to life in her chest automatically at the thought that somehow this colonel may have hurt Conrad too, may have taken pleasure in his pain.

"When his father was deployed to a neighboring planet, Shane brought me home to live with him. Back then it was easier for me to control the glow of my eyes. Easier to believe I was just a regular boy like Shane, a boy from school in need of a place to stay. His mother was a kind woman, but years with the colonel had taken their toll on her mind. She accepted my presence as an afterthought, as though I had always been there. We grew up together, became like brothers. It was a happy time for me. Three cycles after the colonel left, Shane's mother began to grow thick with child. Her husband had been gone for far too long; there was no way he could be the father. We knew what would happen if the colonel found out. He would see her infidelity as treason, and none of us would be safe. Shane made plans for us to leave with the baby as soon as it was safe for him to be parted from his mother."

He looked up at Finn, his eyes going soft again with fondness.

"Family is important to Shane. He saw his brother as a new start, a sign of hope that his family wasn't doomed by the evil deeds they'd wrought. Eventually, his mother told us an Anunnaki had mesmerized her into conceiving the child."

He shook his head as if forcing himself to stay on topic.

"Everything was planned out. AJ was healthy and strong from the moment he drew his first breath and screamed. We were a week away from making our escape when the colonel returned. It was almost as if he knew our plans before we'd even made them. His wife begged him, pleaded for her life, but he executed her like she meant nothing more to him than a rabid dog in the street. He shot her in the head, point-blank, right in front of us. When he came for the baby, Shane and I tried to stop him." He looked at Finn, eyes haunted. "He shot Shane. He shot his own son. You have no idea how badly I wanted to kill him. How many nights I'd spent lying awake and dreaming of doing exactly that. But I owed Shane my life, and he was dying right there in front of me. I used my powers to throw the colonel across the room and carried Shane to safety. There wasn't time to get to AJ."

His voice was hoarse, from the story or the content, Finn couldn't be sure. He hung his head, refusing to meet her eyes, and her heart ached for him—for all of them. He'd saved his best friend's life, the man he called brother. In the same instant he'd lost another, along with the hope of a happy future. The anguish on his face spoke of the guilt that obviously weighed on him.

"It's my fault he is lost to us. Somehow, the colonel knew what AJ was, and he handed him over to the Reliance. They did things to him, horrible things." He gazed into the distance for a time, before seeming to shake himself out of it. "As I said, it's not my story to share. Shane and I spent the next eleven cycles tracking him. When we finally found the facility they had him in, we broke him out, but I'm afraid the damage was already done."

So many thoughts raced through her mind: the turbulent lives these men had led, AJ's torture at the Reliance's hands, Conrad's misplaced but noble guilt. It physically pained her to see him so torn. Finn wanted to reach out and swipe away the frown from his brow, the urge so strong her hand actually lifted before she stopped herself.

"What happened to AJ wasn't your fault, Conrad. You saved Shane's life. If you hadn't, it's possible none of you would have survived. None of the half-breeds on this ship would have lived into adulthood, let alone found a place they could call home." He watched her with that same haunted stare, his expression disbelieving. Finn thought about her next words carefully. "I don't think AJ is a lost cause. Don't get me wrong, the kid is definitely screwed up, but I looked into his eyes. I don't think he had it in him to open that valve, Conrad. He's angry, unstable even, but I'm not ready to say he's a lost cause."

He watched her for a long time, his face expressing some emotion Finn was lost to decipher.

Amazement? Gratitude?

She had little experience with either, and found herself searching his features with rapt attention, desperate to know which it was. They watched each other for a long moment before he finally spoke.

"Every time I think I have you figured out, you surprise me. I look at AJ, my *brother*, and I see a child broken beyond repair. You look at him, your would-be murderer, and you see someone worthy of redemption."

Her eyes darted uncomfortably. He made her sound like a saint. Why couldn't he just see her for what she was, like Shane and Iliana had? He saw her scars, knew the story they and her markings told, yet he refused to treat her any differently, and curse it all, Finn liked the way he looked at her far too much to set him straight.

His hands moved on the mattress, resting on the sheets next to her. For the first time since meeting him, Finn noticed scars on his knuckles.

Had Conrad been a scrapper even as a child? He told her his parents had been married. She wondered what his upbringing had been like.

A happy one, she hoped. Curiosity won out and she asked, "Before—" She struggled to get the question out. "Before you were . . . on your own, were you happy? Was your family happy?"

One long finger traced the edge of the blanket where her hand rested. When he met her gaze, his eyes seemed sad, but then he smiled, and his smile was full of warmth. The effect of which seemed to suck all the oxygen out of the room, leaving Finn dizzy. Whenever he looked at her like that, trapping her in the glow of those beautiful eyes, her mind practically turned to mush. He must have realized it too, because his smile got wider.

"Very. But if you want to know about my past, Hellion, you're going to have to tell me about yours."

And just like that, Finn felt as though he'd dumped a bucket of cold water on her. He seemed to notice the abrupt change, concern quickly replacing the smile on his handsome face.

"Finn, what is it?"

She wrapped her arms around her middle in a feeble attempt to ward off the chill suddenly filling her.

She'd been kidding herself. There was a reason Finn kept to herself, a reason her experience with men like Conrad was so limited. She would never be capable of opening up to him, not in the way he desired. Finn chanced a look up to find him studying her in that same way Grim always did. The one that made her feel like a Reliance experiment.

A pained expression crossed his face when he realized she had no intention of answering.

"Is it so crazy for me to want to know you?"

Finn wanted to scream at him. *YES.* Didn't he understand what he was asking? If he believed AJ to be broken beyond repair, she could only imagine how he'd feel if he knew everything about Finn she was only now starting to remember. Things that were probably better off forgotten.

Nausea churned in her stomach.

"We should get some sleep," she mumbled half-heartedly. "Tomorrow is very important."

Her voice sounded smaller than she'd ever heard it. A parade of emotions danced across his face—disappointment, anger, sadness—before that casual mask of indifference Finn envied took their place.

He nodded curtly and grabbed a pillow, spreading out his massive frame on the cold metal floor. The sudden distance between them left her feeling empty and aching. She recognized it as the deep, unrelenting kind of loneliness she thought she no longer had the capacity for.

Finn lay down and turned her back on him, trying to take deep breaths despite the sharp pains in her chest.

Tiri had been right about one thing: Conrad *could* keep the bad dreams away, seeing as how neither of them would be getting any sleep that night.

TWELVE

Finn paced the length of her room for the eighth time, running the layout of the senator's estate through her mind. She found herself completely unaccustomed to the surge of nerves washing over her. She didn't know what to do with the churning and fluttering in her gut, or the total lack of confidence she felt.

This was a mistake.

What would Finn do at a Reliance ball? She didn't possess the pedigree or the knowledge of how to act; someone was bound to figure her out as soon as she walked through the door. She'd given Conrad a hard time for his carelessness in going through with this job, but really it was Finn who should be worried. She'd spent the last seven cycles on the Mud Pit hanging out with the some of the seediest, most underhanded criminals the Farthers had to offer.

"Will you sit down already? I'm getting dizzy just watching you."

Finn paused mid-stride to glare down at Conrad. He sat on the floor near his pillow, staring at her with an arm draped over his knee, his dark hair mussed from a sleepless night. He looked roguish and grumpy.

That made two of them. Her eyes narrowed on him.

"Then don't watch."

Stretching, he got up from his spot on the floor. He didn't even bother looking at her as he made his way to the bathroom door, stopping just outside. Obviously, he was still upset about her evasiveness the night before. Finn continued her pacing.

"I don't understand why you're so nervous," he mused. "You said yourself; you're a thief, this is what you're good at."

A litany of new concerns had already formed on the tip of her tongue, but when she turned to deliver them, her jaw fell open and nothing escaped but a puff of air. Conrad had removed his shirt, revealing a broad, tanned back stretched tight over hard muscle.

She could finally see the full extent of his markings where they wound a pathway down his spine in an intricate grouping of runes. They formed a pattern of sorts, coming full circle as they spiraled their way up his neck and down both of his shoulders. They were beautiful and formidable, just like him.

The room suddenly felt a lot smaller than it did before.

"Wh—What are you doing?"

"What does it look like? I'm taking a shower. We'll be orbiting Cartan in a few hours. We need to start preparing for the ball."

He finally turned to face her, and Finn made herself look away, else risk getting trapped staring at the lines of muscle covering his abdomen. She knew better than to fall for that trick a second time. His husky laughter hit her a breath later, and she scowled at the wall, refusing to meet his gaze.

"This is *my* room, Conrad."

He didn't answer for so long Finn decided he must be waiting for her to look at him. She could almost *feel* his smug grin from across the room. Gritting her teeth in frustration, she darted a glance over and swallowed hard. Her eyes took their time traveling over his body.

The hard planes and ridges of his abdomen looked just as delectable as she remembered, and she commanded herself to meet his eyes before she had a chance to travel farther down. When she did, all traces of humor had erased themselves from his rugged face. Instead, his jaw tightened and his eyes glowed.

"You have two choices, Hellion. You can go to Iliana's pod and let her help you get ready, or you can join me in the shower. You have ten seconds to make up your mind or else I decide for you."

The hungry look in his gaze bordered on savage, and Finn knew what he would decide. The half-breed had been playing with fire these last few days, and his edges were starting to singe. It served him right. Not that Finn had any room to talk; his husky ultimatum had exploded her flutter of nerves into an inferno. She licked her lips, and his eyes tracked the movement.

For a moment, her mind wandered.

What would it be like to be kissed by a man like Conrad? The heat spreading throughout her body traveled to her face, a warm blush blooming there as her breaths panted in her chest.

"If you want to know about my past, Hellion, you're going to have to tell me about yours."

The memory stopped her fantasy short, leaving her inexplicably hollow.

Finn shook her head and took a few steps back. If her decision disappointed him, he didn't let on. The glow in his eyes remained bright as he gave her a curt nod and went into the bathroom, closing the door behind him. Finn stood frozen in place, watching the space he'd occupied not moments before and wanting to slam her head into something.

With shaky legs, she sat on the edge of her bed. She needed to get a handle on this. If she didn't get her head on straight she would definitely be the reason their job failed tonight. Finn heaved in a deep breath, begging her lungs to cooperate, but the sound of running water from the bathroom shattered her concentration.

With a frustrated groan, she threw herself off the bed and stormed out of the room.

It didn't take long for her to burn a trail down the hall to Iliana's pod, her irritation propelling her faster and faster with each aggravated step. The ship passed by in a blur of gunmetal gray until she found herself staring down Iliana's door.

It made Finn think of two days ago, when she'd been standing in front of the very same door on the Mud Pit, completely oblivious as to what lay before her on the other side. Gods, had that only been two days ago? It felt more like a lifetime.

A shower with Conrad was starting to look better and better compared to quality time with her sister, but Finn had to admit (even though she really didn't want to), if anyone on the ship could really prepare her for this job, it was Iliana.

"Are you going to open the door or ask it to dance?"

Finn nearly choked on her own heartbeat as Lex sidled up next to her, a giant grin eating up her face. She wore her signature pink pigtails and fitted T-shirt, only today she'd opted to add a voluminous pink tutu skirt that she'd pulled on over her suspenders. Finn eyed the pile of ball gowns stacked in her arms warily. Just the sight of all the different shades of material (Finn couldn't name them all, but she noted some silk and lace numbers at the top of the stack) made her skin crawl.

"What are you doing here?"

Lex's amber eyes were a mixture of shock, disbelief, and maniacal glee.

"You thought I was going to miss your first makeover?"

Makeover?

Finn didn't get a chance to set her straight. The tutu-clad ball of hyperactive energy breezed past her in a blur of fabrics. She proceeded to open the door to the pod, calling out loudly,

"Our project just got here."

Finn sped into the room hot on Lex's heels, forgetting her earlier apprehension.

"Did she just call me a project?"

Finn stopped walking when her eyes adjusted to the lighting, slowly taking in the room around her. Lit candles covered every available surface. They even hung from the chandelier, their flames illuminating the orange and red drapery hanging from the walls. Tiri sat in front of Iliana's vanity, lining up brushes and color palettes as she hummed a little ditty to herself.

When she caught sight of Finn in the mirror, she smiled at her baffled reflection.

"No fighting today, Finn," the little girl admonished, "unless it's the bad guys."

Lex and Isis laid out dresses on Iliana's four-poster bed, giggling quietly between themselves as they petted the soft fabrics.

Music played in the background from a box sitting on one of the tables by Iliana's dresser. Finn recognized the contraption right away; Grim kept one in his office. He called it a record player. It surprised her to see Iliana opting to use such an outdated piece of machinery, especially when she could have any of the Union's latest devices.

The music didn't sound familiar. Grim liked to listen to something called jazz, high-energy music with lots of horns and drums. Finn liked it too, but the song currently playing sounded different, the melody pleasantly soft, with a mixture of strings and piano. It made Finn feel strange, like listening to a sad conversation between the instruments.

Looking around the room at all of them, it was as though she'd been invited into a sacred moment. These women, unlike any she'd ever known, shared a kinship with one another—one she'd unwittingly stepped into, and no one seemed to mind. In fact, they seemed genuinely glad to have her.

Finn felt a little like one of the Farthers folks who tried pure Mud Pit moon whiskey for the first time. The only problem with moon whiskey was once you got a taste you always wanted more.

Iliana appeared from what looked to be a walk-in closet, carrying an ornate-looking velvet box to the vanity. She hadn't dressed yet, and Finn found it odd to see her out of her fancy courtesan clothes (not that her floor-length silk robe screamed bottom of the barrel). She looked more like the sister Finn was beginning to remember growing up with, the one who didn't mind muddy feet and soil under her nails.

She caught sight of Finn in the mirror and turned abruptly.

"Finn, you came."

A glimmer of hope transformed her expression. Finn felt it in her gut like the sharp bite of a sword passing through her innards and coming out the other side, taking her sense of peace along with it. The calm mood of the room suddenly shifted, and she crossed her arms to ward off the new feeling of emptiness it brought.

"Yeah, well, don't get too excited. My shower got hijacked."

If Finn's words disappointed Iliana at all, she hid it well. Lex bounced over like a drunken bunny, wiggling her eyebrows suggestively.

"Hijacked by whom? Conrad?"

Finn frowned at her.

"Shouldn't you be flying the ship, or *sedated*?"

Finn shot a meaningful glance at Isis, but the woman merely smiled warmly, returning to her task of folding dresses.

"Are you kidding?" Lex practically squealed. "This is quality girl-time. I am *not* missing out. Jax sends his love by the way; he's pretty peeved he's being excluded."

Finn rolled her eyes, fighting the humor Lex's strange personality constantly seemed to evoke, and searched out the only sane person in the room. The little girl simply waved a purple hand in her direction and continued fiddling with makeup and hair brushes.

Iliana plucked another long white robe from where it hung near the vanity.

"The bathroom is just behind you. We will be waiting out here when you are done."

Finn snatched the robe from her hand, gritting her teeth when she carelessly brushed Iliana's. The smooth silk slipped through her fingertips like the wings of a tambifly.

She is seven years old and crying. None of the iridescent tambiflies flitting around in the air will land on her hands. Above her stands Iliana, brushing the tears away with her fingertips and smiling down at her.

"Chasing that which doesn't want to be caught is like trying to hold the suns in the palm of your hand. You must be patient, let them come to you."

As she watches, Iliana extends an open palm and waits, perfectly still, until a tambifly the size of a large fist and covered in bright purple fur soon lands on it. Her little sister can't hide her shock as her tears dry and her mouth falls open. Iliana grins mischievously and reveals the bud of a bright orange tamborn flower in her other hand. As Kyra inspects her sister's palm more closely, she can see the sweet nectar she has spread there to entice the creature.

Iliana leans in, careful not to disturb the winged insect.

"Of course, a little encouragement never hurt anyone."

They both laugh, causing the tambifly to flutter off into the sky.

How much longer was she going to be a victim to these specters and their whims? Finn avoided Iliana's eyes, almost dropping the robe in her haste to get away.

She locked the bathroom door with a little too much gusto and busied herself with the task of taking the galaxy's longest shower. The longer she could put this off, the better.

She wasn't dreading the ball nearly as much as she was dreading "quality girl time." For a moment there, when she'd first walked into the room, she'd been filled with a strange sense of rightness. That feeling scared her more than any Reliance celebration ever could.

Was it possible a part of her wanted to stay on *Independence*? Finn shook her head and rubbed her skin harder, trying to scrub out the unwanted thought with it. She belonged on the Mud Pit, with Grim and Doc.

She took her time washing her hair and body, using every single soap and foam available in her attempt to prolong the inevitable. Finally, when she couldn't put it off any longer, she dried her damp skin and wrapped herself in Iliana's robe. Finn almost moaned at the way the soft material caressed her skin.

She tied the belt tight around her waist, slipping on her cuffs and gloves. The contrast between the leather and the silk reminded Finn of herself and Iliana. The disparity was almost laughable. Their fates could just have easily been reversed if only Finn had gotten away first. Even as the thought came to her, she dismissed it. Deep down she knew she could never stand in her sister's place, because *she* could never have left her sister behind.

As though on a death march, she made her way back into the bedroom, only to find them all waiting for her on the bed. Iliana had used Finn's absence to get ready, and Finn almost tripped on her own feet when she saw her big sister all dressed and ready for the ball. Iliana looked magnificent. *Staggering.* It was a small but blessed dose of relief amidst the stress of the day. The way she looked, no one at that ball would be paying the slightest bit of attention to Finn.

She wore a deep crimson gown with off-the-shoulder sleeves. It clung tightly to her curves all the way down to mid-thigh, where it flared out in an elegant cerise train. The neckline dipped low, but not indecently so—just enough to have all the Reliance men thinking indecent thoughts.

She'd let her red hair flow free, the long waves falling past her shoulders in cascades of fire. Tiny red and gold crystals embellished the individual locks, giving them an otherworldly glow. An opulent ruby necklace dipped gracefully into the crease of her cleavage and Finn marveled at how her sister managed to stand up straight under the weight of the obscenely large gem. As always, her makeup was applied expertly, her indigo eyes highlighted with smoky shadows and her plump lips painted an alluring shade of scarlet.

Finn's fingernails bit into her palms. It felt strange to hate someone and respect them all at once. If they succeeded tonight, it would be because of this fierce courtesan at their sides.

Tiri drew her attention.

"Finn, come and look at your dress. Iliana says it's perfect for the ball."

Finn made her way over to the bed, the little girl's excitement both contagious and impossible to ignore. All the while she fought her unease at the smiles she received from Isis, Lex, and Tiri. Her eyes landed on a gold satin ball gown embellished with ruby flowers. Finn ran a finger over one of the gemstone petals adorning the bodice.

Dear Gods, her mind could barely wrap around how much gold it would fetch on the Mud Pit. Carefully, as though it might break, she picked the dress up and turned it over in her hands. It was strapless and dipped low in the back, almost to the tailbone, with a full tulle skirt worthy of a princess.

Finn looked from her cuffs to the low back of the dress, the sound of the whip echoing in her ears. Her hands began to shake, her head filling with screams. She tried not to panic by sheer force of will, tried not to let the memories overtake her.

"I—I can't wear this."

She dropped the dress on the bed and began to back away, dread seizing her chest as she consciously ignored the concerned looks everyone threw her way. What had she been thinking accepting this job?

Iliana's eyes appeared directly in front of her own. They held her steady.

"Finn, everything is all right. Tell me what's wrong."

Gods, she hated her, hated that the strength in her voice and the confidence in her gaze had already begun to sooth the rising panic.

"I can't wear that dress, and I can't do this job," she gasped.

Iliana moved to reach out and hold her, but Finn hissed like a feral animal, promising pain if she so much as made a move. Iliana let her hand fall to her side as though she'd been burned, but her face remained calm and in control.

"Explain to me why, please."

Why? Why wouldn't she just back off? Finn needed to get out of here, needed to feel the wind in her hair as she ran in the opposite direction and watched this ship and everyone in it disappear into the distance.

"She needs something with a high back."

It took long moments before Finn finally registered Tiri's small voice, but Iliana didn't miss a beat. If she felt any curiosity or surprise at the odd request, she was smart enough not to ask.

"I have something."

Iliana disappeared into the closet in a blur of red while Finn sought out Tiri, needing her presence to steady her. The child gave Finn an encouraging nod, her gaze far too knowing for her own good. Finn focused on those eyes, letting the rest of the room disappear.

"Finn, it's going to be okay. Trust Iliana."

Tiri's voice echoed in her head, but she'd learned to expect the unexpected when it came to *Independence* and everyone on it, and barely even flinched.

"Not bloody likely."

Tiri had the nerve to sigh at Finn in her own head.

"She loves you."

Finn glared.

"Don't push it, kid."

Tiri scowled right back, her pretty eyes shooting daggers, but she didn't respond. The corner of Finn's mouth quirked a little at the girl's boldness. That temper would get her into trouble someday. Tiri noticed Finn's growing smile and grinned back, making them both look like loons as they communicated silently in a room full of people.

"All right. It doesn't fit the color scheme, but I think it will look beautiful on you, Finn."

Color scheme? She turned to ask, but Iliana's voice had gone soft with emotion, and Finn's eyes locked on the sleeveless dress her sister cradled tenderly in her arms.

The color was a stunning emerald green. The kind of green that made Finn think of ridiculous things, like emerald gemstones and midnight garden parties. Tiny dark-blue sapphires sparkled on the bodice, giving it an incandescent glow. The back stretched high as promised, the fabric reaching up and around the neck into an elegant collar.

There it revealed a semi-scandalous peep-hole at the chest (semi-scandalous for Finn anyway). She'd never worn anything so feminine and revealing. The skirt caught her eye, and she sucked in a breath at the beauty. It clung tightly to the bodice until mid-thigh like Iliana's, where it fanned out to reveal a mixture of dark-blue and emerald-green ruffles.

"It's chiffon. You should find it very comfortable."

Finn doubted if she'd ever feel comfortable in something so extravagant. She looked up hesitantly at Iliana. Her sister seemed as unsure of herself as Finn was. With delicate precision, Iliana placed the dress in Finn's arms, along with a set of very uncomfortable-looking undergarments. Next, she fixed her gaze on Finn's cuffs and gloves.

Finn knew where her sister's mind was headed, and her jaw had already begun to clench in defensive anger. She opened her mouth to tell Iliana she would never take the cuffs off but was silenced by a stern look she recognized from childhood.

"Just hold on for a moment. I noticed you do not like to go without those cuffs or gloves. However, they are not appropriate for a Union ball." Iliana brought a hand out from behind her back and presented the velvet box Finn had seen her carrying earlier. She opened it and held out the contents for her to see. "I thought you might wear these instead."

Finn couldn't help the slackening of her jaw when she saw what lay inside. Folded neatly across the box's blue velvet sat a pair of elbow-length white silk gloves and two diamond cuff bracelets. She'd never seen anything so shiny before; each bracelet had to have at least a thousand glittering diamonds on it. Finn gaped at Iliana, trying to ignore the warm glint of happiness that crept into her sister's eyes.

Iliana cleared her throat.

"You will need some help putting everything on."

Finn turned away from Iliana and glanced meaningfully at Isis.

"Isis, can you help me?"

The slender Aquariian got up from her seat on the bed and glided over while Finn did her best to ignore the disappointment that had transformed Iliana's beautiful face.

"Of course, my dear."

They headed to the bathroom together, Lex's bellow following them as the door shut.

"Don't let her look in a mirror! She can't see herself until we're done!"

The task ended up being less awkward than she imagined. Isis's gentle nature kept most of her panic at bay.

Finn backed up as far as the wall would allow as she fidgeted uncomfortably with the lace undergarments they expected her to wear all night. The blasted things were already killing her.

When the time came to put the dress on, Isis slipped it easily over Finn's head. To her surprise, it fit like a glove, the material caressing her skin in a soft embrace. Isis gave her a knowing smile, but Finn was too busy staring down at the ample cleavage the dress's peephole revealed to ask her about it. She supposed she understood the blasted undergarments now.

Isis kindly turned around while Finn struggled with the gloves, finally pulling them up to her elbows, thankfully without ripping anything or tearing off any of the precious jewels. When she finished, she took a deep breath and let Isis nudge her back into the bedroom. She struggled to walk normally within the tight constraints of her gown.

Everyone grinned at Finn like fools; everyone except for Lex, who squealed at the sight of her like a piglet hearing lightning for the first time.

"Just wait until you see yourself, *Finnie*."

Finn let her know nicknames were *not* on that day's agenda with a scowl that promised agony if she so much as whispered the word *Finnie* ever again. She could tell Lex wasn't intimidated when she responded by sticking her tongue out and thumbing her nose. The next few hours passed by in a blur of commotion. They unceremoniously covered the mirror with a red silk sheet, and everyone got to work on making her look presentable.

Finn let herself shut down, calming her racing thoughts as the gaggle of women around her began fussing with her hair and powdering her face with all kinds of makeup that had her fighting back sneezes. She didn't dare move a muscle, not with Lex threatening to float her if she so much as blinked wrong and messed up the hairstyle she'd spent hours perfecting. Judging by the uncharacteristically hard gleam in her eye, Finn knew to take the pink-haired woman seriously.

Despite the unfamiliarity of it all and her genuine discomfort at being fussed over, Finn felt more than a little concerned to discover she was actually enjoying herself.

Iliana finished lacquering her lips with some shiny gloss and sprayed her with a cloying perfume, announcing they could remove the sheet. Finn took a deep breath and stood tall, facing the mirror like the badass she used to be good at pretending she was.

When Iliana pulled the sheet away, Finn searched the reflection for long moments, confusion furrowing her brow. Then she realized that the beautiful woman in the mirror's brow had furrowed as well.

Wait, is that me?

Her gaze flew to the other women in the room. Each one watched Finn with her own special smile. She took a step closer to the mirror, swallowing the dryness in her throat. She looked . . . radiant.

Lex had wound her waves into an elegant up-do, leaving her slender neck exposed. A few loose tendrils hung free, softening the look. Iliana had carefully placed two sapphire jeweled combs amidst the curls, and they added a noticeable sparkle to her dark auburn locks.

Her eyes looked brighter than she'd ever seen them, whether from Iliana's expert touch with the makeup or her own surprise at seeing herself like this for the first time was anyone's guess. Her cheeks held a rosy glow, her lips shiny with pink gloss, and her eyes fairly glowed in contrast with the dark, smoky shadows they'd applied. Iliana had even dusted her skin with the glittering gold powder so many women in the Union wore to look more like their Arcturian forefathers.

Finn ran her hands over the dark blue gemstones embossing her bodice. She'd been so afraid of this job, so afraid that she'd be spotted for Farthers garbage. None of that felt true right now. She actually looked like she *belonged* in this dress, like she belonged at a Reliance ball.

"You look beautiful, Finn."

Tiri came up to stand next to her, and she returned the child's warm smile. For once, the compliment didn't make her as uncomfortable as it usually did. Iliana cleared her throat, and Finn met her watery gaze. She appeared to be fighting tears as she held out a pair of obscenely high heels. Finn's warm glow immediately dissipated.

"I'm not wearing those."

Iliana's eyes flicked back and forth between Finn and the shoes, as if realizing for the first time that they'd forgotten a very important detail: Finn had never worn high heels before. Suddenly her dress felt too tight and her lungs had a hard time getting air. All their hard work would be worthless because she'd be stumbling around the ball like one of Doc's regulars.

Isis chose that moment to step forward. She calmly took the heels from Iliana's grip, replacing them with Finn's old faithful boots and a pair of clean socks.

"Perhaps we should let Finn walk before she learns to run. It might be nice to have something familiar tonight. Besides, the dress is so long no one will ever see her shoes."

Finn let out a significant puff of air, catching Lex's death glare as she realized the action must have somehow temporarily marred her perfect appearance. She shot the woman a rueful smile and snatched the boots out of Isis's hands. She offered the Aquariian a grateful look as her feet sank into their comforting softness.

She was right: with the ruffles on the train falling gracefully this way and that to the ground, her boots would never be seen by anyone. Finn gave each of them a determined smile, feeling more like herself by the second.

"Let's go to work."

THIRTEEN

sis, Tiri, Lex, and Iliana followed her down the ship's corridor like Finn's own personal entourage. Just minutes before, Lex had run a hand down the walls of Iliana's pod, then announced they were about to enter Cartan's orbit. Nervous energy wound its way too tightly around Finn for her to puzzle out how Lex had known that by simply touching the ship.

Everyone wanted to see them off, their eyes alight with excitement. Finn, on the other hand, found herself anxious to solidify a plan with Shane and Conrad.

As they reached the end of the hallway and turned the corner next to the nearest travel pod, her eyes locked on Conrad's imposing form. Finn hissed in a breath at the magnificent sight before her, his size and black-as-night hair the only things about him she recognized. He turned at the sound, his gaze locking on her. They stared at each other for long moments, both of them dumbfounded.

He'd traded in his casual attire for a three-piece suit in dashing onyx, a few shades darker than his skin. A starched white button-up caressed his pectorals. He'd slicked back his hair and shaved his stubble, his lethal dimple in plain sight tonight, giving his roguish appearance a new, suave facet.

The final touch, however, was a pair of sleek black wraparounds completely hiding his eyes. They looked different from the ones he'd worn yesterday, more stylish and thicker in the areas above and below his eyes. At a Reliance ball, they would never appear out of place, their design perfect for hiding the glow of his cerulean blues.

Someone behind Finn cleared her throat, and she realized she'd been shamelessly staring at him for far too long. She ran her hands down the length of her gown and took a few steps toward him. What did he think of her "makeover," as Lex had called it? With those wraparounds on, she couldn't decipher his expression. Not that she ever could.

When Finn stopped next to him, she glimpsed the muscle in his jaw ticking, his body going stiff. He stared down at her in silence, his unexpected reaction leaving her speechless as to what she should say. Because of his aloof behavior or perhaps in spite of it, her brain landed on the most awkward conversation starter possible.

"How was your shower?"

One eyebrow quirked up over his wraparounds, and his expression transformed, a wolfish grin tugging at the corner of his lips.

"Cold."

Finn grinned back. Hopefully smiling didn't fall under the list of things that would ruin her makeup, or Lex would be trying to float her any second now. After all the times Conrad had caused her discomfort in the last two days, she discovered it immensely pleasing to know she'd affected him in return.

His eyes flitted over her dress, assessing her appearance in a cold, calculated way. Swiftly, her smile fell from her face and embarrassment filled her at the warm glow of anticipation she'd felt at first seeing him.

Finn crossed her arms below her chest and offered him her best steely glare.

"Where's Shane? We need to come up with a game plan."

Conrad opened his mouth to speak, but Lex cut him off, dancing over to stand beside her.

"He's updating the Luminary."

The entire ship seemed to go silent as all eyes honed in on Lex, who seemed to realize her mistake a second too late. A sheepish look began to creep over her face, and she backed away slowly.

"I'm just going . . . to go help Jax." With that, she turned and ran at a full sprint down the corridor.

Finn spun on Conrad, a memory pricking at the back of her mind.

"I've heard that name before. Iliana mentioned it when I first came on the ship. What's going on here, Conrad?"

Instead of answering, the big jerk had the audacity to ignore her, turning his attention to the other women in the room.

"Ladies, please excuse us. Iliana, why don't you go and find Shane?"

Everyone accepted their dismissal without question, leaving Finn alone with Conrad.

"Tell me what's going on right now, Conrad. Who or what is the Luminary, and why am I just hearing about it now?"

Conrad heaved an impatient sigh.

"There's nothing to tell. This has nothing to do with you. You've made it very clear you want nothing to do with this ship or the people on it, Finn. Once this job is over, you're out, isn't that right?"

Her mouth fell open. She'd been ready for a fight, ready to argue her case for information, but she hadn't been ready for that. Her mind raced with thoughts, so fast the room fairly spun with the force of them. That was the plan, right? Once they finished the job, Finn would leave and return to the Mud Pit.

The last few days, that one goal had kept her going. Now the idea of leaving *Independence* and everyone on it filled her with an overwhelming sense of hollowness.

Finn fought back the lump forming in her throat.

"That was the plan."

Conrad's head snapped up so fast, Finn wouldn't have been surprised if he sprained something.

"*Was?*"

She clasped her gloved hands together in fists, fighting the tension working its way up her chest.

"It's only been three days, Conrad. The first of which I stayed here because I didn't have a choice. And it's not like I'm exactly jumping with joy at the idea of spending more time with my sister. Besides, how can I trust any of you if you insist on keeping me in the dark?"

Gods, she wished she could see his eyes. Some of the tension in his body seemed to ease, and he took a step toward her, dipping his head to meet her at eye level. Finn held her ground, fighting the urge to retreat.

"You're right, Hellion. I'm sorry." He ran a hand over his jaw, no doubt missing the comfort of his stubble. "The Luminary is our contact with the Toad. He also happens to be a very good friend to everyone on this ship."

Finn didn't miss his double meaning.

"You mean a friend to half-breeds?"

He nodded slowly, choosing his words carefully.

"The Luminary had a hand in bringing each and every one of us together. He is the reason most of us are still alive. I'm sure you can understand why we would want to keep his identity a secret . . ."

"Unless you were absolutely sure you could trust me," she finished for him.

Their need for secrecy didn't offend Finn. It wasn't the first time she'd noticed their noble intentions to protect one another, and it surely wouldn't be the last.

She thought about the last three days on *Independence*. She thought about Tiri, Isis, Lex, and most importantly, the man standing in front of her. For the first time since boarding, she forced herself to be honest; she wasn't ready to leave them behind. The admission felt momentous, but Finn wasn't quite ready to share her decision with Conrad.

"Let's just get through this job first."

He let out a deep breath.

"I can live with that."

A few awkward beats of silence passed, and Finn remembered he'd yet to comment on her appearance for the ball. Rather, he seemed more than a little displeased with the way she looked.

"Should we get going, or did you want to glare at my outfit some more?"

His brows arched in surprise for a moment before a wide grin spread across his face. Before, he'd been devastatingly handsome. With that grin, he became blinding.

"You can't blame me for that. I asked Iliana to help you blend in. Instead, she brings you out looking like every man's fantasy." He dipped his head, voice going gruff. "Every. Man's."

She caught his meaning and let out a surprised laugh.

Conrad's intense stare held hers. "You look beautiful, Finn," he said.

She didn't have to see his eyes to know they surely glowed behind those sleek wraparounds. His praise seemed to ignite something inside her, an internal spark that warmed her from the top of her head to the tips of her toes. This man had a strange habit of filling up the hollow bits deep down inside of her, making her think impossible things.

He offered her a cheeky smirk.

"I am, however, wondering where in the hell I'm supposed to hide a weapon in that get-up."

As his sentence registered, genuine excitement began to surge through her for the first time in days.

"I get a weapon?"

Conrad's soft chuckle shook his chest. When he next spoke, his voice held an easy note of affection she'd only ever heard when he joked with Tiri.

"You're all dressed up, about to attend your first ball, and the thing that gets you excited is a weapon?"

Finn beamed back, poking her finger at his massive chest.

"Well, if you hadn't taken all of mine away, maybe I'd be able to concentrate on the fancy ball we're about to attend."

He grasped her gloved hand, holding it to his chest in a firm but gentle grip. Her heart almost seized at the contact. He watched her face cautiously, but he'd taken care not to touch her actual skin, making it a tiny first step for both of them.

"And if I hadn't taken your weapons, I'd probably be riddled with bullet holes and knife wounds by now," he whispered roughly.

Finn let her hand relax a little in his hold, instinctively responding to the tenderness in his voice. With her free hand, she held aside the ruffled skirt of her gown, revealing the boots hidden underneath.

"I think I know where we can hide a weapon."

Conrad's answering smile was resplendent, accentuating the dimple in his right cheek.

"That's a very bold fashion choice you've made there."

Letting go of her hand, he moved to a bag lying on the ground and picked it up. Though she found herself surprised to be missing the contact, Finn was eager to see what he had for her. He returned to her side, removing two short wooden staffs with a curved, wooden blade at the top of each. Neither looked particularly impressive. They really needed to discuss his definition of *weapon*.

"That's it?"

Finn got the feeling if she could see his eyes, he'd be rolling them.

"The senator's estate is going to be swarming with Reliance soldiers tonight. They will have scans at every entry point to make sure no weapons are brought inside."

"What about the soldiers? Won't they have weapons?"

"Fortunately for us, the senator's wife considers guns at a party to be a grievous faux pas. She's banned them from the ball. Soldiers will be carrying heavy wooden staffs, all the better to break you with, and their usual stunner gloves."

Finn forced back a shudder. In theory, the staffs didn't seem all that intimidating, but she'd seen a man beaten to death by one of those things firsthand and had found the sight more than a little scarring. The sound of his bones crunching with each striking blow still haunted her. But what really concerned her were the stunner gloves.

Reliance soldiers wore the inconspicuous gloves as part of their uniform. An electrical current powered each glove, allowing the soldiers to emit what they liked to call a *blast*. They sold them on the black market in the Farthers, so Finn had seen her fair share. Once hit with a blast, the stunner glove's victim found themselves down for the count and good for nothing but whimpering and soiling themselves for the next eight to twelve hours. The total lack of control the gloves induced scared Finn in a way no other Reliance weapon could.

Conrad held out the funny-looking staffs for Finn's approval. Upon closer inspection, she could see their sleek black oak handles.

At least they looked sturdy. They couldn't have been more than ten inches each in length. Their sickle-like blades, also made of black oak, curved outward about four inches.

"These are called *kama*. Because they are solid wood, they won't read on the Reliance scans, and, though they might not look it, they can be deadly in a fight."

Finn reached out and grasped one of the *kama* in her right hand. The staff felt glossy and solid in her grip. She examined the wooden blade closely, running a finger over the tip.

"It's sharp."

Conrad's hand covered hers where she held the weapon, and he settled himself into a battle stance behind her. With a swift motion, he brought the staff down in a wide arc in front of them, as though slashing some unseen foe. His warmth against her back lulled Finn.

"I sharpened these blades myself, but that's not their only use. You can use the *kama* to block, trap, or disarm your enemy." He leaned around to meet her gaze as he pushed her arm forward and twisted the *kama* to the right. "Think of the blade as a hook. You can use it to slice and maim if you want to, but you can also leave an armed Reliance soldier confused and empty-handed if you utilize it properly."

Her mind wandered to the soldiers carrying their unyielding staffs at the ball tonight. Conrad was giving Finn her best shot at defending herself. She felt a strange tugging inside her chest and turned in his hold to flash him a giant smile. The action seemed to confound him, and it took a moment before the shock on his face transformed into a grin that matched her own.

"Had I known that weapons would get this kind of a reaction from you, I would have given these to you sooner."

Footsteps down the hall shattered their little moment, and they both turned abruptly toward the sound. Shane and Iliana made their way to them in matching strides, their shining heels and loafers clacking along the floor. They looked like two holograms fresh off the screen and designed by the Reliance itself.

Shane was dashing in a tuxedo that matched Iliana's dress, his starched white shirt in contrast with his dark burgundy jacket and bowtie. Those poor Reliance ladies didn't have a clue as to what lay in store for them tonight. He'd slicked back his dark blond hair and shaved, exposing the sharp angles of his jaw. If not for the calculating glint in his deep green eyes, Finn would have pegged him for a stuffy upper-crust stiff, more than easy on the eyes but stiff nonetheless.

After nodding in Conrad's direction, Shane turned his calculating gaze her way. His eyes promptly widened in surprise. His lips parted when he took in her fancy hairdo, pristine gloves, and borrowed gown. Finally, his eyes settled on the kama she held in each hand, and a knowing twinkle appeared in their depths. Had she not known better, she might have mistaken the look for pride.

"For a second there I thought we'd lost our feisty little stowaway." He chuckled as Finn rolled her eyes and slipped a kama into each of her boots. They fit snugly, and once her ruffles fell back in place, no one would be the wiser. "Glad to see I was mistaken."

Iliana's smile seemed a little strained, but other than the barely perceptible tell, she'd transformed into full-on courtesan mode. Her movements became more deliberate and graceful, her facial expressions more practiced. Even her voice took on a huskier cadence.

"I believe Shane is trying to say you look lovely, Finn."

Finn didn't bother responding to either of them, her mind already focusing on the job at hand. Any minute now they would be heading for the senator's estate. She'd long ago passed the point of no return. Her eyes sought out Shane's as she stepped forward.

"There are a few ground rules we should lay down before we land on Cartan."

Shane cast her an amused smirk.

"More rules?"

Finn ignored his humor.

"I want full disclosure going in. Conrad already filled me in on the Luminary, and I understand why you would want to guard that secret, but I need all the information on this job before I go in there and put my freedom on the line." Shane's alarmed gaze shot up to Conrad where he stood next to Finn, and she rushed to his defense. "The Luminary's identity is still a secret. He didn't tell me. But I'm done being kept in the dark."

Shane did his best to appear calm, but she could tell she'd rattled him. Something flashed in his eyes as he shared a silent moment with Iliana. Finn tried to decipher their wordless communication, but by the time he returned his gaze to her, he appeared calm and collected.

"Very well. In a few minutes, you'll be joining us on a travel pod. We will be attending the ball as two couples. Iliana and myself, and you and Conrad. Iliana is well-known in Reliance circles. She has already spread the word that she will be attending the ball with her handsome upper-caste escort and her cousin." He gave Finn a pointed look. "That's you. You and Conrad are from the remote Inner Rings planet, Glaska. You have never visited Cartan before. You will smile, dance if need be, but you will let Iliana and me do the talking."

Shane lifted the cuff of his jacket to reveal a sleek, black watch.

"Conrad and I each have comms attached to our watches. We stay in pairs at all times, we never go anywhere alone. That way we always have contact with each other and the crew. At the ball, Iliana and I will make nice with the locals while you and Conrad make your way to the senator's office upstairs. The artifact we are stealing is kept in a safe. Conrad knows how to get inside. Your job is to lead Conrad safely to the artifact and avoid the senator's guard. Once you've obtained it, Conrad will let us know, and we'll meet outside at a rendezvous point about half a mile from the estate."

Her mind spun as it ran full speed, attempting to keep up with him and formulate the plan the way he envisioned it. It sounded solid, but it hinged on them not getting caught by any Reliance soldiers or straying partygoers, which meant they needed to be especially good at blending in and allaying suspicion.

"Is that it? Is there anything else I don't know?"

He watched her carefully. Finn felt Conrad shift at her side and resisted the temptation to gauge his reaction. Reading Shane's eyes as he answered seemed far more important.

"No. I've told you everything."

His gaze held hers unflinchingly. If he lied, he hid it well; better than anyone she'd ever met. She shot a glance at Iliana, but her sister darted her gaze away almost instantly. Finn told herself not to base any decisions off of her behavior. She trusted Shane and Conrad more than she trusted her sister. Finn was taking a huge leap of faith going into this job, accepting what they said as truth: her first leap in a very long time.

When Finn inhaled a deep breath and nodded her head firmly in agreement, everyone seemed to let out their own exhale of relief.

Shane's smile returned.

"Are there any other rules I should know about before we do this?"

"Just one," she replied. "I don't take jobs with casualties. Killing isn't in my job description."

The ship got so quiet she could have sworn she heard their heart-beats, tense and steady as she waited for a response. Iliana and Shane exchanged a look of stupefaction. Was her unwillingness to take a life really so surprising? Sure, she liked weapons; what self-respecting warrior didn't? Finn was a fighter, through and through. She had to be to survive in the Farthers. But that didn't make her a killer.

She scowled at all of them as the quiet dragged on. Finally, Conrad broke the silence.

"Easy, Hellion, it's not in ours either."

FOURTEEN

H er stomach dropped through the floor as their pod made its descent to the beautifully landscaped acres of land just outside the senator's estate.

Finn had barely batted an eyelash when Conrad reinstalled one of the missing navigation hubs, flashing a self-satisfied grin. She'd merely rolled her eyes and fought back a grin of her own, causing Shane and Iliana to regard each other with identical looks of bewilderment.

The short ride from Cartan's orbit to the senator's estate filled the pod with a loaded silence. Everyone busied themselves with mentally preparing for the task at hand, Finn included. Several times, she caught Iliana watching her, her eyes filled with a mixture of fear, worry, and sadness. Finn did her best to ignore her and focus on the approaching planet with its lush green terrain and bodies of water as far as the eye could see.

The walls of the pod trembled as they touched down. A topographical map of the planet appeared as a hologram before them, a monotonous voice from the screen in front of Shane announcing, *"Cartan—Population: 2.3 billion. Atmosphere: Oxygenated."*

Her palms began to sweat inside Iliana's gloves. Conrad's playful nature from earlier seemed to have completely dissipated, his mouth set in a serious line and his body thrumming with tension.

Rather than panic, as happened to be her inclination at the moment, Finn forced herself to concentrate. She excelled at this. This was familiar. The setting and the people might be different, the outfit was *definitely* different, but the task ahead remained the same.

Get in. Get the job done. Get out.

Finn took a deep breath as she let those three sentences flow through her in soothing ripples, drowning out the rest of her fears and doubts. When she opened her eyes, she found her companions watching her carefully, seeming to sense that she needed a moment to gather her bearings. Ignoring their cautious gazes, she pushed ahead for the pod's doors.

When they opened in front of her, a burst of pure, fresh air sweeter than any she'd ever tasted hit her in the face. Garish chords of music and harsh peals of drunken laughter echoed throughout the grounds, reaching Finn where she stood. She took a few tentative steps down the ramp of the pod, expecting her boots to sink into the verdant greenery beneath her.

She started when the grass felt hard beneath her boots, barely giving way under her weight.

Her eyes widened then scanned the extensive lawns surrounding her, every inch the same dazzling shade of bright green. The entire grounds of the estate were blanketed with thriving plant life and rolling hills, the intensity of their colors rivaling that of her dress.

Every inch of it was fake.

Finn cast a confused glance to Conrad as he sidled up beside her.

Seeing her look, he said,

"Synthetic grass; it never decays, requires no upkeep. Since Cartan isn't a farming planet and they can get their oxygen through vacuum ultraviolet laser turbines on-planet, most of the wealthier Reliance replaced the real thing as soon as they settled."

Finn felt her eyes growing wide a second before her fingers twitched in raw anger. Some of the more successful peddlers in the Farthers sold synthetic flowers when they could get their hands on them. They paled in comparison to the real thing, but even a poor imitation was better than nothing. These people had the real thing in abundance, and they'd destroyed it.

All of that life erased, and to what end?

Conrad placed a warm palm against the center of her back, both urging her forward and soothing her at the same time.

"Easy. You're going to see a lot tonight you might not like. You need to rein in that anger and use it to get this job done."

Finn nodded, coaxing her emotions to return to their stasis. Iliana and Shane soon joined them. Together, they made their way toward the large manor nestled on the ridge of the hill on which they'd landed. The estate spanned acres, and the manor looked more like a palace than a house.

The structure reached three stories altogether, with massive stone columns around the main entrance. There must have been at least fifty windows, and each one of them seemed to watch the four as they approached like sets of menacing eyes. As they neared, Finn noted the colossal golden fountain with a statue of an Arcturian standing sentry in the center. Water spewed out in grand arches, running down in rivulets to a pavilion filled with gardens of synthetic flowers and domed gazebos.

When they reached the entrance, the sounds of music and laughter increased tenfold, as did the force of her heartbeat. A mammoth Sirian stood guard at the entrance's gold-plated double doors, sizing the group up as they approached.

Like Khaleerians, Sirians were known for their short tempers. However, the races' similarities ended there. Whereas Khaleerians prided themselves on nobility and honor, Sirians lacked such scruples. Canine in appearance, they were big and brutish, with low IQs and light tufts of fur covering their skin, ears, and snouts. Their razor-sharp nails and fangs were lethal, their chilling yellow eyes constantly scanning and hungry for violence.

Naturally, they served as muscle for the Reliance army.

This one wore the army's usual get-up: black trousers and a red coat with a red-and-gold badge over his heart in the shape of the Arcturian eye. Finn only felt slightly relieved to see that his giant mitts bore no stunner gloves (probably because his claws stretched too long to accommodate them). His feral eyes flicked through their group with barely leashed menace before locking on Finn and growling, "Invitations. Now."

Finn felt Conrad stiffen next to her. His aggression flowed from him in steady waves as he regarded the Sirian, but he managed to look casual when he handed over their invitations. The Sirian guard looked them up and down for all of two seconds before grunting and moving aside to let them pass. As they did, she could have sworn the foul beast sniffed her.

When the doors before her opened, sights and smells assaulted Finn's senses from all sides. The interior of the manor revealed a grand white-marble staircase that led to the biggest ballroom she could have possibly imagined. Dancing, laughing, and feasting members of the Reliance filled the space to capacity. Shane and Iliana took the lead arm-in-arm and made their way for the staircase like a couple of professionals. Finn, on the other hand, had begun to panic, and she hadn't even made it inside yet.

She felt Conrad move at her side. Before she had time to shift her panicked gaze to him, he'd looped his hard, muscled arm through hers in a formal yet supportive action. Finn struggled to understand her feelings about the sudden contact. She hated to be touched, but she found this far more . . . welcome. Did he realize how much his touch soothed her? His face continued to scan the estate, but he tilted his head in her direction and spoke quietly.

"Deep breaths, Hellion."

Warmth spread throughout her chest at his words. She did as he said, not at all bothered to follow his orders in this. They caught up quickly to Shane and Iliana, the four taking their place at the top of the behemoth staircase. Finn tried to mask her expression as best she could but found the task somewhat difficult considering all that lay before her.

Several tables draped in red silk dotted the floor in a zigzag pattern. The estate's chefs had stacked them flamboyantly high with fresh ripened fruit, steaming meats, and glittering gold-dusted cakes and pastries. Finn nearly salivated at the sight, but everything looked far too pretty to be consumed.

Handfuls of slaves, painted gold and shaved bald (no doubt to look more like their Arcturian forefathers), stood motionless at the end of each table. Her stomach heaved at the sight of their underfed bodies and emotionless faces. As painfully thin as they were, and draped in shimmering gossamer, it was impossible to distinguish genders. They may as well have been statues.

Conrad's earlier words rang true. She was seeing plenty tonight that made her blood boil. Finn shifted her eyes from the gaudy Reliance feast over to the source of the music. A live band played for the crowd with real instruments. Finn recognized the black grand piano from Grim's books, but some of the more oddly shaped pieces, flashing neon pinks and oranges from their bases as waves of sound filled the air like smoke, looked completely alien to her. The sound mesmerized, reminding her of a manic, tantalizing version of the soft, pleasant strings they'd listened to while getting ready in Iliana's room.

Hundreds of upper-caste men and women, an equal mix of alien races and human, communed and danced throughout the ballroom. Their elegant, and in some cases ostentatious, suits and gowns were cut from every imaginable variation of red and gold. The shades spanned the spectrum; from carmine and amaranth to citrine and golden poppy.

With a sinking feeling in her chest, Finn suddenly understood what Iliana had meant earlier when she said Finn's dress wouldn't match the *color scheme.*

She shot a glare in her sister's direction, but Iliana studiously ignored her. Before she could gain her attention, a disembodied voice echoed throughout the hall.

"Announcing Courtesan Iliana Terrandon of Tesla and her escort, Major Shane Montgomery."

Finn's mouth popped open in surprise before she could stop it. Iliana's title made sense. She belonged to the courtesan caste, and everyone knew courtesans were trained and raised in the Inner Rings territory known as Tesla.

But Shane? A major?

Finn thought about what Conrad had revealed the night before about Shane's father serving as a colonel for the Reliance. She supposed it might not be a crazy leap for Shane to be a ranking military officer, but dear Gods, how many more surprises could she take?

She didn't get a chance to ponder it further before that same disembodied voice continued.

"Announcing Conrad and Finn Marthox of Glaska."

Finn felt the exact moment all eyes shifted to them. The music quieted to dull background noise, and the dancing ceased. Every conversation hushed at once. Conrad gave her arm a reassuring squeeze as he led her down the staircase. She tried to focus on anything but the shaking in her legs or the not-so-subtle way everyone stared at their group.

Many of the men wore wraparounds like Conrad, making their eyes nearly as impossible to read as his. However, the women, as they leaned over one another to speak in low whispers, were not so difficult to interpret.

Finn tore her eyes away to shoot Iliana another dark glower. This time her sister was watching, her stoic gaze focused on Finn's. She could almost feel Iliana's eyes pleading, *Trust me.* They made it to the bottom of the stairs without incident, and Finn sent up a silent prayer to the Gods for that.

Her boots hit the white and gold marble floor of the ballroom, and Conrad released her. He didn't go far, but she found herself missing the contact.

A plump woman in a cardinal-red ball gown with cap sleeves click-clacked her way over to Iliana. The skirt of her dress ballooned out around her in waves of velvet. From the looks of it, she could be hiding at least three slaves underneath its mass. She also wore a number of dark-red feathers sticking out of her graying hair, and several ostentatious jeweled roses adorned the bodice of her dress. She assessed the group with a dark brown gaze, taking extra seconds to examine Finn from top to toe before finally landing on Iliana.

"Iliana, love, I am so pleased you could make it. You look stunning as always."

The woman's falsetto voice didn't sound as unpleasant as Finn had expected, but her affected Reliance tone put her on edge. Iliana took the woman's hand and gave a small curtsy, bowing her head.

"Madam Califax, your home is lovely as always." She spent a long moment taking in the room around her. "And the ballroom! What an eye for detail you have."

Finn leaned closer into Conrad's side as she assessed the newcomer: the senator's wife. The woman smiled widely at Iliana's praise, revealing a row of blindingly white teeth. Then, her penetrating gaze flicked to Finn.

"Darling, you must introduce me to this enchanting creature."

Finn's body tensed as she braced for what was to come. Iliana followed the woman's gaze to Finn's face, and she smiled her best fake smile.

"Of course, Madam Califax. This is my cousin, Finn. She and her husband are from Glaska."

The senator's wife closed in on her, reaching out a perfectly manicured, albeit slightly wrinkled hand. Finn grasped it, mirroring Iliana's earlier actions. Feeling ridiculous, she executed her first curtsy-head bow combination while the whole room watched. She let her eyes focus on the array of massive jeweled rings weighing down the woman's fingers for half a beat before deciding to release her. When Finn returned to the calculating brown eyes watching her, Madam Califax again flashed those strangely white teeth.

"You look positively enchanting, my dear." She leaned in conspiratorially, but she made sure to stage-whisper loud enough for her words to reach the entire room. "Every woman here is kicking herself for not thinking to wear a dress like that. I myself was considering changing up the color scheme. Every cycle it's always the same: red and gold, gold and red. Blessed be our Arcturian forefathers, but it does get a bit stale. You've just given me some fantastic inspiration for next cycle's ball, my dear girl." She turned her head to address the room. "Glaska has always been very fashion forward."

She didn't wait for a response, leaving Finn flabbergasted as she moved on to other guests. Finn got the sense the exchange was somehow important, but the odd woman left her too dumbfounded to understand the whys or the hows. The music and conversation in the room resumed as though some unknown force had hit play on the paused scene.

Every once in a while eyes would scan in her direction, but she no longer seemed to be the sole focus of the ball. Finn let out a relieved sigh and turned to Conrad. She found him smiling, and her eyes widened in surprise.

At her confused frown, he leaned down close.

"There is absolutely nothing I hate more than Reliance gatherings, but you are making this one more than tolerable. You're making it bloody entertaining."

She did her best to glare at him, but ended up fighting back a smirk, feeling herself relax a little in his presence. It seemed hard not to feel anything but warmth when he looked at her as he did now.

An out-of-breath, authoritative voice robbed her of the chance to respond to Conrad's gentle teasing.

"Major Montgomery, it's good to see you, boy. Your presence at these shindigs is quite rare. Was it my wife's unique taste in decor that drew you or the company of your fine courtesan?"

Finn turned to see a stout man in a three-piece golden suit grinning lasciviously at Iliana's breasts. He stood at least a head shorter than her, which put him at eye level with his target. He had a round, ruddy face with more hair in his ears and nose than on his scalp, and his beady little eyes didn't even bother trying to hide where they currently focused.

As if completely at ease with his shameless ogling, Shane and Iliana offered him warm smiles. Shane extended a large hand to shake his.

"Senator Califax, I'd say it was your wife's decor, but we both know I'd be lying."

Finn tried not to gag in response to Shane's cheeky wink. Seeing these two in action was turning out to be quite the experience. One

Finn could have skipped altogether. They certainly looked at ease playing Mr. and Mrs. Reliance.

The senator let out a wheezing chuckle and slapped him on the back.

"You're right about that, my boy."

Next, he bent low to kiss Iliana's hand in a garish display. Finn looked down at his feet to keep from chuckling at the little man's showy behavior, only to discover him wearing a pair of golden shoes. Honest to Gods golden shoes. Seeing them, she couldn't keep the chuckle in any longer. Thankfully, she managed to turn the sound into a cough at the last second. Iliana, Shane, and the senator's eyes shifted in her direction simultaneously, and Finn felt Conrad tense at her side.

She shrugged her shoulders (daintily she hoped) and offered them the most innocent look she could muster. The funny little man's eyes flitted over her with an intense curiosity, making her skin itch. Just like with Iliana, his gaze lingered far too long on her chest, but eventually it returned to her eyes. His face broke out into a wide grin, revealing startlingly white teeth like his wife's, with the exception of two incisors capped in gold.

Dear Gods.

He puffed up his chest and strutted her way, grasping her gloved hand in his before giving her a chance to stop him. He brought it to his lips, and her stomach churned with nausea at his touch. She chanced a glance up at Conrad and was mildly surprised to find his face remained stoic, giving no hint of the barely leashed ferocity his body currently gave off.

The senator finally released her hand and met her gaze, his grin lecherous.

"And who, pray tell, is this stunning beauty?"

Iliana rushed over, placing herself at their sides. Her simulated smile was bigger than Finn had ever seen it, but she still caught the worried shine in her eyes.

"This is my cousin, Finn Marthox. She and her husband are visiting from Glaska."

His eyes never left Finn's. Not even to size up "her husband," who currently outweighed him by at least one-hundred pounds of muscle, and overshadowed him by several feet. In fact, he seemed to conveniently ignore the part of Iliana's sentence that even mentioned the word *husband*. Instead, he continued to watch Finn, not even bothering to hide the lustful haze in his eyes.

"I'm so glad Glaska could bear to part with you. Now, you must appease my curiosity and tell me what you think of this evening's decor."

With a sweep of his arm, he gestured over toward the tables filled to brimming with every kind of tasty treat imaginable. It took Finn a moment to realize his pointing wasn't aimed at the food or the red silk tablecloths. Rather, he gestured toward the slaves where they stood spread out by the tables: motionless, expressionless, barely clothed, and painted gold.

Her blood turned to fire as she fought to keep her serene expression. The slaves were the decor he'd been going on and on about? She longed for the power to breathe fire and burn him to a cinder on the spot. He continued to watch her, his smile growing the longer it took her to answer, as though her appeal only enhanced the lower her IQ appeared to get. Finally, Finn choked out an answer.

"They're positively statuesque."

His heavy brows lifted in surprise for the briefest of moments before he burst out into a fit of wheezing chuckles. Finn tried to ignore the way his round stomach jiggled and strained the buttons of his shirt.

"What a delightful creature you are." He leaned in closer and returned his gaze to the slaves. "The paint we used has real flakes of gold in it, the closest they'll ever come to the stuff. So you'd think they'd be grateful, but no, they lament, crying and carrying on because we shaved their heads. Honestly, the ingratitude is astounding."

It took every ounce of her control in that moment not to stab him with a *kama*.

As though reading her thoughts, Conrad put an arm around her waist and gave her a gentle but insistent squeeze, a silent warning to rein it in. She did her best, nodding back at the disgusting man, but she did not smile. The senator would never earn her smile.

It didn't matter. He appeared oblivious to the twister of emotions he'd created inside her. With another flippant grin, he placed his hand on Finn's.

"My sweet, you must dance with me at once."

Her anger instantly turned to terror. Not only did the thought of the senator putting his hands on her fill her body with disgust, but more importantly, Finn couldn't dance. She'd *never* danced, didn't even know if her body could. Sure, as little girls Iliana and Finn did what all little girls would do: they'd spun and twirled and fallen on their rears, but that was nothing compared to the choreographed, gracefully executed moves the dancers in attendance were pulling off on the dance floor at that very moment.

Her mouth opened and closed as she struggled for a graceful way to decline his offer. Fortunately, Conrad once again saved her, casting the senator a dismissive smile that looked more like a grimace.

"Sorry, Senator, I promised *my wife* the first dance."

Ignoring the senator's miffed frown, he released her waist, grabbed her hand, and tugged her reluctant body to the dance floor.

Finn stumbled to keep up, nearly tripping in her efforts as she bit out a harsh whisper to Conrad's back.

"Conrad, stop. I can't dance."

"You either dance with me or the senator, Hellion. Take your pick."

Finn gulped.

"Is there a third option?" *Preferably one where I break my legs and can't dance with anyone.*

He halted abruptly when they reached the outer edge of dancing bodies, pulling her flush against his unyielding form. The muscles of his hard stomach pressed against her softer one, and his large palms squeezed her waist. She craned her neck to look up at him.

"Time to fit in with the locals. Do you trust me?"

Her mouth dropped open.

"What?"

What did trust have to do with dancing? Finn tried to focus on him, but struggled with the task. As she looked around she realized none of the other dancers were pressed as indecently close to their partners. He tugged on her hips, forcing her to meet his gaze again.

"It's a simple question, Finn. Do you trust me?"

His jaw clenched, making her think she'd somehow angered him. A point further accentuated by the fact that he'd called her *Finn*, something he had a habit of doing when aggravated. He moved her body back a few inches, so he could look into her eyes. She grabbed on to his wide, solid shoulders to keep from stumbling.

Once balanced, she shot him a dark look and rolled her eyes.

"Yes, I trust you. But I don't see how that's relevant in this particular situation, seeing as how *I can't dance.*" The last of her sentence ended on a frustrated hiss, each word punctuating her frustration, but Conrad's growing grin distracted her too much to work up any real anger. "Why are you smiling like that? This is serious, dammit."

His chest vibrated with tiny rumbles in his struggle to hold back laughter. Finn didn't see anything particularly funny about their situation. In fact, in her opinion the half-breed had officially lost his ever-loving mind. She didn't get a chance to tell him so, however, because he was already moving her right hand to rest on top of his left shoulder. Once satisfied with that, he clasped her other hand gently in his larger palm, his free hand gripping her waist in a comforting hold.

Her panicked gaze locked on his as he leaned down to whisper.

"Trust me, Finn."

With that, he began to move. Finn let out a tiny gasp, expecting her feet to get tangled up in her gown as she struggled to keep up with his fluid movements. They never did, because her feet no longer touched the ground. Her boots floated mere centimeters above the marble floor. Not enough to be noticeable, but just enough to make Finn a malleable if not graceful dance partner. She felt her body tingling and realized, with no small amount of shock, that he'd used his ability on her. Instead of feeling her usual anger, she felt nothing but gratitude for the clever half-breed.

Finn looked down between their bodies and then up at Conrad, grinning broadly as he floated her in elegant circles across the dance floor. Gradually, her body began to relax in his hold as she allowed herself to enjoy the sensation of soaring elegantly around the room. This must be what it felt like to fly. Her mind struggled with the contradiction of the big, rough man before her who seemed completely at ease carrying out the elaborate steps and spins of the dance with surprising grace.

"Where did you learn to dance like this?"

His body tensed slightly. She wouldn't have noticed had she not been holding on to him. After a beat, she felt his muscles relax, and he answered casually.

"My mother loved to dance. Even without music, she would dance to songs she made up in her head and take me along for the ride."

His voice softened with fondness, and Finn smiled at the picture of a little Conrad dancing around with his mother, his cheeks probably warm with embarrassment. He would have danced with her anyway, because, as Finn was learning, Conrad possessed an unnatural kindness. Finn gazed up at his wraparounds, barely paying attention to their movements any longer.

"Where is your mother now?"

She felt the change in him right before she saw the muscles in his jaw flex with tension.

"She's dead."

Her grip on his shoulder squeezed of its own volition, as did her heart. Finn didn't know what to say, how to express how deeply she understood his pain.

"I'm sorry."

Her whispered words felt lame in comparison to the swirl of emotions she could feel boiling inside herself, and in him. He must have disagreed. His face instantly softened.

"It was a long time ago."

"Still," she whispered, "I'm sorry anyway."

A shadow fell over his features, and Finn finally took her eyes away from him long enough to realize he'd steered their bodies away from the crowd into a distant alcove. A thick marble pillar stretching high to the ceiling hid them from view. Slowly, her feet lowered until they landed on the solid ground, but Conrad didn't release his hold on her waist. Her lips parted in confusion as she scanned their surroundings. He'd put them close to the kitchens. Not exactly a direct route to the senator's office upstairs.

"What are we doing?"

He continued to spin her in elaborate circles as his head dipped and his hand released her to come down and rest on her other hip. His face stopped mere inches from hers, making her head spin from the sensation of sharing his air. Something pleasant in her stomach knotted at his nearness, a satisfying twist of anticipation that started her knees to trembling . . .

Stepping into her, he pulled her arms back up to his shoulders and placed them around his neck. Heart beating in her throat, she felt one of his hands return to her waist as the other began to stroke her gloved wrist, up and down to the rhythm of the music. With every crescendo of the orchestra's strings, his hand moved a little higher, creeping to the edge of her glove and inching closer toward the bare skin of her arm.

As he moved them in small, carefully choreographed steps, he watched her, their bodies slowly keeping time to a beat only they seemed able to hear. As the next swell of music reached them, his hand approached the edge of her glove, just a hairsbreadth away from the skin at the inside of her elbow. Her skin burned so intensely with anticipation she thought she would surely burst into flames.

He remained motionless for so long, Finn knew he was waiting for her to make a decision. This powerful man, capable of taking whatever he wanted without question, would not make the first move unless he knew she was absolutely ready. Something strange and equally beautiful blossomed inside the black pit of her stomach, illuminating the darkness and warming everything it touched. Finn gave him the slightest nod.

The subtle acquiescence all he needed, he let his fingers continue their exploration, burning a pathway of sensation across the skin of her arm. The contact sent jolts of electricity coursing through her veins, and Finn reveled in the warmth of his skin against hers.

It ended up being the last thing she felt before total darkness consumed her.

FIFTEEN

Finn blinks her eyes, no longer feeling Conrad's strong arms gripping her or the tender heat of his skin against hers. As she looks around, panic starts to take over. She is somewhere small and dark, sitting with her legs crossed. Her knees are pulled protectively to her chest. She hears a whimper and looks down.

A small boy sits to her right in much the same position as her. The tiny space pulses with his fear. She can feel it. Suddenly a small door opens and Finn realizes they are nestled within the hollowed-out innards of a wall. A stunning woman's face shoots in, her dark eyes alight with alarm and worry as she calls to the little boy on a whisper.

"Conrad, you must be silent, my brave boy. Not a peep, no matter what happens." She reaches her hand inside and caresses his dark hair. "I will always love you."

Did she say Conrad?

Finn looks at the boy more closely. He can't be more than seven or eight, long-limbed and lanky. His dark hair hangs in his eyes. As he watches his mother shut the wall behind her, tears flow freely from their glowing blue depths. Oh Gods.

Conrad.

Finn tries to call out to him, but no words escape her mouth. He doesn't even look her way. It's as though she's not there.

Her heart seizes in her chest, and she fights another wave of panic as a huge, resounding boom sounds from the other side of the wall. Conrad jumps and inches toward a metal grate, peering through it to see to the other side. Finn follows him, seeing the interior of a modest single-story cottage. The walls are a deep shade of burgundy brick, with lovely emerald throw rugs covering the floors, and a cozy fireplace in the corner.

A scream pierces the air, and the beautiful woman is thrown on one of the rugs Finn has just been admiring. Her long black hair, Conrad's hair, obscures her face. Her sobs reach Finn clearly behind the wall.

Suddenly there is a roar, and a large man thunders into the room. He is built like Conrad, tall and muscular. He turns rage-filled eyes on some-one Finn can't see: rage-filled eyes that glow a familiar cerulean blue. His entire body is covered in the same runelike markings adorning Conrad's back and shoulders. They even wind their way up his face, shadowing his eyes and jaw. They too are glowing in that same otherworldly blue as his eyes, stark against his dark skin.

Without warning, several Reliance soldiers burst into the room, beat-ing the man with staffs and blasting him with stunner gloves. He fights bravely, tossing handfuls of them to the ground using both his feet and fists, and the power that lies within those strange runes and glowing eyes. He is so caught up in his rage to protect his wife that the blasts don't down him at first. Finn screams for them to stop, her hands banging on the wall, but no one turns. No one hears.

Little Conrad whimpers at her side. His fingers dig into his legs so hard he draws blood. Finally, when the man is down and no longer fighting, a Reliance soldier comes forward. He walks slowly, purposefully, as if savoring the moment. His badge marks him as a colonel.

He motions to someone behind him, and a blond boy steps forward. He is dressed in a red coat like the other soldiers, but he can't be more than eleven or twelve cycles. His worried eyes scan the room. He wrings his hands nervously, looking for all the worlds like he would rather be anywhere else: anywhere but here.

The colonel places a hand on the boy's shoulder, but he is too busy staring at the wall to feel it. His wide green eyes are focused on the metal grate. Finn looks down and sees Conrad, his fearful glowing gaze locked on the boy's. Oh Gods. She has to intervene. She has to do something. Before she is given the chance, the young boy in the red coat places a finger to his lips, indicating for Conrad to remain silent. Then he turns to the colonel.

The man motions toward the other soldiers present, and two of them fall upon Conrad's father, stabbing him with blades from their belts. Another soldier, this one a Sirian, lunges at Conrad's mother as she weeps on the floor. He sinks his fangs and claws into her flesh and tears. Her agonized screams fill Finn's head until all she can do is wrap her arms around herself and pray for it to end.

"Finn?"

Finn opened her eyes to find Conrad watching her with concern. Sensation hit slowly, then all at once: his warm hands, the pillar at her back, the music still playing loudly in the background intermingling with laughter and conversation. Finn pushed words out of her mouth, expecting her voice to sound raw and hoarse from all the screaming. It didn't.

"How did you do that?"

Conrad's brows furrowed in confusion.

"Do what? What happened? One minute you were with me, and the next it was like you went somewhere else."

She tried to back away from his grip, but the pillar and his unyielding hold gave her little room. Her mind spun with confusion. Fear clung to her, to the air, *his* fear. It felt so real, like a third presence in that tiny wall. Finn put her hands to his chest and pushed, but still he didn't budge. She could practically taste the terror on her tongue, and no matter how hard she tried she couldn't seem to get it to dissipate. She glared at him in accusation.

"Why would you show me that? Why wouldn't you at least warn me first?"

Conrad's body stiffened, and his face became utterly still.

"What are you talking about? Show you what?"

Her hands turned to fists on his chest as she worked to put her whole body into pushing him away. Her anger gave her added strength, and she moved him a few inches before he stilled.

"You made me watch your parents die," she hissed. The back of her throat burned while she struggled not to cry, her body still recovering from the trauma of being forced to relive Conrad's nightmare. She'd had no control over her emotions, no way of hiding from the fear and terror of that memory. He'd done that to her.

Conrad stepped back as though she'd slapped him, his face twisting in agony at the mention of his parents.

"I made you *what?*"

He sounded so disgusted, so appalled, Finn found herself retreating from the severity in his gaze. Even behind those wraparounds, she could feel it burning her with its intensity.

"I—I saw your parents die. You were hidden inside a wall when Reliance soldiers broke in. A boy saw you, but he let you live."

Conrad's face looked like it could be carved from stone. His jaw clenched in a terrifying display of raw anger. After what felt like an eternity, his face softened and his head dipped. He stopped just before his forehead reached hers, exhaling a deep, heavy sigh.

"Shane. Shane saw me and let me live. Finn, I don't have the ability to show you my memories. I couldn't do that even if I wanted to. And believe me, I wouldn't if I could. I wish to the Gods you hadn't seen that. That was the worst day of my life, and I would never ask anyone to relive it. Least of all you."

Her stomach fluttered as soon as she registered what he'd said, as well as its meaning, and Finn alternated between tiny pulses of relief and sheer terror. Shane saved him. Shane was the little boy with the worried green eyes. No matter how Finn had felt about him in the past, from this day forward she could only look at him with gratitude.

Just one thing didn't add up and therefore caused her increasing panic.

"If you didn't show me, then how did I see your memory?"

"There you two are. I've been looking everywhere. Get your shit together and get going. In case you've forgotten, we have a job to do."

Finn tried not to jump out of her skin at the sound of Shane's irritated yet carefully controlled voice right next to them. Conrad didn't even bother looking up at his brother, his face locked on hers as he spoke carefully.

"We're going now, Shane. Don't get your fancy panties in a twist."

Shane looked livid, his green eyes burning, but he did his best to hide it and appear amiable considering they could have an audience. Conrad gave her one last squeeze and grabbed her hand, leading her toward the back of the grand ballroom. Finn tripped over her feet, struggling to keep up with his longer strides, before finally getting her head in the game.

If ever there was a time to compartmentalize the feelings and confusion roiling through her, this was it. Finn wouldn't think about how she'd seen Conrad's memories, or the way his gentle touch had sent her heart pounding into erratic beats.

They could put the hard part behind them. They'd played dress-up, danced around like fools, made introductions, and pretended to be impressed by the Reliance frivolity surrounding them.

Now came the part Finn could handle.

Now came the time to be a thief.

SIXTEEN

Finn followed Conrad down a long, candlelit corridor, a strange yet familiar sense of calm washing over her as they began to put more distance between themselves and the party guests. Lush red velvet carpeting covered the floor beneath them, and the holographic flames of synthetic candles in towering wall sconces bounced and reflected off of golden walls. The effect gave the hall a hypnotic glow.

To get them this far, Iliana had chatted up the two guards blocking the entrance to the corridor. They'd been putty in her capable hands as she subtly led them away with a seductive sway of her hips and a dip of her ample bosom. It gave Finn and Conrad plenty of time for escape.

When they reached the end of the hall, Conrad's large frame stopped in front of her. She peered around him, glimpsing three golden doors. He shot a questioning glance her way. Recalling the manor's layout, she motioned with her head toward the farthest door to the right. He gave her a barely perceptible nod before opening it, leading her up a set of service stairs for slaves and housemaids.

The stairway reared ahead, narrow and dark. The air tasted stale. Finn felt her heart pounding with the familiar sensation of claustrophobia. She did her best to focus on navigating and not what would happen if the already tapered space constricted any farther.

The estate's layout flashed through her mind, images rushing behind her eyelids as they continued to climb. When they reached the third floor, Finn placed a hand on Conrad's shoulder and squeezed, breaking off from his lead and heading toward a dusty oak door on the left. He let her take the lead for only a moment before

gently pushing her behind him again as he turned the handle and
pulled the door open.

Conrad peered around the frame, his eyes scanning for any movement that might indicate guards and spell trouble for their plan.
After a breath, he moved through the doorway and into another synthetic candlelit hallway almost identical to the one downstairs. Finn
followed closely behind.

"This one looks exactly the same as the last," he groused on a whisper. "How the hell can you tell where we are?"

Finn tapped her forehead.

"Amazing, remember?"

In truth, the new hallway had a few modifications the other
one lacked. In addition to the red velvet carpeting and candles, an
array of paintings adorned the golden walls. Some of them, like
the portrait of the senator and his wife, left a sour taste in her
mouth. Others, Finn found so breathtaking she forgot to keep following Conrad.

However, it wasn't until she caught sight of a red mahogany book-
case at least two heads taller than Conrad that she completely lost
focus, her feet frozen to the floor. Books of every size and color imaginable filled the shelves to the brim. The sheer volume of literature
exceeded Grim's collection on the Mud Pit many times over.

She felt a hand wrap around her wrist, breaking her out of her
thoughts, and turned to find Conrad's eyes on her. She could feel
his expression, soft and warm behind his wraparounds, but his body
remained tight with tension, letting her know they no longer had
time for breaks to examine the hallway's contents.

Her eyes shot back to the books, and she felt an overwhelming
surge of outrage. So many people would never have the good fortune
to understand the beauty that lay inside each one.

Why? Because the Arcturians and upper-castes deemed them infe-
rior and unfit to appreciate it?

Finn thought about how Grim's face would light up with pure
joy if he could see all of them, shoved tight, cover to cover. He

would probably lock himself in his office for hours, hunched over an ever-growing stack as he tried to scour through each one.

And what about Tiri?

The girl spent her entire life on *Independence*, separated from the worlds a group of golden egoists had created, and she possessed more of an artist's eye than anyone Finn had ever known. She wanted to share these books and so much more with the little girl who saw beyond any other child her age.

She moved with lightning speed over to the shelf, causing Conrad to bite out a harsh whisper.

"What are you doing?"

Glancing back over her shoulder, she reached up and tugged a thin and nicely compact red leather-bound book from the middle of a center shelf.

"I'm taking one."

The corners of Conrad's lips quirked in a half-smile as though he found her actions adorable. She glared back at him, but it did nothing to ease the humor around his mouth.

"I can see that, but the question is *why* are you taking one?"

Finn decided to ignore the amusement in his voice in favor of focusing on her task. They did have other things to do after all.

"Because it's beautiful, and people should have the chance to read it. It shouldn't be wasting away in some stodgy senator's estate. I mean, why should anyone get to decide which castes can appreciate art anyway? The lower castes are just as capable of seeing something for what it is as the upper castes are. Need I remind you, we are not the ones who got rid of all the plant life on Cartan? If that's not a travesty, I don't know what is."

Finn realized she'd been waxing on, but she'd become too busy shoving the small book into the side of her boot to prevent herself from blathering like an idiot.

Conrad's deep chuckle reached her as she finally got the book settled in place, and she swung around to face him.

"What are you laughing at? This is serious."

He crossed his arms at his chest and continued to grin. Gods, he was handsome.

"I suppose when the Toad mentioned what a talented thief you were, we should have taken him a little more seriously. Are you sure you don't want to grab some candlesticks on the way out, perhaps some of the gold filigree?"

Now came her turn to cross her arms. The look she gave him aimed to incinerate on the spot. However, he didn't look intimidated in the slightest.

"I'm not taking the book for money. I already explained that. Now, are you going to try and stop me?"

With that last question, Finn raised an eyebrow, daring him to do his worst. If possible, his grin widened even farther.

"One: that's the most I think you've ever opened up to me in one breath, and I'm not complaining, so don't look at me to stop you. Two: I agree with you about the castes, Hellion. If you want to stick it the Arcturians and steal a book, you've got my full support." He leaned in. "And that brings us to three: I've been waiting to get another good look at you from behind since the day I caught you on your knees looking for wires in the escape pod. You won't catch me objecting to the view."

At this last point, his grin faded, a new heated look taking over his face. One that sent warm ripples throughout her body and down her legs.

He leaned in even closer, his breaths fanning her cheek. "So why don't you bend down and make sure you've got that book in there nice and tight?"

His heat enveloped her, dissipating her anger and leaving her a puddle of mush in its wake.

"You are such a pervert," she mumbled under her breath.

His answering chuckle washed over her like a caress, and she fought back a sigh in response.

"Now that you've got your book, do you mind telling me where we're going next?" he asked.

"The senator's office is the last door on the right."

They made their way silently down the corridor, creeping along at a steady pace. Just before they reached the door to the senator's office, Conrad's watch began to blink before beeping twice. He let out a frustrated growl and lifted his wrist. Flipping a latch on the watch's face, he pressed a button on the side and whispered harshly.

"This better be important."

"Well, hello to you too, Big Guy."

Finn recognized Jax's voice laced with amusement. Conrad tensed and held down the button on the side of the watch again.

"What's going on? Is everyone okay?"

"The senator's place is rigged with cameras. You and Sexy Stowaway almost put on quite a show for the Reliance guard."

Conrad's jaw clenched forcefully. Finn's eyes scanned the hall for any sign of cameras. She couldn't see them anywhere. They must have been expertly hidden.

"Is this your way of telling me the problem is solved?" Conrad asked.

"I believe the words you're searching for are 'Thank you, Jax. We are forever indebted to your generosity and wisdom. If she has the chance, Sexy Stowaway will give you a lap dance post haste.' Does that sum it up?"

"Jax—"

Conrad's warning growl sounded ferocious, and Finn almost snorted in laughter. Jax gave a long suffering sigh, followed by a snicker. Then Finn heard Lex pipe in.

"Hey guys, the cameras have been disabled, and all traces of you have been erased. You're in the clear. Now, Finn, you've got to give me some details. I'm dying up here. What are the dresses like? Is there a ten-tier cake? I heard they serve a ten-tier cake glazed in *gold*."

Conrad's face shot heavenward and then down to Finn as though she knew how to save him from this nightmare. She gave him a half-grin and shook her head. He slammed his hand on the button and bit out, "We're signing off now."

Her body shook with barely concealed laughter. Conrad gave her a look that suggested he didn't find the situation funny at all. He snatched her hand and pulled her through the door into the senator's office: an office at least ten times the size of her tiny apartment on the Mud Pit.

Like the rest of the estate she'd seen, the same red, velvety carpeting covered the floor. Even more paintings covered the walls, and a long, ochre couch sat in the far corner with beaded burgundy pillows on each end.

A warm, crackling fire burned in the fireplace across from the couch, as though the room had prepared itself for its master's return. The standout piece of the area, however, had to be the giant desk sitting toward the back of the office, centered beneath a spacious window displaying a view of the entire estate. It appeared to be solid gold and looked like it weighed a ton (possibly two). How they even managed to lug it up here in the first place remained a mystery of epic proportions. Feats of the impossible made her think of the twins, and she called to Conrad in as loud a whisper as she dared.

"How were Lex and Jax able to disable the cameras and erase our footage?"

Ignoring her, Conrad moved toward a painting just to the left of the fireplace. She watched in silence as he tugged on the frame. She opened her mouth to speak, but to her surprise, the frame swung outward and revealed the front of a wall safe.

Curiosity propelled her to Conrad's side, her eyes examining the cool metal door of the safe.

"The twins have a way with technology," he said, answering the question she'd already forgotten asking. "Some might call it a gift."

The meaning wasn't lost on Finn. The twins were obviously half-breeds, and now she knew where their talents lay. A thought struck her as she remembered the renovations on the escape pod.

"Are they the ones who modernized the escape pod's flight tech and screen ports?"

Conrad merely grunted a response, his focus on the safe's numbered lock and his gaze so intense Finn doubted he would even notice if her dress suddenly fell off. Slowly, the lock began to turn clockwise on its own, or, Finn suspected, with a little help from Conrad's half-breed abilities.

She'd worked with safes and combinations before. Ironically, the higher-tech safe models that had come with Arcturian unionization could be easily hacked with the very same tech used to make them "safe." Over the last few cycles, though, upper-caste well-to-dos had reverted to using older-model safes with cylinder locks from centuries ago. Their antiquity meant most people had no real way to electronically crack them.

Some crews preferred to use explosives to get in, opting for the loudest, messiest means to an end possible, but they usually wound up getting caught after one or two jobs. Others, when they could afford it, used what they called a *Breach*, a very rare individual skilled in cracking the antique safes. In this instance, Finn felt sure she was dealing with the latter and knew he would need her absolute silence so he could concentrate.

She put a lid on the conversation and held her breath. She heard a barely audible click as the lock hit on the first number. Her heart pounded in her chest, the drumbeat so loud she thought for sure he could hear. A few moments passed and a second click sounded, indicating another correct number. The lock went on its third spin around and Finn held her breath, waiting for the third and final click. Seconds stretched into infinity before she heard it, and she released her breath on a loud exhalation, causing Conrad to turn and give her a satisfied grin. His hand went to the lever at the side of the safe's door and pulled, opening the heavy metal and revealing its insides.

Finn felt the tension in her body deflate. The thing sat almost completely bare, save for a few rolled-up pieces of paper, a holopad, and a blue velvet box. She'd never seen a worse take on a safe job in her entire career as a thief.

"Well, this is disappointing."

Her grumble earned Conrad's attention, and he turned around to stare.

"Excuse me?"

Finn waved her arms toward the belly of the safe, expecting that to explain it all. When he still didn't seem to get it, she rolled her eyes.

"Conrad, there's nothing in there. After everything we've seen in this estate, I was expecting to find it stuffed to brimming with jewels, or ancient books dipped in gold. Not a piece of paper and a holopad. Not to mention, I don't see any artifact to take back to the Toad."

He watched her for a long time, his face giving nothing away. Slowly, he took a small black device out of his pocket. Lifting the holopad from its resting place inside the safe, he set it gently in her hands.

"Not everything of value sparkles and shines, Hellion."

With deft fingers he attached the little black device to the side of the holopad and began typing away across the top of the clear screen as she held it steady. Before long, three-dimensional images appeared in the space above. Conrad swiped impatiently through pictures, memos, and videos before finding what he wanted.

As Finn watched, a list of alien races and descriptions hovered in front of their faces, along with locations and names scribbled off to the right of each one. Conrad pressed more keys, and the list began to download, most likely onto the little device attached to the holopad.

Finn finally got over her shock enough to speak.

"What am I looking at, Conrad?"

He didn't bother glancing up as he continued to type, his eyes on the progress bar of his download.

Twenty-two percent.

"It's a list of every half-breed in Reliance captivity."

Her eyes swung to him. She felt the instant all the warmth drained from her chest as a new, cold tightness took its place.

She'd thought she knew everything about this job.

She'd been wrong.

She pushed the holopad back into his hands and took a step back. Finn expected her voice to boom, but it escaped her throat no louder than a whisper.

"*What?*"

She watched the progress bar in a daze.

Fifty-eight percent.

"The Reliance has been capturing half-breeds for decades," he stated flatly, "Enslaving and experimenting on them for their own gain. This list contains the location of every single one."

How could any of what Conrad said be true? The Reliance killed half-breeds on sight.

"I don't understand, this doesn't make sense—"

"Do you really believe the Reliance would eliminate something that could be used for their gain? Regardless of the risk?"

Like one of the thousands of brainwashed, illiterate Mudders Finn was constantly berating for their mindless acceptance of Reliance propaganda, she wanted to quote the signs posted to every wall of her planet's crumbling ruins. Only days ago, she'd mocked Nova for buying into all the garbage they spewed about half-breeds, and yet all this time Finn had just accepted the Reliance's claim of hunting half-breeds to the verge of extinction as truth.

She tried to swallow the lump in her throat, processing this new piece of information, information Finn should have been given a hell of a lot sooner than in the middle of a high-risk job.

Finn decided to push those questions down for now in favor of a more important one. One that had her palms itching and her throat burning with nausea.

"What does the Toad want with the location of a bunch of half-breeds?"

Conrad gave her a look that suggested he'd seriously begun to question her intelligence.

"Don't look at me like that," she snapped. "Up until two days ago, I thought most half-breeds were dead. And up until two minutes ago,

I thought we came here for an artifact, not a list of alive-and-well half-breeds."

Something like pain slid across his face.

"They're alive, but I doubt very much that they are *well*." Her stomach dropped as he continued. "This kind of information would be worth its weight in gold to the right buyer. The Toad knows that, so he wants it."

Something cold and ugly wormed its way up her spine as she assessed Conrad with a sharp gaze.

"You said you told me everything. Well, this is a pretty significant piece of information to leave out, don't you think?"

His body stood ramrod straight, more tense than she'd seen him in days. She should have known better than to ask, but curse it all, they'd yet again withheld information. Didn't he understand how hard it had been for her to trust him?

He turned then, finally giving her his full attention. When he did, she wished he hadn't. His body thrummed with irritation, the muscles in his jaw ticking wildly.

"Listen carefully. Lex and Jax will make him an encrypted copy with a virus that will be activated when he tries to decode the list. He'll never see a single name on this holopad."

He turned back to the progress bar, and Finn's mind swam even as relief filled her.

Eighty-eight percent.

"At least tell me what you and Shane want with the list."

"We know what we're doing, Finn. You said you trusted me. Now is your chance to prove it."

"And look at where trusting you got me. Just tell me the truth for once, dammit." She meant the words as a demand, but they came out as a plea instead.

He stared at her for several long moments, neither one of them saying anything. Eventually his eyes dimmed and he turned back to the holopad. He had no intention of answering, that much was clear. Pain sliced into her chest, rendering her body immobile.

Unable to do much else, her eyes flew to the list that appeared to float above the holopad. At least fifty half-breeds flashed there. Finn took her time reading each one, finding comfort in the mundane, as the rest of her found it hard not to fall apart.

Breed: Sirian Location: Arcturus Name: James Jessup
Breed: Xandar Location: Arcturus Name: Alastair Temple
Breed: Teslan Location: Aquarii Name: Demetrius Florax

On and on it went. Her unease grew as more and more breeds, locations, and names began to pile up. When she got to the last one, her heart stopped.

Breed: Khaleerian Location: Cartan Name: Emerson Califax

"Conrad, there's a half-breed somewhere on this estate."

Not just any half-breed; a Khaleerian half-breed. Finn thought of Grim and the raw anger she'd see in his black eyes if he knew all that she'd just discovered. The holopad beeped, the progress bar showing a completed download.

Conrad removed the device and placed it back in his pocket. Carefully, he set the holopad back in the safe exactly as it had been and shut the door. Without his touching it, the lock spun rapidly left then right to reset itself. Without so much as a glance in her direction, he grabbed her forearm and dragged her to the window.

Finn pulled against his hold, raising her voice to get his attention. "Did you hear what I said, Conrad? The senator has a half-breed here."

He continued to pull her to the window. *Curse him for being so strong*, she could do nothing to stop him. When they reached the glass panes, he finally faced her.

"I know."

Finn felt the blood drain from her face at the coldly stated fact. *He knew.* Part of her wanted to collapse to the ground and cry, an action so weak she couldn't believe she even considered it. The other part of her wanted to tear one of the *kama* free from her boot and stab some sense into him.

He must have read the violent thoughts on her face, because his gaze hardened and he bit out a harsh *"Don't."*

She was just beginning to contemplate the consequences of scratching his beautiful eyes out when his watch beeped and Jax's voice rang out. It still sounded cheerful, but a little more businesslike than before.

"Shane and Iliana are almost to the rendezvous point. You've got two guards headed your way on rounds. Now would be the time to make your great escape, Big Guy. Oh, and don't forget about my lap dance."

Both Conrad and Finn glared at the watch this time. His apathetic gaze met hers again, as if waiting for her to make a decision: stay and get caught by Reliance soldiers or go with the big jerk she was fairly certain she had feelings for but couldn't trust.

Finn chose option three and decided to ignore him completely. She made her way to the window, suddenly even more grateful than before to have her trusty boots on her feet instead of some fancy pair of neck-breaking heels.

She felt his heat at her back and tried her best to ignore how nice it felt or how what they were about to do made her stomach queasy. They were going to leave a half-breed behind. A week ago, the idea wouldn't have given her too much pause. Now things were different. *Finn* was different, and she had thought Conrad was different too.

Footsteps sounded outside the office doors. They both turned abruptly. Her heartbeat thudded in her ears as she saw the golden handle move down. The door didn't open. The handle moved up and down more rapidly, muffled voices outside the room beginning to whisper harshly to one another.

Finn chanced a glance up at Conrad and found his eyes glowing eerily, visible even with the wraparounds. His stare fixated on the door. She didn't waste any time watching, hurrying to the window and sliding open the panel on the far-right side. Pushing the glass out, Finn created a space big enough for them both to climb to the roof.

She crawled out first, biting her cheek in frustration as Conrad's hand clasped her waist to steady her. He followed closely, putting pressure on her spine. When they made it outside, he pulled them both down onto their stomachs in a prone position on the roof. He closed the window behind him just as two guards stormed into the office. Conrad's heavy bicep settled over her back, his hand resting next to her head.

They waited in silence while the guards stomped around the room, looking for signs of an intruder. After what felt like an eternity, the two men gave up the ghost hunt and returned to their rounds, grumbling something about "old manors" and "tricky locks."

Finn shifted as she moved to get up. Before she could, however, he'd already yanked her to her feet, his face close to hers.

"I have never in my life met anyone as stubborn as you."

Finn backed away, too angry to care that they remained on the roof several stories above the ground.

"Trust me, the feeling is mutual," she bit out.

"What do I have to do to convince you I'm not the villain in this story you've made up in your head?"

"How about you go back in time and tell the truth?"

His answering sigh was heavy, and Finn snapped her mouth closed. Narrowing her eyes at him, she refused to speak any further.

Gradually, he seemed to remember their precarious situation, and shook his head. Reaching out, he pulled her struggling form into his, dragged her to the edge of the roof, wrapped his arms around her waist, and jumped them both over the side.

The wind rushed up around them, whipping the free tendrils of her hair around her face and stealing her breath. Her stomach dropped so quickly, she didn't have the chance to scream as she felt her body free-fall to the ground. Her nails bit into Conrad's biceps, holding on for dear life.

Suddenly, when only about fifteen feet separated them from their demise, their bodies slowed and they began to float like two leaves falling gently from a tree readying for the winter cycle.

Her eyes shot up to Conrad, expression no doubt full of shock and fear, only to find his lips upturned in a mocking smile. His focus remained on the air and ground around them, using his abilities to keep them steady. Slowly but surely, they floated to the earth, their descent calm and almost pleasant save for the pounding of Finn's heart in her chest. When her boots touched the synthetic grass, she slammed a fist into his chest.

"You did that on purpose."

Gods, she hated him. Finn mentally took back every good thing she'd ever thought about the man. In fact, she planned on beating the half-breed jerk to within an inch of his life just as soon as the feeling returned to her legs and they stopped quivering like jelly.

He didn't deny it. Most of the anger seemed to have left his face, a calm mask of indifference taking its place. He watched her with detached amusement, and her fingers itched to feel the weight of the *kama* between them. Instead of giving in to the urge, Finn stormed off in the direction of the rendezvous point.

She knew where she needed to go. Conrad had landed them on the darker, outer edge of the estate, where they'd be less likely to be spotted. She didn't bother waiting for him. She found herself too consumed in her anger, still trying to get her heart rate to return to normal. Unfortunately, every time she passed a fake bushel of roses or a synthetic bonsai tree, her blood pressure skyrocketed further.

After several minutes of stomping, Finn passed through a clearing and caught sight of the tail end of their travel pod in the distance. She released a frustrated breath.

Finally, this mess can be over.

On that final thought, she heard the cocking of a gun's hammer as two steel bands wrapped around her midsection.

SEVENTEEN

Finn granted herself only a moment of hesitation before her sense of panic kicked in and she began to fight off her attacker. The steel bands tightened around her middle, their hold unforgiving. The breath cut off from her lungs in one harsh squeeze.

Whoever held her possessed unbridled strength, even more so than Conrad. She tried to tamp down on the terror clawing its way up her chest, but she could feel her unknown assailant's hands crushing her ribs in an inescapable hold. The sensation sent an involuntary rush of bile up her throat.

A shadow moved to her left, and Finn caught a glimpse of the shining barrel of a gun right before she locked eyes on one of the Toad's bodyguards—one of the Toad's giant, freakishly strong bodyguards.

Finn didn't know their names; for all she knew, they didn't have them. They looked almost identical in appearance, though as far as she knew they were not blood relatives. One of the unfortunate downsides to the contents of the little yellow vial promising strength: when a user dosed with Yellow Faze and dosed as often as the Toad's meteorhead bodyguards, they began to notice unintended side-effects.

Yellow Faze was used for an increase in strength and reflexes. Frequent use led to the expected increase in both, but it also began to change other aspects of the user, from their physical appearance to their speech and thought patterns. Yellow Faze wasn't as addictive as some of the others in circulation, so most people spaced out their doses to avoid such negative effects. But by the looks of the Toad's hired muscle, he hadn't given them much of a choice.

Meteorhead Number One towered over Finn, his back to the clearing and his gun pointed directly at her face. He stood at least six and a half feet tall, his build even more muscular than Conrad's, with a thick neck and veins bulging from his massive exposed biceps and shoulders. His skin had taken on a sallow yellow hue from the tips of his fingers to the top of his bald head, the color nearly identical to the canary irises of his lifeless eyes. Those dead eyes watched Finn calmly as Meteorhead Number Two tightened his viselike grip around her.

When Number One spoke, his voice sounded rough and garbled, as though he'd recently chosen to rinse with a shot of acid.

"The boss wants the list now, and he wants you with it."

Had she been capable of breathing, she would have sucked in a shocked gasp. The Toad wanted Finn to come with him? Her stomach roiled with revulsion as she thought about all the consequences to that new bit of information.

The Toad might find her useful for a number of reasons, and none of them bore thinking about. Finn wouldn't last long in his employ, especially if she found herself there against her will. There was no way she'd let that happen.

Apparently, she wasn't the only one. Her eyes followed Conrad, looking particularly ferocious as he prowled through the clearing. He approached Number One from the left.

Oh Gods, what did he have planned? Number Two hadn't clocked him yet, but it was only a matter of time.

He could get one or both of them killed. Finn tried to make eye contact with him and communicate that very fact, but his focus remained squarely on Number One. He surprised her by speaking to the brute directly, and even she cowered at the steely tone in his voice.

"She's not going with you. Tell your meteorhead partner to take his hands off her, or I'll rip them off."

The Toad's bodyguards didn't seem all that intimidated by his threat, but they should have been. Finn could see it in every molecule of Conrad's body. He thrummed with wrath, his muscles practically itching for violence. In that moment, she didn't doubt his ability to rip off more than just Number Two's hands.

Number One turned to face Conrad, his expression unchanged and dead as ever, but his body had tensed, ready for a fight. Finn took a moment to appreciate the fact that his gun no longer pointed in her direction.

Then he spoke in his low, hoarse voice.

"If you give me the list, I'll kill you quickly. If not, I'll make you watch while we take turns ripping her apart."

Something slimy wormed its way across her skin, and Finn genuinely fought the urge to throw up as Number Two snickered in her ear and tightened his grip. She looked at Conrad and promptly forgot her desire to vomit. She'd never seen him look so savage.

Number One appeared to be struck momentarily speechless as well. Apparently he'd chosen the absolute wrong thing to say and was just now beginning to realize his error.

Conrad's fists clenched at his sides, and his muscles rippled and strained under the material of his suit.

"Killing you would be too easy," Conrad snarled with menace, "I'm going to enjoy kicking your ass." Without warning, Number One's arm flew out to his side, his fingers unfurling one by one as the gun dropped from his hand. He didn't get a chance to absorb this development because Conrad was already charging him, in the process of tackling him to the ground.

Their bodies collided with a sickening thud, and Conrad rolled them into the synthetic grass. It surprised her how easily he took the big man down. As it turned out, no matter how much Faze he had pumped himself with, the Toad's bodyguard still posed no threat for the ferocious half-breed. Conrad landed two bone-crunching punches to his jaw before Number One seemed to get his wits about him, launching Conrad into the air.

Finn started squirming in Number Two's hold, slamming her head back until she heard the satisfying crunch indicating her skull had connected with his nose. She fought to gain leverage in his arms while keeping an eye on Conrad and Number One.

They launched themselves at each other again, both out for blood; their savagery permeated the air. Conrad headbutted Number One, and Finn almost stopped struggling for a moment to watch in amazement as an arc of yellow blood sailed from the monster's nose and mouth. He didn't take long to recover though, and, to her horror, threw his body weight into Conrad. The impact sent him careening into a synthetic Eucalyptus tree, nearly felling the thing with his momentum.

Terror gave Finn added strength. With a brutal kick to Number Two's kneecap, she finally propelled herself out of his arms. Landing in a crouch, she lifted her skirt and pulled both *kama* free from her boots. Her eyes darted to find Conrad. Number One still pinned him against the tree, his huge hands at Conrad's throat. Finn didn't think, just acted, throwing herself at the yellow beast's massive back.

She didn't get far before something grabbed a fistful of her hair, yanking her backward. All of the air left her lungs in a loud *whoosh* as she landed on her spine on the hard ground. Number Two stood over her, his straight nose now crooked and dripping yellow blood. A look of raw fury lit his face. Finn didn't get a chance to roll away. His large palm closed around her throat and lifted her into the air with one hand, her feet dangling helplessly.

Finn wheezed, her lungs struggling to take in air. His fist squeezed her neck, her feet kicking out in a feeble attempt to dislodge his hold. As her vision blurred, she started to lose sight of Number Two. In the distance, Finn heard Conrad roar her name, and in some foggy recess of her mind, she remembered the *kama* still clutched in her hands.

With all the strength left in her body, she swung her right arm up in an arch like Conrad had shown her. Her eyes widened in horror as the *kama*'s blade sliced into Number Two's face, spraying yellow gore over both of them like a gruesome fountain. His scream of agony rang so loud, so gut-wrenching, that she found herself unable to look away. Blood covered his face where she'd slashed him, leaving a gaping hole where his left eye had been.

With another bellow, he threw her through the air. Finn landed on the far side of the clearing. She hit the ground hard, her stunned and aching body unable to do more than lay there. After a few beats, she finally drew in shallow pants of air, her throat burning and throbbing from the sensation. She forced her body to roll over, despite the pain in her side and lower back.

Eyes rolling, Finn glanced up to see Number Two stomping toward her. Apparently, the loss of his eye did nothing to alleviate his anger or sap his strength. Her hands reached desperately for the *kama*, but she must have lost them at some point during her flight. She heard Conrad yell again, and her gaze shot to him across the clearing.

He grasped Number One by the neck, the bodyguard looking a lot bloodier and much worse for wear after a throwdown with the big half-breed. With a single precise strike, he head-butted Number One then let his big, body fall to the ground in a boneless heap. Still in the throes of his wrath, he began sprinting toward her through the clearing, his face set with determination as he closed the distance between them. She wondered if he'd make it in time. He had to be too exhausted at this point to use his abilities and Number Two already prowled above her, his remaining yellow eye promising death.

Finn could recall very few instances in her life when time seemed to slow down. As she watched her would-be murderer's hands reached for her, her impending death a very real possibility, everything around her seemed to stop. It really didn't seem fair, all things considered. If her future held a painful death, she'd much rather it happened in fast-forward than slow motion.

Finn became so busy irrationally contemplating the injustice of the situation that she didn't notice the movement to her left or the red material of a dress as it passed by her.

Number Two noticed. He stopped short, his remaining eye blinking in shock.

Finn watched in a fog as she realized Iliana had appeared out of nowhere, placing herself between her would-be murderer and Finn. As she blinked, still in a daze, Iliana lifted a dainty gold-dusted hand and placed it on his cheek. If Finn hadn't been watching with rapt attention, she might have missed her sister's harsh whisper. But she didn't; she heard it loud and clear.

"You will pay for touching my sister."

The visceral cruelty in her tone made Finn sit up straighter in the grass, her dizziness fading. At the contact of Iliana's palm against his cheek, Number Two's remaining eye went wide, his body becoming rigid and immobile. Finn watched in stunned silence as he began to tremble in genuine fear, his wide gaze never leaving Iliana's.

After a few beats, her hand released him, and his large body fell to the ground. When he hit earth, he curled into the fetal position. Slowly, he began to rock himself back and forth, emitting a low keen of terror.

He did not get up.

Finn felt Conrad's hands under her arms, lifting her to her feet.

"Steady now. You okay, Hellion?" he whispered into her hair.

She wanted to answer but couldn't do anything more than gape at Iliana's back and the once formidable Number Two as he lay crumpled on the ground.

What had she done to him?

She'd merely touched him, and he'd been reduced to a shriveling mess on the grass. Finally, Iliana turned to face her, her gaze fierce as it looked Finn up and down.

"Are you all right?"

Finn's round eyes shot back and forth between Iliana and Number Two. For the first time, she found herself at a loss for words in her sister's presence. Movement out of the corner of her eye caught her attention then, saving her from having to formulate a response.

Shane strolled up to Iliana's side, a large, limp body balanced over his right shoulder. His hard stare scanned the scene, passing over Conrad, Iliana, Finn, and finally landing on the defeated bodyguard's writhing form. Finn watched as his face tightened in anger at the man's terrified squirming. Carefully, he set the body on the ground and bent over Number Two.

Finn stopped watching him then, too busy staring at the unconscious figure he'd just set at her feet to pay much attention to what he did next. The young man in the grass appeared to be asleep, a wave of light-brown hair falling over his brow. Two long, black horns curled around his head, the tips only slightly obscured by his soft locks of hair. His face looked troubled in sleep, the parts of his skin not mottled by fresh cuts and bruises appearing pale, not dark red like she'd expected.

The Khaleerian half-breed.

She turned to find Conrad watching her, his face inscrutable. Her mouth opened to speak, but she couldn't decide on what she wanted to say. Another first for her. There was still so much she didn't understand about these people and their intentions, but as she gazed at Conrad's powerful frame, and her eyes moved over to Iliana, she decided she would be giving them a chance to do just that. No more running and no more pulling away.

Something about her decision must have shown on her face. Conrad's expression immediately softened, and he took a step toward her.

"Finn—"

She really wanted to know what he meant to say, but Shane cut him off before he could finish.

"We need to get to the ship. The Toad double-crossed us sooner than I would've expected. I want to put some distance between us and him."

"He wanted Finn."

All heads turned at Conrad's gruffly spoken revelation. Shane raised his brows.

"What?"

"He sent the meteorheads for Finn. The Toad wants the list, but it would seem he wants her more."

Conrad's ominous tone sent shivers down the back of her neck. Wherever the Toad was right now, she pitied him a little.

Shane turned to Finn, his features lightening with affection.

"Well, he isn't going to get her."

Something warm bloomed in her chest, and she didn't try to fight the awkward lopsided smile that appeared in response. Shane shook his head, grinning as he leaned down to heft the unconscious half-breed over his shoulder.

They moved at a fast clip to the travel pod, leaving Number Two to writhe in misery alone. Finn felt Conrad move to her side, and some of the tension left her body. She allowed herself a moment of relaxation before her expression sobered. She didn't plan on making this easy for him.

"Now that I'm staying, you do know you're going to have to explain everything, right?"

"You're staying?" His lips lifted into a glorious grin she found herself helpless not to return.

"Don't act like that's such a surprise. Now, the truth. All of it."

"I'm looking forward to it," he said.

Finn felt a warm shiver of anticipation steal through her body.

EIGHTEEN

As the pod docked with *Independence*, a panting AJ met them at the door. All thoughts of relief fled when they found his normally angst-ridden features pinched tight with worry.

His dark eyes immediately sought out Shane.

"We've got company. Lex and Jax spotted the Toad's ship heading this way. It looks like he's coming in hot."

Dread turned her blood to ice. Shane's eyes flitted briefly to hers, and he gave her a short, reassuring nod before turning back to the others.

"Everyone get to the bridge. Prepare for impact."

No one seemed to be in the arguing mood, and they all filed out one-by-one into the hall. AJ, Iliana, and Shane, still carrying the unresponsive half-breed, went toward the elevator off to the left. Conrad, bless his soul, led her to the steel ladder ahead. With a gentle push, he sent her climbing above him, following closely on her heels.

"Don't worry, we'll be safe on the bridge," he said, seeming to sense her anxiety. "Jax and Lex had the whole thing renovated two cycles ago, just in case we ran into something like this."

They'd almost breached the floor leading to the bridge when the entire ship shuddered and the lights around them began to flicker. The warning gave her only a moment to grip the rungs of the ladder tighter. A second later, a loud crash sounded, and the ship shook, throwing Finn violently to the side.

Despite her efforts to hold tight, she went flying, her grasp on the ladder completely lost. Conrad's strong arm reached out and grasped her around the middle. As though she weighed nothing, he pulled her flush against him and continued to climb.

Finn let out a deep breath.

"The crazy scum-sucker is firing on us, isn't he?"

Conrad didn't answer. He merely tightened his jaw and lifted her up onto the metal grate flooring. Once he'd pulled himself up alongside her, he snagged her hand, tugging her in the direction of the bridge. Her skin itched with awareness, the fine hairs on her arms screaming *Danger* as they sprinted down the halls. Finn struggled not to topple over when more loud crashes filled her ears, and the ship tumbled left then right with the force of the enemy blows.

The door to the bridge already stood open, and they charged through, breaths heaving in their chests as they took in the room. Seeing it for the first time during her stay, Finn understood what Conrad had meant earlier by Lex and Jax's "renovations." More spacious than any she'd ever been on, the Dogwood's bridge had enough reinforced seats for the whole crew, not to mention several flashing panels and consoles at the helm making up the most impressive battle station she'd ever seen. The Khaleerian half-breed still lay unconscious, his large body securely buckled into a seat. Relief caused her to sag when Finn spotted Isis and Tiri in the seats next to him. Both looked no worse for wear despite their precarious surroundings. AJ stood silently against a far wall and Shane and Iliana were seated next to Jax and Lex in their positions at the helm piloting the ship. The twins' bodies strained as they fought to keep *Independence* steady.

Another massive shudder rocked them, sending sparks flying from the access panels above them. Everyone ducked low, looking up cautiously to see if anyone had been injured. Panic squeezed Finn's chest when she made contact with Tiri's terrified gaze.

Finn couldn't let these people die for her.

With shaky legs she took a few steps toward Shane, yelling to be heard over the crashing and shaking of the walls around her.

"Just hand me over, Shane! He's going to kill us all if you don't!"

Finn tried to ignore Conrad's angry shout: "Over my dead body!"

Finn yelled back at him, "That's what I'm trying to prevent, Conrad!"

Shane barely spared her a cursory glance over his shoulder before returning his full attention to the screen in front of him. He calmly assessed the damage to his beloved ship while shouting instructions to Lex and Jax.

Finally, he gave her his full attention.

"That's not going to happen, Finn. You're one of us now. Stop trying to get out of it."

She could hear the smile in his voice and couldn't quite believe his audacity, joking at a time like this. Didn't he understand how dire their situation was? The ship was literally falling down around them.

Jax turned from the control panel in front of him and flashed Finn a grin.

"Seriously, Sexy Stowaway, sit back and enjoy the ride. There's no way I'm letting you die when you owe me a lap dance."

Her jaw dropped. Completely unaffected, he returned to the controls, his hands moving faster than she could track. Worked up now, Finn marched back to Conrad's seat with angry strides.

"You're all cracked."

Apparently she *was* the only one who realized how dire the situation was. Conrad merely winked at her, refocusing his attention to the ship's controls. That left Finn with the unwitting Khaleerian, Tiri, Isis, and AJ at the back of the bridge. The half-Anunnaki appeared to be frozen in his spot against the wall. He still hadn't taken his seat and she tried to ignore his shell-shocked eyes as they watched her, by focusing on the twins and their progress at the ship's helm. They held their heads close together and appeared to be involved in a deep, hushed conversation. The ship rocked again.

Shane looked back once more, his eyes catching Finn's and widening.

"Buckle the hell up, Finn!"

Without warning, Lex and Jax joined hands, a look of complete calm on their faces despite the jarring and rumbling of the ship around them. Finn stared in fascination as their brows furrowed and they began to move in synchronized motions. Had she not been watching with her own eyes, her hands clutching at the walls around her for leverage, she might not have believed what she saw next.

Those strange fish markings on their cheeks began to glow, their free hands dipping into the ship's console. As she continued to watch in stunned silence, *Independence*'s wiring began to wind its way around them. Like the body of a snake, it slithered up their arms and shoulders until the twins had become one with the ship. She was so busy staring, she forgot to buckle into a seat as instructed.

The air around them stilled, everything going quiet for the briefest of moments. The fish markings on their cheeks flared even brighter as *Independence* seemed to heave a large sigh, surging forward at hyperspeed. Everyone but the twins flew back against their seats from the force of the rapid change in velocity, debris from the ship falling down around them. Finn tumbled to the ground and rolled.

She watched a large piece plummet toward AJ, who had also been thrown to the ground in the chaos. Without thinking, she forced herself to her feet and sprinted at him, shoving his body out of the way. She barely managed to dodge the falling metal herself before landing hard with her back against the wall. A rush of air left her lips when she hit, something wet and warm blooming around her stomach.

Great, now the ship is leaking?

Jax yelled triumphantly in the distance, his joyful whoops mingling with Lex's happy squeals.

"Smell you later, Bug Breath," Jax cheered.

Finn tried to get up to check on AJ and everyone else, but she couldn't get her legs to move, most likely the aftereffects of adrenaline, shock, and that incredible hyperjump they'd just made. She decided to wait until they wore off.

They'd survived. Everyone cheered and smiled with relief. Everyone except AJ, who watched Finn, his eyes widening on her stomach with dawning horror. She followed his gaze down.

A shard of jagged metal debris protruded from the center of her abdomen, the widely spreading dark-red stain ruining her beautiful gown. She searched his face, confusion coloring her own. Finn didn't know how long they watched each other, both of them too scared to move. It felt like hours, but more likely only seconds passed. Eventually, something seemed to click in his frantic gaze, and he turned his head.

"Conrad. Isis. Someone, please help."

All at once, chaos exploded, and her vision blurred as all the voices around her began to blend together. Finn heard Conrad's voice above all the others. A second later, he knelt in front of her, his big hands holding up her head as gently as possible.

"Finn? Finn, stay with me."

She tried to respond, but her tongue felt heavy, too heavy for the momentous task of speaking. Instead, she did her best to focus on him, did everything she could to stay with him as he'd asked. Her lids fluttered like moth's wings, but she fought to keep them open.

Everything within her body felt weak. An overwhelming sense of numbness had washed over her limbs, making her chest ache with rising panic. If she'd possessed the strength, she would have flailed with the increasing sense of dread, but there was no strength to speak of. If not for Conrad's hands holding her in place, her head would have lolled to the side by now.

Movement behind him caught her fading gaze, and she stared past his face at the young girl watching her solemnly. She wore a pink gown, her long blond hair falling past her shoulders in soft waves. She stared at Finn with large, sad eyes, one blue and one white. Like Finn, a dark red stain was spreading on her dress.

Finn felt tears clouding her eyes and falling down her cheeks, her words a hoarse whisper as she cried,

"I'm so sorry, Sophie . . ."

Confusion knit Conrad's brow, replaced by sudden recognition.

He turned to look over his shoulder. His eyes landed on Tiri, who now stood in the young girl's place watching Finn with a horrified gaze.

"AJ, get Tiri and the boy out of here. Now."

AJ threw the big Khaleerian half-breed over his shoulder in a surprising show of strength and grabbed Tiri by the wrist. He stared down at Finn one last time, a strange look of disbelief on his face, before all three disappeared around the corner. With a will of their own, Finn's eyes started to roll back in her head, and she struggled for long seconds to get them to refocus on Conrad.

"Isis, hurry, we're losing her." His voice sounded garbled, far away.

When she finally opened her eyes again, Isis and Shane had joined Conrad. All three of them looked dire. They began to talk amongst themselves, seeming to forget Finn's presence.

"Can you heal her, Isis?"

Shane sounded worried. Finn would have felt worried too, but she couldn't seem to feel much of anything anymore. Well, that wasn't entirely true: her hands were cold. She could at least feel that.

"We must move quickly. Once we get the metal out of her, she will bleed out. I can try to heal her, but it will be close, and it will take a lot out of me. She is very near death already; I can feel it. Once it is done, one of you will need to get me to the Sanctuary immediately."

Shane nodded and turned back to Iliana where she still stood by the ship's controls.

"You should go and join Tiri. You don't need to see this."

Her face had gone pale. She wrung her hands in the skirt of her dress until they became stark white from the tension, but determination sparked in her eyes as she seemed to come unglued from her spot and made her way over to them.

"I am *not* leaving her, ever. Now stop wasting time and save my sister."

Isis rubbed her hands together as though warming them up. Finn wished she could do the same; hers felt frozen.

"Shane, Conrad, you need to pull her from the metal and lay her on her stomach. Try to do it as fast as possible. The sooner I can heal her, the better."

Finn was beginning to have trouble following the conversation. Everything sounded muted and distant, like the way the world might sound to a fish swimming underwater. Conrad placed his mouth against her hair before whispering in her ear.

"I'm sorry for this."

Sorry for what?

She didn't get the chance to contemplate it further. Each of them grabbed one of her shoulders and tugged. Suddenly her body was on fire, needles stabbing her from all directions.

Finn let out a bloodcurdling scream.

She didn't have time to process the transition from her back against the wall to lying facedown on the floor. By the time her cheek hit the cool metal grating, the blessed numbness had returned, her wet tears falling through the slats on the floor and intermingling with her blood.

Finn felt someone tear at her dress, baring her back, and cool air brushed her skin.

Someone cursed.

Someone else whispered,

"Dear Gods."

Dimly, Finn realized they were seeing her scars for the first time, and her fingers curled with the desire to hide them from their gaze.

Then Conrad growled, and the menacing sound soothed her fading but rapid heartbeat like a lullaby.

"No one says another word."

His sweet command was the last thing Finn heard before a bright blue light filled the room, and her eyes finally slid shut. She would miss the stubborn, fierce half-breed.

NINETEEN

Finn knew she must be dead before she opened her eyes. The pain from before was gone, and brightness burned the backs of her eyelids, the atmosphere around her tranquil. She wanted to open her eyes and look around, but the sound stopped her—the sound of someone singing. The voice was nothing short of angelic, soft and lilting, achingly pure as it hit the high notes. Finn decided to see what death looked like later, keeping her lids closed and enjoying her own personal lullaby.

When the mystery voice hit the beautiful final note of its melody, Finn let her eyes flutter open and scan her surroundings. It all seemed rather ordinary. Death looked an awful lot like Iliana's pod on *Independence*. Her gaze took in the red-and-orange silk, the oak bureau, and the candles lighting the space.

She took a moment to wiggle her toes, getting a feel for her body.

Dead people shouldn't be able wiggle their toes, should they?

Although it must be said, the mattress was soft enough to belong in the heavens.

The mattress in question shifted next to her, and Finn looked up to find Iliana seated on the edge of the bed and watching her with worried eyes. She looked down and realized she was propped in a nest of pillows, no longer dressed in her fancy ball gown. Someone had changed her into a pair of soft gray pants and a matching long-sleeved shirt. They'd replaced her cuffs, but her gloves were noticeably absent.

She lifted the shirt's hem to examine her stomach where she'd been impaled. Her fair skin appeared unmarred, nary a scratch to be

found on the surface. Her gaze flew to Iliana. Her sister's hair hung
loose at her shoulders. She too had changed into a pair of pants and
long-sleeved shirt. Finn had never seen her dressed so casually.

"Does this mean I'm dead?"

Iliana's eyes widened in shock and then narrowed infinitesimally.

"Of course you aren't dead. Why would you think such a thing?"

Finn watched her for a long moment, taking in the welcome news
that she had, in fact, survived. Her sister looked so indignant, Finn
couldn't help but flash a grin. It reminded her of the way Iliana used
to look when Finn would come home from playing in the mud with
the piglets. She'd always show up at dusk, covered from head to toe
in muck. Iliana would level her with a glare that she didn't really
mean, ranting and raving about how Finn had no sense of cleanliness
or pride in her appearance. Then she'd hose Finn down and give her
a bath. In the end they'd always wind up laughing and splashing each
other with the soapsuds. Deep down, Finn thought Iliana secretly
enjoyed her little sister's forays to the barn.

Now Iliana's eyes traveled down to Finn's grin and softened, tears
pooling in their depths. By the time they made their way back up to
her face, they appeared tormented.

"You frightened me, Little One. If Isis hadn't been able to heal you,
I don't know what I would have done."

Something heavy lodged in Finn's throat and refused to go down,
the backs of her eyes burning with emotion. She did her best to
speak around it, her voice whisper soft.

"Sorry, Li-Li."

As soon as the words left Finn's mouth, Iliana let her tears fall, a soft
smile playing at her full lips. She seemed to let herself enjoy the moment
for a few seconds, and Finn watched her, finding that she enjoyed it too.

Iliana took a deep breath, her face returning to its serious
expression.

"We need to talk."

She felt the heavy weight in her throat drop down into her stomach, suddenly wishing she could close her eyes and go back to playing

dead. She knew what Iliana wanted to talk about, knew it needed to happen, but she also knew she was nowhere near ready for it. Iliana must have read her hesitation, because that light of determination Finn was growing to resent settled into her eyes.

She decided to change the subject.

"How is everyone? Is the ship okay?"

Iliana arched a brow, subtly letting Finn know she was on to her game, and got up from her spot on the bed.

"The ship is fine, as is the rest of the crew. They are more worried about you than anything. I asked for some time alone with you, else the room would be filled with visitors."

Finn let that information process as she watched Iliana make her way to the oak bureau across from the bed and pull out a drawer. She bent down and lifted something out, but kept her back to Finn. When she returned to the bed, she placed a bundle wrapped in a white cotton blanket there. The cautious way she observed Finn set her nerves on edge, as though she'd just placed a bomb next to her and now waited for it to detonate.

When Finn didn't make any move to touch the bundle, Iliana gave her a slight nod.

"Open it."

Finn didn't know why she became so afraid to look inside, but it felt as though the blanket concealed a severed head or a vial of deadly poison, so deep went her fear. Her heart beat so fast she forgot to breathe. Finally, she forced her shaking hands to unwrap the soft material and reveal what lay inside. For a moment Finn just stared at the blackened doll the blanket revealed, confused by how anticlimactic the moment had ended up being.

"I feel like we've done this before," she quipped. She looked up at Iliana and stopped cold when she saw the look in her eyes. Her sister looked anguished; the pain Finn glimpsed in their indigo depths was like a living thing as she spoke.

"I'd made arrangements for us to escape that night. I would have done anything to get us away from *him*." Her voice hardened on the last word, and Finn knew whom she referred to. She let Iliana continue, even as her own pain burned a pathway up her chest. "I found someone willing to take us to Tesla. I was to make our payment that night, and he would send someone for you, to bring you to us. I refused to leave you alone, but he told me it was the only way, told me only I could make the payment. He vowed that you would be brought to me safely, and I believed him. I know it was foolish. I have no excuse." Her arms wrapped around her stomach protectively as her eyes begged Finn to understand. "I was desperate and so painfully naive.

"I waited for you for what seemed like hours. Finally, a man came, but he was alone. You weren't with him. He handed me your scorched doll, told me that Uncle Henry had burned down the barn in a fit of rage with you inside when he discovered me missing. When he said you were dead and it was my fault, something inside of me broke. I tried to go back to our farm. I wanted to avenge you, but they took me away. They made me go with them on their ship."

Her eyes flared with desperation as her wet tears fell freely down her cheeks. She leaned her face close to Finn's, her gaze searching.

"You have to believe me, Finn. I never would have left you behind."

Finn's mind scrambled to adjust to all the information she'd just been given, even as her heart felt as though it would burst from her chest. Iliana hadn't left her behind. Finn's hands shook even harder as she gazed down at her dolly, running a finger over its charred face. When she looked back at Iliana, shiny tears of her own pooled in her eyes.

"I believe you."

Iliana seemed to deflate before her, all of the tension leaving her body as she fell to the bed beside Finn, a sob heaving from her chest. Finn could see she wanted to reach out and hold her, but she held back. Finn felt gratitude for her restraint, not quite ready for the contact. She compromised, moving on the bed until they faced each other, cross-legged.

"Iliana, what happened to you after you went on their ship?"

Her sister's eyes darkened, and she gained control over her sobs immediately, her beautiful face tightening.

"That is a story for a different time."

Finn wondered if she realized how much hidden pain her behavior revealed and decided that her time for telling said story would come sooner rather than later. If someone had hurt her sister, Finn wanted to know about it.

Iliana interrupted her dark thoughts when she placed a hand next to her leg on the bed.

"Finn, there is a reason I tried to get us out when I did. Uncle Henry was planning to sell us—"

Finn interrupted her before she could finish, already uncomfortable with where the conversation was headed.

"I know what his plans were, Iliana. I was there, remember?"

She didn't mean to sound terse, but the memory of waking up that morning to find her sister gone, to find soldiers in her home waiting to mark her, burned fresh in Finn's mind.

Iliana's eyes closed in pain and then opened, focusing on her with a startling intensity.

"No, you don't know all of it. Uncle Henry found out what we were, what we *are*."

Something cold slithered up her spine.

"What do you mean, 'what *we* are'?"

"Mother died before you were old enough to remember much of her. I only remember bits and pieces myself, and the Gods know Father never spoke of her. He did his best to keep us isolated on the farm and hidden from others. To keep us safe. Even though we seemed to take after him, he was afraid that we might show signs of taking after Mother. All those cycles, never letting us out of his sight, never letting us leave the farm or explore the towns around us. I never understood why until the day I came to him on his deathbed. He told me what we are, what our mother was. She didn't die of sickness, Finn. Our mother was killed, murdered for falling in love with a human."

Finn's entire body pulsed with recognition, even as her mind rebelled against what Iliana said. Then her sister looked Finn dead in the eye as she spoke the words that would turn Finn's world upside down.

"Finn, *we* are half-breeds."

Finn struggled for breath, but her body became paralyzed. Iliana offered her no pity, continuing to fill her with so much unwanted information, her head spun.

"You belong on this ship. You belong with me. I must say, your ability to glean and retain information with merely a touch is quite remarkable. I've never heard of our people being able to do such a thing, but you can do so much more than memorize maps and navigate spaces, little sister. You can navigate minds. Our mother was a Teslan. Her people, our people, have only to touch someone and they can access the furthest reaches of that person's psyche, even their deepest, darkest memories. I am assuming that is why you never knew the true extent of your abilities." She looked down, suddenly saddened. "The abilities only manifest from skin-to-skin contact. I know how much you dislike being touched. Perhaps it has been your way of protecting yourself from the truth."

Finn floundered for some kind of response, anything at all, but her mouth continued to flop open and closed, no sound escaping.

How could any of this be true? Their mother was a Teslan?

Finn searched her mind for anything she knew about the species. The answer was next to nothing. They were one of the Arcturians' most formidable opponents during the initial unionization, and because of their abilities nearly overthrew the golden gods.

Nearly.

The close call scared the Arcturians so much they'd executed almost every single Teslan they could find. The rest went into hiding and hadn't been seen in the Union since.

Finn tried to remember something about her, some tiny insight into what her mother looked like or sounded like, but her memory banks ran dry. She'd always thought of her ability to memorize maps and navigate spaces as a gift.

Could it just be part of some half-breed ability she'd always possessed?

Finn felt sick. One touch from Conrad had propelled her into reliving the worst day of his life. Her half-breed abilities had been the cause of the anomaly all along. She thought about all the times her sister had "accidentally" touched her during her short stay on the Dogwood, and the ease with which each gentle contact would send a specter of the past flying free from the dark recesses of her memory.

Suddenly Finn remembered Iliana's run-in with Meteorhead Number Two. How she merely touched a hand to his cheek and rendered him useless. Could it be true?

Her eyes shot to Iliana as another thought hit her.

"Is that why you became a courtesan? Is that how you help Shane? You let those people touch you so you can invade their minds?"

"I don't expect you to understand, Finn, but my station allows me access to the kinds of people who are privy to information we need. Letting them touch me is a necessary evil. The Luminary helped me understand that. He helped me find my way to Shane, helped me achieve my status so I could find others like me." Her eyes met Finn's. When they did, Finn noticed they burned. "He helped me so that I could avenge you." She leaned in even closer, the fire in her eyes dimming just a little. "The Kyra I remember is gone now. I understand that. But you and I, we can start together anew. I can teach you how to use your gifts."

For the first time, her gaze remained open as it held Finn's, all of her emotions there plain as day for her little sister to see: hope, excitement, sadness, fear, and overshadowing it all . . . *love*.

Of all the things Finn had dreamt of, all the things she'd spent nights lying awake hoping for, she never imagined the future Iliana proposed could be one of them: a fresh start with a family of her very own. Yet here that family sat, for all intents and purposes reaching out for Finn with open arms. She was wanted. She was *loved*.

Her mind rebelled against all the information flooding it. Half-breed abilities she didn't understand and couldn't decide if she wanted. With them, a heritage she'd known nothing about and a future more uncertain than anything she'd ever envisioned. But as Finn looked at the raw love and resolve in her sister's eyes, just as she remembered seeing it every day of her childhood, she knew she'd willingly venture into the unknown to experience a fraction of that love again.

Finn nodded her head, unsure if she was capable of speech at the moment. Iliana seemed to understand her meaning and released a deep breath, a glorious smile overtaking her face.

It lasted only a moment before her brows puckered with something that looked like concern. Her body tensed, and Finn felt herself go rigid in response, small shock waves of warning crawling across her skin.

"Finn, I need to know what happened to you after I left."

Her hand inched closer toward Finn's on the bed. Shock left Finn frozen for only a moment before she scooted back on the mattress.

"No, Iliana. What's done is done. Leave it in the past where it belongs."

A look of gritty resolution manifested itself on her sister's face, and terror unlike anything Finn had ever known began to fill her at the sight. With wide eyes, she watched her sister's hand slowly begin to move again. Like the coiled body of a serpent, it slid its way over the sheets to Finn's hand, stopping just before they touched.

"Please understand, Finn."

Tears Finn could no longer control ran down her cheeks. She couldn't let this happen, she needed to get away, but Iliana's eyes held her captive in their stare. Her dread burned hot in her chest, making her voice a choked whisper as she pled with Iliana.

"Please leave it, Iliana. We'll never be able to start over if you do this."

Iliana's hand latched on to Finn's, her soft voice washing over them both as the room went black.

"Don't you see, Little One? I'll never be able to forgive myself if I don't."

TWENTY

Sophie's whimpers wake Kyra in the middle of the night. She cuddles up closer to Kyra who reaches out her free hand to pull the girl's tiny form closer. They sleep on their sides facing each other. They prefer it this way, as they both have nightmares.

"Kyra, I can't see."

Sophie blinks slowly, her cheeks wet and her eyes unfocused. They used to be a clear blue, like the sky. Now one of them is milky white and opaque from one too many beatings. She can't see out of it anymore. Sometimes she forgets when she first wakes up. Her skin is pale and Kyra knows hers must look the same. It has been so long since either of them has felt the sun on their face.

"I'm here, Sophie. It's okay."

She grips Kyra so tight it hurts, but Kyra doesn't mind. Her sleep has been fitful anyway. She is still recovering from her latest whipping. It pleases the chancellor to punish his slaves, and he does so often. Kyra has been whipped, beaten, and burned so many times her back has become nothing but a mass of scar tissue.

It has forced him to become creative in his punishments.

Kyra studies Sophie's unblinking white eye. They had both arrived at the chancellor's estate on Aquarii around the same time three cycles ago, and immediately clung to each other.

Kyra's back burns where her shirt sticks to her healing wounds. She tries to adjust herself, but the manacles around her right wrist and ankle prevent her from doing much.

They are both bound in chains more often than not these days, but Kyra is grateful if it means she doesn't have to look at her markings and remember the day she got them. The day everything changed.

In the beginning, she would struggle against her bindings, breaking the skin and causing scars. This angered the chancellor and earned her extra punishments.

She learned quickly.

Sophie whimpers again, and Kyra can feel hot tears on her shoulder. She hugs her tighter, even though it presses on her bruises.

"Shhh. Everything will be all right, Sophie. You'll see. Let's pretend we're somewhere else."

Sophie lifts her head up just far enough that she can speak without her words getting muffled.

"Somewhere far away?"

Her words end on a hiccup, and Kyra's chest aches.

"Yes, somewhere far, far away," she forces herself to whisper back. "Somewhere green with lush fields and blue skies. We have our very own farm and two rocking chairs. Every day we run through the fields and climb trees. And when we're too tired to run anymore, we sit in our rocking chairs and watch the sun shine, and the plants grow."

Sophie sighs and relaxes against her.

Sometimes Kyra finds herself thinking about Iliana, wondering if she is out there somewhere, looking for her baby sister. Most of the time, Kyra believes in her heart of hearts that Iliana never would have left her to this fate. Other times though, when things are really bad and she finds herself alone in the dark with her thoughts, Kyra wonders if she might be wrong.

A sliver of morning light begins to creep through their tiny window. It is the only source of illumination in the sparse room. Many days, when they lay like this in the dark, she wonders how it is possible that they have not gone mad from deprivation. If it weren't for one another, they probably would have by now.

A knock on their door precedes three Aquariian maids as they enter with a basin, towels, and steaming water. Their tall, robed forms nearly take up the entire room with their sheer size. Sophie and Kyra exchange a look of shared horror. They only bathe the slaves when the chancellor is planning a special visit.

He likes them to be clean before he bloodies them up. Kyra is confused. She is still healing from his last visit.

The chancellor is a sick man. Something inside of him is twisted, and he delights in finding new ways to cause pain. It's almost as though he is looking for something. Behind every scream, every drop of blood spilled, his cunning eyes are always searching. For what, Kyra does not know.

He seems to know just how far he can push the girls while still keeping them alive. Sometimes she finds herself wishing he would slip up and just kill her, ending her nightmare, but then she remembers that Sophie needs her and she tries to be strong.

The maids start with Kyra, gently removing her clothes. She has long since lost any sense of modesty or shame. They carefully sponge around her injuries, soothing her in a language she doesn't understand. The hot water feels good, but it does nothing to ease her rising panic.

She knows what is coming.

Finn came out of her memory on a gasp, her wide eyes seeking out Iliana's, even as she tried to ground herself in the present. She was not Kyra, not anymore. Kyra was dead.

My name is Finn.

Iliana's hand still grasped hers tightly, a look of grim resolve furrowing her brow despite the tears running down her cheeks.

Finn locked gazes with her.

"Please stop, Iliana. Please."

Her hand squeezed Finn's tighter, and the room went dark again.

He is coming. They've removed the chains and given the girls special dresses to wear just for him. It makes Kyra feel queasy. Just the thought of him makes her sick with fear, and she knows Sophie feels the same. More and more lately she's been getting this far-off look in her eyes, as if she's going somewhere else, and even Kyra can't reach her.

It feels like she is losing her only friend. Kyra cannot survive here without her. If only she could find a way to escape. Maybe then there could be hope for them.

The door opens and he walks in, a cruel smile playing on his thin lips. His black eyes find Kyra first. His smile widens, revealing a row of too-white teeth, and her stomach clenches in fear.

She has always been his favorite.

"Are we feeling stronger today, little dove?"

His thinning hair is slicked back. His gray suit is pressed and immaculate, as usual. He removes his black-and-gold cloak from his shoulders and approaches her with purposeful strides. He is a big man, and the closer he gets, the tinier she feels.

When he is in front of her, he backhands Kyra across the face.

Hard.

He has not removed his rings, and she feels a line of blood running down her cheek from where one has cut her. Tears sting the backs of her eyes, but she doesn't let them fall. Kyra knows this is just the beginning of the pain he has planned for tonight.

"I asked you a question."

Sophie is crying softly in the corner.

"Yes, Chancellor."

He runs his hand across her cheek, smearing the blood there.

"Good girl."

Kyra's fists clench in a bid to hold down the tiny meal she had eaten earlier. The chancellor begins to remove his suit jacket, rolling up his shirt sleeves. He takes a gun from his belt and lays it down on the table next to her.

Her eyes widen and her chest tightens. He doesn't usually bring guns in with him. Next, he takes out his whip and sets it down. The whip she knows well.

"Are you familiar with the art of gambling, dove?" When she doesn't speak, he lifts his hand as though to strike her again, and she hastens to answer him.

"N—no, sir."

He lays out a few other nasty-looking tools before motioning for Kyra to sit on the bed. She obeys quickly, and he smiles.

"Funny, your uncle knows the game well enough. And tonight we are, as a gambler might say, upping the ante."

Despite the terror his attention brings, Kyra is grateful that he is leaving Sophie alone for now. She huddles in the corner with a lost look in her eyes. Kyra closes hers. She pretends she is back on Gliese, lying in the cornfields, the sun on her face. She can almost feel Iliana holding her hand.

"Open your eyes."

She obeys, afraid of what will happen if she doesn't.

Her heart pounds. She hears him remove something from his belt, but doesn't look down. He runs it down her face, stopping just above her collarbone. It is a blade. Kyra struggles not to cry out when he increases the pressure just enough to break the skin. It burns, and she can feel the blood pooling. She tries not to swallow, afraid it will only push the blade in deeper.

At his chuckle, her hands fist in the blankets beneath her. She feels his hot breath in her ear.

"I've been very patient, dove, but I'm afraid I've plumb run out. It's long past time for you to show me what you're capable of, don't you think?"

Kyra can no longer hold back a whine of fear. The knife moves lower, stopping at her sternum. He flicks his wrist, and it slices deep. She screams, her voice cracking from the force of it.

"You can stop this, child," he whispers. "All you have to do is show me what you are."

He is still busy cutting when Kyra hears a click. She opens her eyes and looks up. Sophie is standing behind the chancellor, pointing his own gun at his back. Tears are streaming down her face and her hands are shaking.

He turns and growls at her.

"What do you think you're doing, you little bitch?"

She sobs and looks at Kyra with wild eyes.

"Kyra . . ."

Kyra sits still, too shocked to move. Sophie doesn't notice that the chancellor is stalking toward her. She is crying too hard and doesn't seem to be able to make the gun fire. The chancellor's spine is rigid, and Kyra can see he is beyond angry. Sophie will suffer for this interruption. When he reaches her she breaks down, dropping the gun and falling to her knees.

His roar fills the room and snaps Kyra out of her stupor. He throws Sophie against the wall, his hand gripping her throat tightly.

"You will pay for that."

Sophie can't breathe. Her face is turning purple. At the sight, anger unlike any she's ever known fills Kyra, and she gets up from the bed. He doesn't notice her creep over and pick up the gun. He doesn't see her pointing it at him. It's so heavy her arms shake just trying to hold it up.

"Leave her alone."

He turns and bares his teeth at her in a cold smile, bringing Sophie in front of him. She is gasping for air, reaching out for Kyra, but he holds her tight.

"That's right, dove. If you want someone to stop, you have to make them. Show me what you are."

He moves toward her slowly, Sophie still in front of him. All she can do is take small steps backward to maintain her distance.

"P—please stop. Don't come any closer."

He doesn't listen, just watches Kyra like the predator he is as he stalks closer and closer still. Sophie is crying out her name, and Kyra can't stop the tears flowing down her cheeks. She doesn't know what to do. He's getting too close. She takes another big step back, hitting the bed and losing her balance. Her finger slips on the trigger.

There is a deafening crack, and Kyra is thrown backward. She lays in stunned silence for a moment. Then she sits up, her eyes searching to find Sophie's. When she does, she can see they are dull and glassy. She is staring into nothingness, a red stain blooming on the front of her pink dress. The chancellor's brow is raised, but no anger flushes his face. He lets out a surprised chuckle. Finn barely hears him over the pounding in her ears.

"That's not exactly what I had in mind."

He drops Sophie on the floor. She hits with a thud, unmoving. Kyra's throat feels dry, and she is having trouble getting air.

No, she can't be dead. Kyra didn't kill her . . . she didn't!

"Sophie! Sophie, wake up!"

There is a high-pitched wailing filling the room. After a moment, when her throat starts to burn, Kyra realizes the sound is coming from her.

Sophie doesn't move, doesn't even blink. No breaths enter or leave her gaping mouth.

He kicks her body with the toe of a black boot.

"It's a shame. I paid good money for her. Oh well, there's always more where she came from."

His eyes are gleaming, and he's walking toward her, hands reaching out to touch her. The room spins. Her body is starting to tingle all over, like maybe this is all just a dream. Her legs feel like they're going to give out, but she can't let them. He's still coming.

Kyra raises the gun again and aims it at his chest. He stops and raises his hands in supplication. She doesn't think, just pulls the trigger. The force has her stumbling backward again. When she lifts her gaze, he is on his knees, clutching his bleeding chest. For the first time in two cycles, Kyra sees fear in his eyes.

Kyra takes in the scene before her with a silent scream, allowing one last look at Sophie's lifeless body. Her only friend is dead. She killed her. She is a monster, just like him. She chokes back a sob and drops the gun. Then she runs through the open cell door.

The girl runs, and she doesn't look back. She's not sure how she manages it, but by the time she finds a way off planet, she has no name. She can't even remember what she is running from, only knows that she can't look back.

TWENTY-ONE

Finn felt the exact moment Iliana released her hand. Almost immediately, the room around them began to come into focus, but the horrors of the past still clung to her with a tight grip that refused to let go. She felt dizzy, as though stuck in a brutal tug of war between past and present.

Hot tears burned her cheeks. She could still feel the heavy weight of the chancellor's gun in her palm. Finn choked on a sob, wrapping her arms around her body in a feeble attempt to block out the memory of Sophie's lifeless eyes and bloodstained dress.

"Finn . . ."

Her gaze shot up to find Iliana watching, her eyes wide with horror. At the sight, pain erupted in her gut so intense, it felt as though some beast had clawed its way inside and yanked. Her sister had seen her greatest sin, and it horrified her. Worse, she'd forced Finn to relive it. Now they could never start over.

Pain and anger intermingled, creating a cacophony of fire and destruction inside of her until she felt as though she would surely explode from it. Finn wrenched herself from the bed, unable to control the sobs wracking her body.

"Why couldn't you just leave it?"

"Finn, I didn't know. That man was—"

Iliana reached for her, but Finn released a savage snarl promising pain if she came close.

"Now you know. Now we both know. I'm a murderer."

Hatred spewed from her like a dragon breathing fire; whether hatred for her sister or hatred for herself, it was impossible to ascertain. Iliana's mouth dropped open, pain lighting her face, but Finn didn't give her a chance to speak. She ran from the room as though the chancellor himself chased her.

Her tears clouded her vision as she ran down corridors, not even caring where she ended up. She called on the dark pit of her memories, begging it to take back the look in Sophie's eye as the chancellor held her by her throat. She prayed with everything inside herself for the blessed numbness to take over and never leave, but it was to no avail. Every memory, every emotion burned hot, the flames licking and growing with each step as she sprinted down the hall.

They consumed her so wholly she didn't see Conrad coming until she slammed into the hard wall of his chest and his unyielding arms wrapped around her. She pushed against him, panic giving her added strength as she screamed,

"Don't touch me! You'll see what I've done. Please, don't touch me!"

To her shock, his embrace merely tightened. Her frantic struggles soon ceased, exhaustion taking over. Finn let her legs collapse, and he gently took them to the ground, cradling her in his lap. She felt one of his large hands cup the hair at the back of her head, tilting it up. The glow of his eyes landed on her face. She knew he saw the tears soaking her cheeks, but she couldn't bring herself to meet his gaze.

"Please don't touch my skin, Conrad. I don't want you to see what I've done, who I am. I killed her; I killed my only friend."

She was as helpless to put a stop to her tearful rambling as she was to staunch the tide of emotions swirling around inside. Iliana's invasion had torn open a wound that had been festering for the last eight cycles.

"Finn, look at me."

Finn clenched her jaw and focused on his chest, refusing to look up. When she didn't obey his command, his hand left the back of her head and found her chin, lifting her head.

Their eyes met, the intensity in his gaze freezing her movements. The glow grew so potent that for a moment she became lost in it, a blessed reprieve from her pain.

When he seemed confident he had her attention, his hand left her chin to rest against her cheek, soaking up the tears he found there. As the warmth of it seeped into her, she began to feel a wave of calm wash over her body.

"It wasn't your fault."

His voice, gentle and gruff with emotion, touched her, but she couldn't let him believe something that wasn't true.

"You don't know what happened, Conrad."

His thumb swept at another tear as it fell from her eye.

"I do."

At his admission, Finn felt as though all the oxygen had been sucked from the room. Her heartbeat raced, and her brows knit in confusion as she waited for him to continue.

"That first day, when you fought me like a hellion, I held your wrists to keep you still. It was the barest hint of my skin against yours, but it was enough. You showed me your memories. I saw a man beating and whipping you. The way you were screaming . . ." His eyes flared as he recalled what he'd seen, his jaw clenching in raw anger.

More tears streamed down her cheeks, and his face softened, his mouth quirking up in a half-smile as his thumb caught them. "Then I had to stop you from shooting holes in Shane when he told you the pods needed repairs."

Finn just barely stopped herself short from gasping at his joke. These people made an odd habit out of finding humor in serious situations. He noticed her disapproval, but didn't seem to care.

"I touched you on purpose then. I shouldn't have done it, but you called me a *mutt* and I was angry. I saw Sophie, the little girl with the blue-and-white eyes. I saw that man cutting on you again, and what happened when you grabbed the gun and tried to protect her. You tried to bury it deep, Finn, but you've been carrying it with you everywhere you go."

Her body began to tremble at his words. He'd seen everything. Conrad had known her deepest, darkest secret that very first day. Her head swam, fresh spurts of shame and guilt pouring from her open wound. She tried to pull away from him, but he held her tight.

"Hear me now. What happened that night wasn't your fault. You didn't kill your friend, that evil bastard did. You were a scared little girl trying to protect someone she loved."

Finn shook her head, wishing she could shut out his voice, but it surrounded her. She could feel his warmth, his strength, and it called to the broken pieces of her battered soul. She didn't know if she could believe him just yet, the pain was still too fresh, but she also didn't have it in her to let him go.

He'd known all along, and it never mattered to him.

"I don't know how to control this. If you touch me, I don't know what you'll see."

At her softly spoken words, the tension he'd been holding in his body seemed to ease.

"I'm tougher than I look," he quipped softly.

Finn watched Conrad's slow grin spread across his face as he helped her to her feet. She wanted to see that grin every day, but could she really stay? Especially now, after everything she knew?

That thought led to Iliana, and she forced herself to stop before the idea of being in the same room as her sister sent her into a frenzy.

"Conrad, I don't think I can stay here. Not with Iliana. Not now."

He regarded her seriously for a moment, his mind hard at work for a solution.

"It's a big ship, Hellion. And we have a new crew member to assimilate. I'm sure we can come up with plenty to keep you busy and far away from your sister."

She wanted so badly to believe him, but she couldn't just disappear without seeing to Grim and Doc first. "There are people back home on the Mud Pit. People I need to talk to . . ."

"It sounds like you've made a decision."

"Maybe," she allowed.

Conrad looped his arm through hers, interlocking their elbows as he began to lead her down the hall toward the bridge.

"Where are we going?"

He smiled down at her.

"I promised you answers, Hellion, and I intend to give them. The Luminary has been waiting to see you. He's had a hand in bringing all of us together in some way or another."

"So you keep saying," she grumbled.

They reached the bridge, and Finn could hear hushed voices inside. She tried to pause, to prepare herself for whatever lurked inside that room, but he didn't give her any leverage. Pulling on her hand, he swung them inside.

"We've been trying to reach you for days. Why haven't you returned contact?" Shane asked a hulking form dressed head to toe in black. A hulking form Finn instantly recognized. Even from behind, she could see his black horns and red skin.

The air went stagnant and the voices quieted as they made their entrance. The figure in black turned, and Finn felt her world unraveling.

His black eyes flickered over to her, glittering with the same calculation she knew from so many of their meetings.

Her voice came out a choked whisper, her heart thudding in her chest at the implications.

"Grim."

She doubted anyone heard, but Conrad must have felt her tension. He finally stopped moving, and she felt his hand tighten. Across the bridge, Grim took two steps forward, his heavy black boots thudding against the metal floor. Finn took an involuntary step back. He saw it, and pain flashed in his gaze.

"I don't understand. Are you here for me?" she asked.

Grim's dark eyes answered her question. No. She realized then that *she* was here *because of him*. He had sent her to steal his precious necklace, and now he was *here*. Her mind whirled.

"*Dhala.*"

At the endearment, something inside her broke irreparably, all of the shards rearranging themselves into jagged, mismatched order. The events of the last few days flashed behind her eyes as she remembered her last meeting with the man she'd trusted above all others. The man who, despite her best efforts, had become the only constant in her out-of-control existence; the man whose lies now burned deeper than she'd ever dreamt anything could after all she'd been through.

Conrad's words echoed in her head.

"The Luminary is our contact with the Toad. He also happens to be a very good friend to everyone on this ship."

Grim is the Luminary.

The realization squeezed the air from her lungs.

"Please tell me this isn't happening."

At the raw anguish in her voice, Shane stepped forward, confusion setting his mouth in a hard line.

"I don't understand. You two know each other? Did you know she was—?"

Grim barely spared him a cursory glance, cutting him off with a curt, "Not now, Shane."

"Was there ever even a necklace?" She managed to choke out the question past the rapidly growing lump in her throat.

His gaze was careful, but she caught the guilt he tried to hide as he reached down into the neck of his singlet and pulled out the chain of a necklace and the attached charm. A Khaleerian gemstone sat dead center inside of it.

"There was always a necklace, but that was never the reason I sent you here. Please understand it had to happen this way."

Finn felt cold. He'd sent her to this ship *knowing* what would happen when she got there?

"Why would you lie to me?" she bit out harshly.

"*Dhala*, there is a bigger mission at stake, one you are needed for. I couldn't tell you until I knew for certain that you were ready. I am sorry to have deceived you. You will never know how much, but this was the only way."

She'd always wondered how much Grim kept hidden from her, despite how close they'd grown over the last seven cycles. Now, she realized, she didn't really know him at all. Their friendship, his mentorship, everything had been a lie to serve his own end. Grim was a lie. This man before her now, this *Luminary*, was a truth she'd never been privy to.

Her gaze shot to Conrad, nausea churning deep in her gut. Had they all known from the beginning? He and Shane looked just as confused as her, but she'd trusted them before and gotten burned. What if this whole thing had been a setup since the day she first set foot on Iliana's pod? The idea reeked of paranoia even to her, but she'd left logic and reason behind the second she walked into the bridge and saw Grim standing in the Luminary's place.

Finn felt the warmth that had been flourishing inside of her the last few days die a quick, painless death as a wave of numbness stole over her.

Grim's sharp eyes noticed the abrupt change, and he took another step forward.

"*Dhala*, these cogs have been in motion for decades. I waited to bring you in because you are only just now ready to play your part."

Her back straightened as she stepped away from Conrad.

"Ready to be your puppet, you mean? You sound just like them, Grim. Just like the Reliance."

His face hardened, but he didn't defend himself.

Whatever Grim's motivations for keeping her in the dark had been and whatever part *Independence*'s crew had played in it, she no longer cared. It was his silence that made her decision for her.

Finn started running. Her feet carried her with swiftness to the nearest travel pod. She heard the pounding of boots behind her, but she didn't slow.

Her need to disappear granted her inhuman speed.

She reached the pod and locked the door, typing in the first destination she could think of. It disengaged from the ship before Grim or anyone else could get inside. A loud bang sounded on the door, followed by Conrad's desperate yell.

The floor shook beneath her. The pod surged forward and away from the ship.

It wasn't until she'd made sure no one followed that she finally allowed herself to cry.

TWENTY-TWO

When Finn's escape pod touched down, she threw herself from it as though the thing were on fire. Even now, Grim and Shane could be following, tracking her down to bring her back to their ship. The ship she never wanted to set foot on again.

Finn's boots hit mud with a sickening *squish*, sinking down almost to the ankle.

Welcome home, she thought bitterly.

The Mud Pit looked just as gray and unwelcoming as it had when she'd left it four days ago. When the smell reached Finn's nostrils, she gagged. After five cycles in the Farthers she'd grown accustomed to the stench of rot and mildew constantly wafting through the air. Four days in space and exposure to the sickeningly sweet air on Cartan had spoiled her; the smell of wet wind, unwashed bodies, and decaying food wreaked havoc on her senses.

The Mud Pit may have looked the same, but Finn had changed.

Had she really only been gone four days? The thought made her want to cry again, but she'd already done enough of that on the trip here to last a lifetime.

As though on a mission to bring Finn to her knees, her brain called up images of her time on *Independence*.

Tiri's smile.

Iliana's smooth, beautiful hands reaching out for Finn's.

Conrad's fingers, butterfly soft over her skin.

Grim's glittering eyes as his betrayal sank in.

Grim. Rage exploded in her chest the moment she thought his name.

"Dhala, *these cogs have been in motion for decades. I waited to bring you in because you are only now ready to play your part.*"

Play her part?

What a joke. He had the entire crew of *Independence* eating out of the palm of his hand like a Reliance master with his slaves, and now he wanted Finn to *play her part?* Grim had kept Finn safe, nurtured her broken mind and body for seven cycles only to turn around and prove himself to be a liar.

All this time she'd thought they'd been looking out for one another, Grim had only been looking out for himself. He'd had plans for Finn, plans she would never know, and it was that uncertainty that haunted her as she put distance between herself and the escape pod.

She wondered how many contacts Grim had out there in the Union who only knew him by his secret identity.

The Luminary.

Finn felt like a fool, raw and wounded from her time away from the Mud Pit, away from the muck-covered streets and worn-down bodies that felt like home. Her days on Shane's ship felt more like a dream than anything else. A hazy moment in time Finn could soon forget.

A dream and nothing more.

"*Nightmares are nothing to be ashamed of, Hellion.*"

Conrad's voice rang loud in Finn's head, as though in fervent denial of her hope. Her hands shook from the weight of it. No matter how hard she tried, she couldn't block them out, couldn't block out the man who had made her wish for things that could never be.

Trudging through the mud into the crowded streets, Finn resolved not to think about any of them: Lex, Jax, AJ, Shane, Isis, Iliana, Conrad. Not even Tiri, though her heart ached at the thought of shutting the little girl out too.

She stopped at her apartment first, avoiding her reflection in the mirror as she slipped on an extra pair of thick gloves. There was no way she'd risk touching someone after what happened with Iliana and Conrad. Finding out she was half-Teslan only furthered her resolution to distance herself from everyone and everything. She possessed so little knowledge of her abilities, so little control. She could end up showing someone her deepest, darkest secrets merely by brushing against them skin to skin, exactly as she'd done with Conrad.

Finn slammed her hand down on the sink in frustration. Only ten minutes since determining to never again think his name, and here she stood thinking about him.

She strapped every weapon she owned to her body, tugging on a heavy, hooded coat to cover them. Then, taking one last look at the tiny, squalid room she'd been calling home for the last five cycles, Finn left.

Her mind focused on recalling all the places she'd chosen to hide gold over the years. There were about ten in all, and Finn planned on hitting every single one of them that day. A lifetime ago it seemed, she'd promised Sophie they would build a farmhouse somewhere far, far away and spend their days basking in the warmth of the sun. She intended to make good on her promise.

Sophie, her only friend in the darkest hour of her life, and the reason she could never forgive herself. Sophie may be dead now, but Finn still had every intention of keeping her word.

Two hours later, she'd consolidated ten bags of gold into one. Lugging it over her shoulder, Finn did her best not to sink deeper into the mud with the added weight. She toyed with the idea of saying goodbye to Doc and seeing the Dirty Molly one last time, but Grim had forever tainted the glow she used to feel about them both. For all she knew, Doc had been in on Grim's twisted plans from the beginning.

She made her way through the city at the fastest pace she dared, not wanting to call unwanted attention to herself. Just as always, vendors draped in their customary dirty rags called out to Finn as she passed their carts. An Anunnaki held up brass teapots and candleholders, her voice husky as she dared Finn to make eye contact. She thought about AJ and his almost successful attempt on her life with those strange swirling eyes.

She wouldn't make that mistake twice.

Her mind wandered to the way those same eyes had looked, filled with fear and confusion as he'd watched her bleed from a hole in her stomach.

Gods, why couldn't she stop thinking about them? Everything here seemed to remind her of the people she'd run from, calling up memories she didn't care to revisit.

"Finn."

A small voice, so hoarse she almost missed it, called out to her from the side of the Anunnaki's cart. Finn's gaze shifted downward of its own volition, finding Nova in the mud propped against a wheel. Her face was a swollen mess of mottled flesh and purple bruises, a gash with crusty dried blood jutting down her forehead. Finn only recognized her by the hooded cape she wore, the one Finn had bought her only four days ago.

"Nova, what the hell happened to you?" Finn rushed to Nova's side and helped her to her feet. The doxie smiled and then immediately winced.

"I got a little cheeky with a soldier who refused to settle up his bill."

Finn glanced over at several Reliance soldiers standing at their posts all throughout the streets, stunner gloves covering their hands and standard-issue firearms tucked into their belts. Her hands itched to pay them a little retribution, but she was severely outnumbered, and Nova couldn't stand on her own.

A group of them kicked at a huddled mass of Mud Pit slaves, throwing blows with their wooden staffs at their already prone bodies, and Finn shielded Nova with her mass as they shuffled their way past, eventually finding safety in the alcove of a brick building. Every once in a while the leader of the soldiers would laugh, yelling out, "You should've found another place to die!"

The slaves' tattooed wrists and exposed forearms wrapped around their protruding ribs to block the blows.

Tattooed wrists like Finn's.

When they didn't move fast enough, the soldiers began hitting them with blasts from the stunner gloves. In the distance, the crack of a whip echoed through the air around Finn, followed by a desperate scream. The sound mingled with the moans and shouts of the slaves on the ground.

Finn backed up against the crumbling wall of the building, her bag of gold suddenly too heavy on her shoulders. Her legs gave out slowly beneath her as she and Nova slid to the ground in a crouch, the girl still leaning fully in her arms. Wet, sticky mud clung to her backside, but she couldn't force herself back up.

"Get up," she whispered. *"Get up."*

Her breaths heaved and burned in her chest, heart pounding to the rhythm of the screams filling the streets.

Could she really leave and live out the rest of her life in practiced ignorance? Could she sleep beneath a clear, pollutant-free sky knowing there were half-breeds on every Inner Rings planet in the Union, suffering at the hands of the upper castes?

Could she die, decades from now, pretending she didn't remember every detail of the senator's estate; from the synthetic grass and trees to the hollow-eyed slaves he'd shaved and dusted gold?

Something strange flowed through Finn as she reasoned it all out in her head. Something stronger than rage. It swam through her veins with ferocity, lending strength to her ragged body and filling her with something she'd never before experienced.

Purpose.

Half-breeds and their location flashed across her mind like a recording on a holojector. She'd memorized the information without even realizing it. Resolution filled Finn as she recalled the first few names and locations.

She might not be able help the lower castes, but there were over fifty people spread out across the Union that she *could* help. It didn't hurt that her plans would throw a wrench in Grim's decades-old cogs either.

A flutter of anticipation lit her belly. Was she really considering this? As if in answer, Finn's legs straightened of their own accord, pushing her back up onto her feet as a wave of calm rushed through her veins.

Without a backward glance to the melee on the streets, Finn made her way down the darkest alleys of the Mud Pit with relaxed, steady strides. Nova kept pace beside her, not bothering to question their destination.

She could think of only one place her gold would be well spent on this planet.

The black market.

If you enjoyed

RELIANCE

look out for

DISOBEDIENCE

Book Two of the
Reliance Trilogy

by Kaitlyn Andersen

Finn No Last Name turned away from the shadowed alcove shielding her from view. With her red velvet cape, gloves, and copper-colored silk shirt, she blended in just as well as any other member of the Reliance.

The population on Arcturus nearly exceeded 4.7 billion. In their midst, she found she floated by like a drop of water in a vast sea. After spending endless cycles too terrified to return to the Inner Rings, Finn now found it more than a little exhilarating to discover how utterly invisible she was.

Making her way past sweeping glass skyscrapers, and flashing holojectors, her eyes remained focused on the planet's tallest, twin towers and the giant Arcturian eye nestled between their peaks. The headquarters for Arcturus' hand-selected, cream of the crop council was nearly impenetrable. Trying to break through their security to rescue the half-breed inside would be considered a suicide mission by even the most capable of thieves.

Something heavy settled just below Finn's chest, webs of pain spreading from its center.

Two half-breeds suffered imprisonment on Arcturus.

One tucked away in a sprawling countryside manor, the other within the heavily guarded confines of the Council Headquarters' domed building.

Finn would only make it off this planet with one.

It wasn't so much that she feared death. The strange sense of resolve she'd found on the Mud Pit's streets so many weeks ago made such worries seem inconsequential. But the cold fact remained: Finn couldn't help anyone if she was dead. Now, the time had come to face the hard truth she'd been avoiding. The truth she'd known the moment she realized one of the captive half-breeds lived within those impassable walls.

I can still save one.

She repeated the sentence in her mind, rubbing away the sting as she continued down the busy street avoiding eye contact with the upper-caste passersby as she went.

Despite the ease with which she'd adapted, part of Finn felt blanketed by a constant state of paranoia at the idea of casually walking through the streets of the Arcturians' home planet. More heavily guarded than any other Inner Rings planet; Arcturus was populated by the most important, influential members of the Reliance, and Finn planned to steal a half-breed right out from under their haughty noses.

Maybe her newfound detachment wasn't purpose. Maybe it was insanity.

When she'd found the infamous James Jessup her first day on planet, it had only taken one look at the puritanical leader of the Union's largest house of Arcturian worship for all thoughts of indecision to flee her mind.

She watched him for days as he casually strolled from one of the four Houses of Arcturian Disciples in his unassuming burgundy robes, surrounded by half a dozen Reliance soldiers serving as his personal guard. A golden ring with a ruby centerpiece and a tattoo of an eye marking the center of his forehead were the only adornments on his surprisingly powerful body. People stopped him on the streets, requesting blessings and prayers on their behalf. He always obliged, his carefully masked features the picture of tranquility. Some of the more dramatic members of the upper castes cried freely when his ringed hand rested atop their heads and his eyes closed in prayers of benediction.

His humble demeanor only made Finn loathe him more, because she knew something the rest of them didn't. Jessup, masquerading as a pious man of the Gods and emissary for the Arcturian forefathers, held a half-breed captive somewhere on planet. A half-breed she intended to find.

She would not leave Arcturus until she had robbed him of his prized possession.

It would have been easy to lose him in the ever-changing tide of red and gold, as the upper crust of the Reliance hustled and bustled from one glass-plated skyscraper to another. The way they carelessly meandered through their sprawling metropolis, spending the gold the lower castes broke their backs for, nearly penetrated Finn's wall of calculated dispassion.

She kept to the shadows, never letting Jessup stray far from her line of sight. Each day, when the three suns orbiting Arcturus rose, she followed, and she watched, learning about Jessup as she did.

The longer she followed, the more she witnessed.

Every day Arcturus's masses held feasts and buffets with enough food to feed the Farthers for a whole cycle. Each meal preceded by a prayer first to the Gods, then the Arcturians. As it turned out, the upper castes prayed to the Gods and the forefathers in equal measure. Seeing the sickening idolization of the golden prigs up close, and with such brutal relentlessness, chipped away her veneer of calm piece by piece.

On the Mud Pit, she'd worried that a life of peace stood out of reach because of all that her time on Shane Montgomery's ship had revealed. Now, she knew it without a doubt; Finn would never be able to block out the images of the things she'd seen here. No matter how hard she tried.

A body slammed into her hard, distracting her from her thoughts, and she caught herself before the force sent her to the ground. Strong hands held Finn above the elbows, steadying her. She glanced up under her lashes at a senior-ranking officer of the Reliance guard, his barrel chest bursting at the seams of his deep-red jacket. He barely gave Finn's bashful act a cursory glance, before letting her go and moving away with a stern, "Pardon me, Madam."

She pretended to blush, slipping a hand into the pocket of her burgundy trousers.

"I am terribly sorry, sir."

With a nod at her husky apology, he moved off to join the other guards surrounding James Jessup as he made his way through crowds of the admiring masses. Finn trailed them at a safe distance, pretending to be one of his marveling followers.

On and on he walked, the crowds thinning the farther away from the city center he went. Gradually, she separated herself, ducking into the shadows and pausing around corners. The guards reached a sleek, black pod designed to look like an old-timey carriage—complete with silicone wheels—and large enough to fit ten men inside comfortably. They ushered Jessup in.

Once he was settled, the senior officer from earlier called out an order to the six synthetic horses attached to the carriage by an assortment of rainbow-colored wires. The pod was more than capable of operating on its own, but Finn had learned that Jessup—like so many other members of the Reliance—leaned toward the ostentatious when it came to methods of travel. Red eyes flickered open and iron hooves began to shift as their inner mechanics whirred to life.

Trailing behind the giant beasts as they sped off into the distance, Finn jogged at a brisk pace. Together, they traversed five kilometers of rocky, unpaved terrain, the steady rhythm keeping Finn at a healthy distance. After the fourth kilometer, she finally began to feel winded, but kept stride, knowing they would soon reach their destination.

Moments later, the carriage stopped. Finn slowed her steps, breaking through a grouping of synthetic cherry blossoms just in time to watch the horses pass through massive iron gates. Moving with silent steps past rows and rows of hedges, her eyes tracked Jessup as his guards led him past the towering cement walls surrounding his three-story manor.

Everything looked calm, as it had the last six times she'd followed him home.

Finn reached into the pocket of her trousers and fingered the ID chip she'd swiped from his senior officer.

Tonight, Jessup would regret his imprudence.

CPSIA information can be obtained
at www.ICGtesting.com
Printed in the USA
LVHW110848010820
662145LV00002B/360

9 781937 868734